Where Shadows Fall

Where Shadows Fall

Shades and Shadows Book 3

Natalie J. Case

For the resistance.

Chapter One

Zero's entire body reverberated with the message, "Salt in the water! Warn them!" and she sat up, knocking Alaric and Raven both away. Alaric's head snapped up and he was half way out the door before Zero had processed the input crashing into her and got her shields up.

Raven stopped at the door to the room, leaning out for a long moment into the hallway before she was throwing clothes at Zero.

The village was under attack, and the chaos swirling around her was almost too much and she had to double up her shields to function enough to struggle into the jeans. Maddie was there suddenly, her face worried. "We have to go."

Somewhere in the distance an explosion sounded, and the building trembled around them. Zero shoved her feet into her broken-in tennis shoes and followed as Raven led them toward the back of the building.

Alaric hadn't finished the work to completely free her mind, but he'd broken down most of the walls and seemed pretty confident that there were no more traps waiting to spring on her. It had left her off kilter and reeling under the sudden expansion of the gifts her father had hidden away from her.

Everything seemed set to the highest volume and her shields were failing to keep the world at bay. She let Raven guide her out a back door, where they paused, listening to the chaos.

Zero knew it was 8th Battalion, not her father. While he had been a part of the inception of the military group, he'd lost control when he had underestimated the religious fervor he had unleashed. The air smelled of fire and gasoline. Alaric's voice filled her head, telling her to run.

Maddie appeared beside her, grabbed her hand and Zero nodded. Together, they took off running into the woods, Raven coming behind them. There was no pursuit that she could detect. Raven stopped them when they couldn't see the buildings of the town or hear the shouting.

"Catch your breath." Raven said as she glanced around them.

"We need to keep going." Maddie said, her voice filled with fear.

"We're safe enough for now." Zero replied, her own voice sounding deeper than she was used to. "No one is coming this way. They're after Mason."

Raven looked up at her, frowning. "Why Mason?"

Zero shrugged. "Not sure, but it's reverberating in the air, like all of them are thinking it at the same time." She let go of Maddie's hand and moved to lean against a tree. After laying in a bed for several days, the running was exhausting.

She rubbed at her head, shoring up her shields. She had access now to most of her memories, and she wasn't sure anymore that was a good thing. Scenes from her father's experiments kept playing through her head, her voice screaming as they filled her body with his serums, cutting into her over and over again.

Zero pushed the latest of those memories away and tried to bring her focus back to the situation at hand. She stood away from the tree, her eyes wide. They weren't alone.

Zero crossed to Raven, and grabbed her arm, pushing the information across into Raven's head. They moved slowly and quietly, taking up positions to attempt to defend themselves.

A few seconds later, Zero relaxed. Two boys ran past them, fear streaming off them. Behind them a man followed, a Shade she vaguely remembered from the village.

"Connor." Raven said, stopping all three of them in their tracks. The boys looked from Raven to Zero and then Maddie. "Are you okay?"

He nodded and held out a hand for the boys. They came without question. "I think so. We were starting breakfast."

Raven nodded and looked around them. "We don't seem to have any one following."

"Not yet, anyway." Connor agreed. "Any idea who else got out?"

Raven shook her head and looked at Zero. Zero closed her eyes and dropped her shields a little, reaching out for Alaric. She got an impression of where he was and who he was with. "The Shadow got his people and maybe five Shades." She spread her senses around the village. "Manny took a group south, through the woods."

The strike force was moving through what was left of the town, searching through buildings before setting fire to them. Dead bodies of Shades lay in the street, salt burns covering their skin. There was a truck filled with Shades, maybe ten of them.

Zero reached for Raven's shoulder to steady herself. "They have prisoners. They're searching the town for more. We should keep moving."

Raven nodded. "We're going to need a vehicle."

"Where are we going to go?" Maddie asked. "They'll just find us again."

"I know a place." Raven said. "It's a long walk, but we have most of the night." She pointed and started walking. There wasn't much they could do but follow.

Zero took up the rear, keeping her attention split between making her way and listening behind them for pursuit. She was tiring quickly. Maddie moved closer, sliding an arm around Zero's waist. Her strength was surprising. "Thanks." Zero muttered.

Maddie didn't respond, just kept them both moving behind the boys' backs. As her body tired, her control on her thoughts frayed. She gave up listening for pursuit and fought the tide of memories. Alaric had been helping her build walls of her own, natural walls that kept information organized, not hidden, but Mason's distress had interrupted them.

She needed time and quiet and safety to get herself back to fully functional. She snorted at the thought. It wasn't likely to happen anytime soon.

* * *

The sun was starting to rise, Zero could sense it even though the trees still provided some shelter. They were going to need to find someplace to wait out the sun, and soon. The boys, Liam and Parker were dragging. Raven's worry that the sun would burn them dry was loud in her head. Connor's concern was strongly tied to the boys.

Zero needed time to adjust to all of the new noise in her head. She caught Raven watching her and nodded. Even with her limited perception of what the Shadow had done, Raven knew that this running was the last thing Zero needed right now.

They were close to reservation land, though Zero wasn't sure how she knew that. Reservation land meant dry, arid expanses that the sun baked hard. Not exactly terrain made for a Shade. Raven stopped them where there was still a little cover from the trees. She chewed on her lower lip, her thoughts skipping between some place on the reservation and the relative safety of the woods.

She turned to the others. "Okay, our options are to double back to that hollow tree and build a shelter, or we keep going about a mile west, where there is a shed, or what's left of one. It should be enough to keep us out of the sun for the day."

Connor leaned out of the tree line and squinted up at the sky. "Sun's going to be up in less than a half hour."

Raven nodded. "If we can get to the shed, come sundown I can get us to a friend's place.

He'll have food and water. We can figure out where to go from there."

"I say we keep moving." Zero said. "Going backwards is dangerous without knowing where that strike force is."

Raven nodded. "Okay, stick close. We're crossing onto Zuni lands." She pointed to the west. "Our destination is just on the other side of that rise."

The group set out at a fast pace, as fast as their exhaustion would allow. They'd still get a larger dose of sun exposure than was good, but once at the shed, Zero assumed the Shades would be safe enough.

Behind them, the sun kept creeping higher. Connor moved Liam and Parker in front of him, using his own body to shade them. Zero and Maddie moved in closer to Raven try to provide what shade they could with their shadows.

When they finally came in sight of the shed Raven had talked about, Zero wrinkled her nose. It was barely standing, one wall was all but collapsed, the roof leaning off to one side, pulling the opposite wall into a precarious looking angle. Zero jogged ahead of the others and ducked inside to see if it was safe.

Inside there was just enough room for the four Shades in the dark corner, if they didn't mind getting close together. There was a hole in the roof that would let the light shine in before too long, restricting the amount of space they would have.

Zero emerged and nodded, ushering the boys in first. She and Maddie waited until the others were inside before following.

Raven stood holding her phone, staring at it, her thoughts about whether it was safe to use or not filling Zero's head. She thumbed it on and shook her head. "No signal." Of course, even if they'd had enough signal to call someone, Zero wasn't sure who. There was Darvin, of course, but there was no guarantee he could do anything if they managed to get him. Raven stuffed the phone back into her pocket.

Maddie and Zero watched as Connor got the boys settled in to try to sleep, then looked at Raven. "You should rest." Zero said. Raven was feeling the expectations of leadership, and it was wearing on her. Zero crossed to put a hand on her shoulder. Thoughts spun out from her, fear, the lack of direction, the not knowing who else had survived, the idea that someone had told the 8th Battalion how to get to them.

Zero sent a wave of comfort, blanketing over the swirling chaos. After a moment Raven smiled and nodded her thanks. Raven turned to find Maddie stripping out of her clothes. "What are you doing?"

"I can handle the sun. I'll stand guard."

Before Raven could respond, she dropped her shirt into Zero's hands and shifted. Raven heard the boys gasp and looked their way. When she looked back, a large black cat had taken Maddie's place, deep green eyes meeting hers.

Raven nodded her acceptance. "Wake me if anyone gets too close." She ducked her head and crawled into the dark corner, laying down beside the boys and arranging her body to keep it away from the spot of sunlight that would move closer as the sun moved across the sky.

Maddie sat in the doorway of the shed, and after only a moment, Zero sat beside her, the pair of them staring out into the bright light of the day.

Behind them, Zero could feel Raven's thoughts winding down, and turned her mind to her own chaos. Memories churned in disconnected streams of agony, pulling her from one moment of terror to the next if she let them.

She needed to get some control. That's what Alaric had been helping her do before the town fell siege. Her shields were still ravaged and needed work as well.

With the solid mass of Maddie's cat beside her, Zero turned her attention inward.

Chapter Two

Zero woke from a light doze, startled by something she couldn't see or hear. Beside her, Maddie was at high alert, staring out into the setting sun. "You sense that too?" Zero asked, climbing to her feet.

The little bit of sleep she'd gotten had helped, but she was still on edge. Zero cast her senses out around her, trying to find whatever had awakened her. No one was nearby though. The nearest person she could sense was at least a mile away.

She stretched, moving slowly to warm up her body. She focused her attention back the way they came. There was no sign of the 8th Battalion. Reaching a little further, she found Alaric, but she recoiled quickly as pain lashed through the connection, seeming to hit her square at the base of her neck.

Zero grabbed her neck, half expecting to find blood. Her knees folded, and she grabbed the side of the shed as she went down. With the distance, she couldn't tell if it was Alaric himself who had been shot or someone close to him. She panted through the pain and pushed herself back up to her feet, struggling to close up her shields to block him out.

Maddie stood a few steps away, lifting her muzzle to sniff the air. A low growl escaped her, and she moved back toward the door of the shed. Inside, Raven was awake, Zero could hear her shifting around. That wasn't what had Maddie growling though.

Zero turned toward the feeling of someone approaching. Maddie's hackles were raised, and she was poised to jump at anyone who might attack them. Zero could sense no malice however, and her hand descended onto Maddie's head to calm her. In the distance, a dust cloud lifted, and a small, black dot was moving in their direction.

Raven joined them as that small dot became a truck coming toward them. There was only one person in the vehicle, a man. Zero couldn't tell much else about him without trying, and she was too tired to try too hard. The truck rumbled to a stop and the man emerged from the cab, taking a few steps before stopping, his eyes on Raven.

He was middle age, gray starting to stripe his long black hair. His skin was deeply tan, dry, like he'd spent most of his life in the desert sun. His eyes skipped to Maddie before returning to Raven.

"I heard there was a panther out here. I thought to myself that it was an odd place for a panther. Didn't expect to find a Raven too."

"Hello, Lonan." Raven said with a smile. "I find myself once more needing your help."

"The winds say Shady Lake has been burned to the ground. I wondered if I would see you."

"The winds say that?" Zero asked, her eyebrow lifting in disbelief.

"Sure they do. Smoke rides the wind, and the radio news tells of 8th Battalion raids." He responded with a chuckle. "You must be dry. Climb in, I'll get you to some water."

"I'm not alone." Raven said, glancing over her shoulder.

"So I see. I don't have much room, but my wife is cooking dinner."

"I appreciate it Lonan." She turned to Maddie. "Why don't you go get dressed."

Maddie looked Lonan over, like she didn't trust him, but went back into the shed as Connor and the boys emerged.

"Lonan, this is Connor, and his son Liam. I don't know if you remember Aliyah, but this is her son Parker. This is Zero, and the Shifter is Maddie."

Lonan nodded his greetings and opened the passenger side door. "You boys hop on in here. I reckon the grownups can handle more sun than you."

Maddie emerged as Raven and Connor climbed into the bed of the truck, her eyes skipping to Zero's. Together they climbed up to sit beside the two Shades, just as Lonan shook out a blanket for them to hide under. "I imagine this won't be the most pleasant ride for you, but this should help."

Zero and Maddie helped them get the blanket tucked behind them and draped over their heads. The truck lurched as Lonan got behind the wheel and set them off back along the dusty trail.

Everyone was quiet, but she could feel the exhaustion pulling on Maddie. The Shifter hadn't slept in well over twenty-four hours. She was going to crash soon, now that the adrenaline that had fueled their escape was wearing off. Zero looked to Raven, who was as pulled into herself as Zero had ever seen. She too was exhausted, the few hours of sleep not enough to erase the sun exposure and apprehension caused by their current situation. Connor seemed better rested, or at least better adjusted, but he too was weary and feeling the effects of the sun setting somewhere ahead of them.

Only the boys seemed to be largely okay. The shock of their escaping the village had mostly worn off, and there was a sense of adventure coming from them. She sensed that Lonan was telling them some story.

Zero turned herself to the work that still needed to be done in her head. She had worked to shore up her defenses around the last of the damaged places and used the tricks Alaric had taught her to set up a sort of alarm system, so that she would know if someone else came snooping through some hidden back door they hadn't found. She was cautiously optimistic that she wasn't going to suddenly snap and become a puppet for her father's plans.

What was left behind was a terrifying mess of memory. She hadn't expected the memories to be so intense, but then, she hadn't remembered even half of what had been done to her in the time since her mother's death. She would be furious at how much of her life he took, once she got past the terror at what he had done to her.

She was pulled from her inner thoughts as the truck rolled to a stop outside a small clapboard house. The sun was brilliant on the horizon, and a woman emerged from the house, wiping her hands on a towel. She raised an eyebrow as Lonan helped the boys out of the cab but held the door open as he hurried them inside.

Raven and Connor kept the blanket over them as they climbed out of the bed and followed, with Maddie and Zero bringing up the rear.

They entered a small kitchen that smelled of spices and cooking meat. "I wasn't expecting so many." The woman touched Lonan's arm. "But you are welcome."

"Raven, and everyone, this is my wife, Tusa. Tusa, my childhood friend, Raven and those who escaped the burning of Shady Lake. They have need of shelter, and water."

"And food no doubt." Tusa replied, a smile tugging at the corners of her mouth. "Come, sit. Lonan will pour you water."

Zero followed Raven as they were led into a slightly more spacious living room, dropping to sit on the floor near the chair Raven chose. Maddie circled the room, her eyes scanning the pictures on the walls before she came to sit beside Zero.

Tired pulled at her, but Zero pushed it away. They weren't safe yet. She didn't dare sleep until she'd managed to get some distance from the suddenly fresh and horrifying memories that filled her head.

"Do you have any news?" Raven asked as Lonan handed out glasses of water from a wooden tray.

"Not much. Many escaped on foot. The town is now ash."

"What about the 8th Battalion?" Connor asked.

Lonan shrugged. "It is said they only pursued one group who escaped in vehicles."

"Jerah." Zero murmured softly. She felt eyes on her and looked up. "They were looking for him specifically. Someone…" She dug for the thought, something she heard or read from Alaric. "The 8ᵗʰ Battalion was looking for him. The raid was…not specifically for him, but once he was spotted it was like the thought swept through the strike team." She reached for Alaric again, and recoiled as she encountered a wash of pain, fear, then came the sound of gunfire and a sharp crack of pain, like before, a replay of something he'd experienced. She grabbed at the back of her neck, fighting to disengage from him.

She was panting as she broke free. It took her a second to open her eyes, surprised to find everyone staring at her. She licked her lips and blinked, parsing through the input. "I think Riley is dead."

Zero had never really interacted with him much, but she'd liked him well enough. Alaric, on the other hand, had loved him like a brother. The pain of the impact had reverberated through him as though it was Alaric himself who had been shot.

She could still feel an echo of the pain in her neck. "He's with Jerah. They were attacked." Most of what she'd gotten was disjointed images and a whole lot of fear and pain. "I think…" She shook her head, trying to understand the images. "I think they got away, but Riley was shot in the back of the head."

Zero could feel Connor watching her, his suspicion bleeding out around him. She blinked and looked up at him. To his credit, he didn't say anything, only looked away. "We should try to round up the other survivors." Connor said. "Figure out what to do next."

"First, we get some rest, and make sure there aren't any watchers lingering. We don't need to present them with another target." Raven said.

"And before that, you eat and hydrate yourselves." Tusa said as she came into the room with two plates. "Let Lonan and his friends seek out the others for you."

Zero took her plate and disconnected from the room. She needed time to sort through the input of the last forty-eight hours and figure out how to function with all of the new memories and the sudden influx of power.

* * *

Ice raced through her veins from the place where the needle entered her arm, forcing the serum into her, disconnecting her from her own abilities and preparing her for another assault. She tried to summon fire to thaw the chill, but nothing would come. Fingers held her eyelids open and a light shined into them. "I think we're ready."

Screams echoed around her, screams that sounded strange and familiar at the same time. Disjointed thoughts darted through her as she was cut open and sewn together, as He forced his way into her brain and broke down the door to her inner self.

She couldn't stop him, but she felt every touch of his blade on her skin, every stab of the needle, everything he did in her head, until her body began to shake from the cacophony of it all. "Control her."

"It's too much, you need to let me give her something for the pain."

"No. Pain is part of the process. I'm nearly done. Hold her down."

Some part of her recognized the screams now as her own. They filled the space and bled out until the darkness came. Even then there was no escape from the agony in her body. It pulled her through the dark and wound around her tight, dragging her from the dark danger of her memory into an even darker room.

Color began to swirl around her, loosening the grip of fear as the room solidified and she knew she had left her own mind and was now in someone else's, dropping from her nightmare into his, into the boiling cauldron of his grief.

Mason Jerah was dead.

Mason Jerah was dead. The thought echoed through her as she woke, her clothes soaked through with sweat and her head pounding. Zero sat up, looking around the small loft she had been sharing with Maddie. The cat was gone, and she was alone.

Her throat was dry and sore, making her think the screams hadn't been kept to her dreams. She pushed the blanket off and put her feet on the floor. Zero pulled a hand over her bald head and took a deep breath.

The "treatment" in her dream had only been one in a long line of agonizing experiments. One of the earliest. It was meant to provide her with more Shadow abilities than she'd already had as her birthright.

She pulled on her jeans and her shoes. It had been nearly a week of waiting. The Shades gathered, they talked, they looked at her like she was an alien. She couldn't blame them. It wasn't their fault she was a freak.

Alaric's grief was still spilling through her, making it harder for her to sort out her own emotions. Taking a deep breath, she pushed everything down and back behind a wall. She couldn't function with it all sloshing around inside her.

Zero stood, crossing to the ladder down into the barn. It was nearly morning. Somewhere to the east of them, Alaric was wallowing in his grief. Somewhere to the west, the 8th Battalion was planning its next move.

It felt an awful lot like she was stuck there in the middle, with no way out. She didn't like the feeling.

Chapter Three

Mason Jerah was dead.

Those four words echoed around his head, long after he had ripped the knowledge from Bryan's mind. It was the only thing he could think, the only coherent thought in his head. Everything else was noise, static.

Alaric knew he'd blasted his grief out to his people, knew Bryan had been forced to knock him out to keep him from hurting anyone. His touch had not been gentle, and Alaric's head still resonated with the residual effects.

It was Mason's death that saved them, kept the strike team from coming after them.

Alaric sat up slowly in the gloom of the borrowed bedroom, blinking as he looked around the room. His hand still held the pendants and he lifted them, letting the sensation of Mason fill his senses. He could almost believe Mason was alive, but he knew, he'd seen the memory of Bryan's escape, he knew what Mason had showed him.

There was no way he had survived.

He could sense Bryan and Sahara, the old man and his daughter. They weren't far. He wasn't sure how much time had passed as he had lain in his grief, submitting to it as if it were a physical thing, put under by Bryan, but kept from surfacing by his own pain.

Alaric stretched and stood slowly, feeling through the soreness and working out the kinks. Bryan was instantly aware he was awake, a product of their connection, and as he turned to the door, Alaric realized that Bryan had also planted a line, through which he'd been monitoring Alaric.

He snipped the line and the door opened. Bryan looked him over, nodding a little. Alaric wasn't in the mood to be coddled. He pushed past Bryan and into the hall. Bryan followed, stopping before he would have followed him into the bathroom. Alaric relieved himself and considered his options.

Mason would have wanted him to get back to his people. He could already tell his mother wanted the same thing. Bryan hadn't completely relinquished the wall he'd put up to keep Alaric from broadcasting his anguish, but his mother had found a way through.

He washed his hands and splashed water over his face. What he wanted was to find the men who had killed Mason, and make them pay for it. In fact, he had already decided that he would. Alaric looked at his reflection and carefully secreted that thought away, building a secure wall to protect it from those who might stop him.

He opened the door to find Bryan had been joined by Sahara. He didn't look at them, just nodded. "I need to get to the globe. There's work to do."

"Just waiting on you." Bryan said.

"And stop babying me. I'm fine." Alaric pushed through them and headed out to the kitchen.

Barbara nodded to him, holding out a bag. "Should be enough food to get you through to Virginia, if you manage to get past the road blocks."

"It won't be a problem." Alaric said, nodding his thanks.

"Dad filled your gas tank. You're good to go."

Alaric nodded. "Let's get moving then."

"Don't you think you should maybe take a minute? Eat?" Bryan said beside him. "You've been down for three days."

"No, I'm fine."

Bryan dropped the wall suddenly and all of the unfiltered input slammed into him, like it would drive Bryan's point home. Alaric grabbed the table as he adjusted, breathing through the onslaught. There was a lot of chaos, his clan was scattered.

All the more reason to leave.

"I'm going. You can stay if you want." Alaric said, holding out his hands for the keys. Bryan stared at him, clearly disagreeing with him and not afraid to tell him so. Sahara cleared her throat, putting one hand on Bryan's shoulder.

Bryan shook his head. "I'll drive. You just woke up."

He led the way out to the truck. Alaric settled into the passenger seat, while Sahara climbed into the back seat, behind Bryan. Once they were moving, Alaric turned his attention to the chaos in his head, acknowledging concerns and letting his presence be known. Once he'd weeded through most of it, he reached out for his mother, letting her presence fill his mind, her touch comforting. She soothed him, wordlessly salving over his pain in the way only a mother could.

Bryan angled them north and east, skirting around Dallas to avoid any road blocks that would close the city off. They found back roads to take them from Texas into Arkansas. It was Memphis where they found their first barricade, manned by state troopers. Bryan smiled at the woman who approached them, and Alaric could feel his *push* that she let them through. It was a strong compulsion.

Bryan drove them through and stopped them at the first gas station. "We need to fill up."

They had no money to pay for gas, but Alaric nodded and climbed out of the truck to head inside.

Once upon a time, using his gifts the way he was about to would have been a step over the line, an act he wouldn't condone. He told Bryan to get ready to pump and went into the small station store. There was no one around but the cashier, a young kid of maybe twenty.

Alaric approached the counter, reaching out for the unguarded mind. It wouldn't take much to deceive the young man, who was already distracted by his phone. He lifted his hand, a smile on his face. "Hi, I'm going to fill it on pump two." He made contact with the kid's hand and his mind used the connection to convince him that the piece of paper in his hand was a fifty-dollar bill.

"Pump's on. Come in for your change when you're done."

"Thanks."

Alaric let Bryan know to start pumping and stayed a moment longer to be sure that the trick held. When Bryan signaled they were done, Alaric left and got behind the wheel to take over the driving.

They didn't have time to obey all of the rules. He half expected Bryan to give him a hard time, but he said nothing as they headed east.

It was after midnight when they reached the next blockade, at the crossing into Virginia. Once it had been a simple checkpoint between states, but with the current tensions between the southern states and the federal government, it had grown to nearly mirror a border checkpoint. It wouldn't be long before it was a border, if the news he was hearing rang true. The southern states were ready to declare their independence from the federal government once more.

They approached the only lane open at that hour and a tired looking man leaned out of the booth. Alaric wasted little time getting a hold of him. He pressed the lie into the man's head, that he had checked their papers, that they were free to cross.

"Have a good night."

He held his breath as the gate opened and they eased through it. About a hundred feet away was another crossing gate. He prepared himself to repeat the performance as the border agent stepped out of her booth. "Where are you coming from tonight?" she asked, leaning into the open window slightly.

Alaric reached for her mind, but was surprised to find that she was a Shadow, her mind strong, with shields and walls and she raised an eyebrow at his touch. "Can you identify yourself?"

He inclined his head, and opened his shields enough that she could confirm his words. "Alaric Lambrecht. My Keepers, Bryan and Sahara."

She nodded knowingly. "I've been wondering when we'd finally see you. We've been keeping someone on duty here who would recognize you." She stepped away, reaching in to the booth and coming back with a map in her hands. "You'll find a couple of routes marked out. We have some interesting militia folk thinking they can block off roads. Follow one of these and you should avoid them."

He smiled. "Thank you."

"Drive safe now."

Alaric handed the map to Bryan. Alaric glanced over at it as Bryan opened it, his fingers tracing the yellow highlighting some of the roads.

He could tell that his mother had taken the globe to an old clan homestead not far from the line between Virginia and West Virginia. They'd spent time there in the summers when he was a kid. It had been in her family nearly as long as her family had been on American soil.

They'd be there in a few hours. Then he could connect with the globe, bolster his strength so that he could begin looking for the men who had killed Mason. Not that he had a plan, exactly, for how to go about doing that, but he'd find a way.

He couldn't be the leader his people needed until that was done.

* * *

Alaric pushed all of his thoughts of vengeance behind a wall as he greeted his mother and submitted to her embrace, followed by more food than they could eat and a thousand reassurances that he was in one piece.

She had kept the others away, knowing him well enough to know that he would want solitude until he'd spent time alone with the globe.

"It's been charging in the sun the last two days." Emily said as Alaric pushed back from the table. "It's in the old chapel."

"Good." He looked at Bryan and nodded. "Be sure I'm not disturbed.

"Don't you think you should sleep first?" Emily asked as he stood.

"I've slept long enough." He kissed her forehead. "Besides, an hour with the globe is better than a whole night sleeping."

"Any idea how long you'll be?" Bryan asked, looking up at him. Alaric could tell he still wasn't happy.

"As long as it takes," he answered. His voice softened, and he let some of his pain spill over his otherwise impervious shields. "Just, give me a little time."

Bryan didn't answer, just stood up to pour another cup of coffee. Alaric took it as acceptance and let himself out onto the porch.

The sun was high, and the land was a familiar place, a welcome that almost made him smile. He shaded his eyes against the sun, turning his gaze out past the old tire swing and the vegetable garden that had gone to seed over the winter. There was a path that cut through the middle of that garden, out past the run-down barn and into the woods.

Alaric stepped off the porch and set foot to that trail. He could feel the pull of the globe, even as the wards and guards that had long been a part of this land opened for him. This was sacred ground.

The grove of oak trees had come from acorns brought from the old country. They had stood as far back as the very first of his people who had come across the oceans in search of freedom. In the center of that grove was the place they called the chapel.

It was no building of wood or stone, but it was a vessel of energy, the site of weddings and birthings, the place of rituals and devotions. Until his family had moved west, it had been the place where the orb lived.

He paused as he reached the barrier. Energy sentinels stood at the four corners and between them the power of the globe cast itself, a glamor of sorts to protect it from those not of the clans. Anyone without the blood would walk past, never knowing it was there.

Alaric raised a hand to the barrier, exhaling slowly and bringing the skin of his palm to press into it. The skin tingled slightly, and the barrier opened to allow him inside. In the center of the clearing the globe pulsed, a welcome from an old friend.

He circled it several times, coming closer with each pass until he was but a breath away. Closing his eyes, he centered himself, cleared the rage and pain and slowly leaned into the energy of the globe.

It enveloped him, buoying him up and cradling him. He was filled with the sensations of hundreds of kin offering him comfort, and he let them for a time.

Eventually though, he separated himself from them and settled in, connecting with the energy of the globe itself. He opened up to it, letting it fill him, clear the cobwebs, approach the problem of finding the men who had hunted them in Arizona. He didn't have much to go on. He had the idea that they were betrayed and that the strike force had been after a particular Shade, not just looking to destroy the village. He had the few voices he'd heard as they'd raced to get to Mason and get them out of the village and his own suspicions, the glimpses any of them had gotten of the men attacking them.

He sent it all out into the globe and let it filter through his input and begin collating corresponding information from the scattered clan. He sat still within the energy and images, voices, places started to pop into his attention. Slowly at first, but gradually growing in number and speed, hints and threads came to him, creating a timeline of sorts and a map of faces.

Building from every mind the globe could connect with, anyone who came from his clan or those like his, minds that could be gleaned, the globe helped him place people in the chain, following it back to the very place he'd first met Mason.

Shallon. The colonel who had tortured Mason was the man behind the strike force.

Alaric inhaled and filed all of the information into neat drawers that would be easily accessible to him later. He slowly withdrew from the globe, letting his energy separate and integrate back into an individual.

The world tilted a little and he nearly passed out. A few seconds later, he felt Bryan and Sahara. "Easy." Bryan said.

Alaric opened his eyes and squinted at Bryan. He looked older than Alaric remembered, the gray that painted his hair thicker now, his face gaunt and haunted. He felt a pang of guilt, knowing that some of that was his fault. His stomach rumbled loudly, and Bryan helped him stand.

"Your mother is going crazy." Bryan said as Sahara supported him on the other side and they got him moving back toward the house.

"How long?" Alaric asked, his voice dry.

"Almost two days." Sahara said.

"I hope you found what you were looking for."

Alaric nodded. "Yeah, I think I did."

His mother had food on the table as they came into the kitchen and he could tell without a word that she was worried about him. "I'm okay." He thanked his Keepers with a touch and they left him with his mother.

"You are going to sit there and eat until I'm satisfied you've had enough, and then you are going to bed. And you're going to deal with the things that need to be dealt with and you are going to give me a few days of not worrying about you. Do you hear me?"

He smiled and nodded. "Yes ma'am."

"Good." She put a plate of old fashioned chicken casserole in front of him with a glass of milk before she took a seat beside him. He could feel her trying to decide how worried to be, her thoughts rubbing along his as he picked up a fork to eat. "I really am fine." Alaric offered after he'd eaten a few forkfuls.

She looked at him, her eyes sad. She knew he was lying, but she took his hand and nodded anyway. "Eat."

* * *

He let her mother him for several days while he spent time contemplating his course of action. By day he would spend time with his mother and his Keepers, and spend several hours attending the basic business of being the leader of his people in a time of turmoil. His people were scared, and uncertain where to go. It was work to calm them and set up plans to keep them safe.

By night, he would drop into meditation to play through everything he knew, and when he would finally fall asleep, he would dream.

Sometimes they were sweet dreams of time spent with Mason, memories of things they had shared, of his life before they met. Sometimes they were filled with Mason screaming himself hoarse. Sometimes they were repeated images of Mason dying, and killing.

He had been in the old house over a week the night he slipped from meditation into sleep, only his dreams became more like visions.

Memory not his own spilled out, images taking shape of a time nearly lost to history. It was family legend, myth more than truth, or so he had always thought. Long before the clan had come to these shores, a leader of their clan had been left bereft, her children and sisters murdered, her husband dragged to his death.

As if he were there, Alaric watched her approach the globe, roaring out her anguish, demanding of it a means to take her vengeance. Her mind opened, and she took…everything.

As a leader of the clan, a Shadow has access to all the gifts within the living clan, all those whose blood is tied to his or hers. But that night, as she screamed her pain into the bright light of the orb, all the gifts ever given were hers to command, from the time when the orb was first used. Death was no boundary. She could see things, know things, she could turn minds, plumb the depths of the souls of her enemies. She could vanish from memories and sight. She could use the dead or living as puppets of her will. She was unstoppable and the vengeance she took was unthinkable.

Alaric sat up in his bed, his body covered in a cold sweat. A plan filled him. It was not something he would ever have considered before, but the world he faced now was no longer the same as it had been.

He told himself that he wouldn't take it as far as she did, but if he accepted that kind of power from the globe...He stood and paced a bit. He even knew where he should start. There was the man that Mason had worked for in D.C. Mason knew there were people other than Shades who worked there.

Alaric just needed to find Adam Darvin and convince him to let Alaric in, let Alaric find Shallon. Let Alaric kill Shallon.

He shoved his feet into his jeans and then his shoes and checked the time. It was barely one in the morning. If he moved quickly, he could be gone before anyone else was even awake. He threw together a change of clothes, his wallet, finding an old army duffle bag in the closet, he shoved everything in it.

Then he pulled his presence in tight so that his movement wouldn't disturb the sensitive people sleeping around him. He snuck down the hall and down the stairs, into the living room. The floors creaked, and he stilled, listening to be sure no one had heard.

When he was sure, he continued out the door and into the cool night. It still bothered him that even with all the globe had helped him learn, he hadn't deciphered the identity of whoever had betrayed them in Arizona. All he had were vague ideas.

But he had Shallon's name. He'd focus on that. He would find Shallon, and before he watched him die, Alaric would take the information he wanted from his mind. The globe glowed softly, making the way to it easy. He dropped his bag outside the barrier and made his way inside.

He stopped short of touching it. He needed to ready himself first. He inhaled deeply and held it, gathering all of his thoughts and needs, all of the emotion that drove him and pushing it out with his exhale. He needed to be clear going into this.

Slowly, one by one, he dropped all of the walls, all of the shields that controlled his gifts, that kept him from fully taking what the globe could give him. It was terrifyingly vulnerable, and he shivered in the chill air. He was half sure that Bryan would feel what he was doing and try to stop him.

Alaric spread his arms wide and leaned inward, falling into the globe.

Everything went white, hot and furious, scrubbing at his every particle until he felt himself come apart. Energy raced through him, coming back again and again, slamming into him and tossing him around inside it until he was screaming silently.

Images slammed through him, memories, emotions stretching back in time, snippets of lives, the past, the present, random glimpses of possible futures. Voices whispered, yelled, turned him around and dropped him to his knees with their screaming.

In the middle of all of it he saw Mason.

Alaric grabbed onto him, onto the reason he was doing this and let go of the fear. His body trembled as he was put back together and expelled from the globe.

Its light had diminished greatly when he finally opened his eyes. If it hadn't wakened the others, they would know soon enough that he had done something unimaginable. It would recharge in the sun though, and dawn was only an hour or so away now.

Alaric climbed to his feet, still catching his breath. Power flowed through him, his skin glowing with the residual energy. His perception was altered in ways he couldn't even articulate. It was like nothing he'd ever imagined. He stepped out of the grove and gathered his bag, pulling a mantle of near invisibility about himself as he headed for the main road.

Knowledge filled him, a heady mix of history and the ability to gather information from the world around him without effort. He spared a glance at the house. His mother would worry. Bryan and Sahara would try to find him. Control him.

Let them look. It would keep them out of his hair for a while. He was too far beyond controlling. He knew what he had to do, and he was ready now.

Chapter Four

Raven pulled the phone out of her pocket, staring down at it for a long minute. Adam had told her to wait at least two weeks before using it. Despite everything that had happened, they weren't quite there yet.

The night was still around her. Maddie was out in the dark, hunting. Zero was in the loft of the barn, though Raven doubted the girl was sleeping. She didn't sleep much anymore.

With a sigh, Raven thumbed the button to dial the only pre-programmed number in the phone, not surprised when Adam didn't answer. She shoved the phone back in her pocket and turned to look around her.

The land around them was not the most hospitable for Shades, and she knew they were not safe there, despite Lonan's assurances that the tribe would shelter them for as long as they needed.

The night felt vast, and despite the people around her, she felt small and alone. Her grandfather's death had hit her harder than she had let on. She was the last of her line. Inside her the memories of her family lived on, but they were little comfort for her as she stood under a canopy of stars that multiplied the feeling of loneliness.

With Mason gone, she was also the last of Adam's Shade operatives. Somehow, in the chaos following the destruction of Shady Lakes, she had become the de-facto leader of the survivors from the village. In the last two nights, more of them had found their way to the reservation. Aside from Connor and the boys, three more adults and two more children had found them.

All of them seemed to be looking to her for guidance. The problem was, she had no guidance to offer. She turned as she felt Connor approach. "Was wondering where you went." Connor said, his voice soft.

"Just getting some air." Raven responded.

"It was getting a bit much in there." Connor stuck his hands in his pockets and turned his face up to the half-moon. "They aren't wrong though."

She nodded, turning her own face up to the light. "I know."

Someone had betrayed them. Someone had told the 8th Battalion where to find them. They had no way of knowing who. The town had always been a safe haven, a place where Shades could live in peace, but someone who knew the town had told the 8th Battalion where to find them. And there, they found Mason, if Zero was to be believed.

The trouble was, she couldn't begin to rule anyone out, not even the survivors inside the small house behind her. Not even the man standing next to her. He had, after all, only come to Shady Lake a few days before she had shown up with Mason and Zero. It could even be someone she had never met.

"Charlie told me that you worked for the government." Connor said, his tone light.

She crossed her arms and turned to look at him. He was taller than her by at least six inches, his hair a dark red that spoke of his Celtic roots. A few days growth covered his jaw, and his blue eyes were still turned toward the moon. "I did. But that seems like another lifetime now."

They stood silently for a long moment, letting the moonlight bath them. Behind her, Raven felt something building, then claws dug into her brain seconds before a scream split the night air. She turned, racing for the source, Connor a half step behind her. Zero's mind surged into hers, dumping adrenaline soaked terror that nearly dropped Raven to her knees. She reached for Connor, who supported her and helped her climb the ladder into the loft.

Zero was tossing on the cot, the smell of sweat and urine filling the air. She was still tightly in the grip of the nightmare as Raven reached her, sinking to kneel beside the cot and tentatively reach a hand for the girl's head. "You might want to stand back," she said over her shoulder to Connor.

She heard him shuffle back as she wiped a hand across Zero's forehead, pushing past the terror to try to find the controls that would bring her some calm. She was dropped almost instantly into the landscape of the dream, a blood-soaked room where Zero stood, strapped to some contraption that held her upright while needles pierced into her back, feeding something into her. Fury flooded her, keeping pace with her fear and the pain of wounds Raven couldn't find.

The walls were splattered with blood and Raven couldn't initially tell where it had come from, until Zero's head turned. There was a pair of boots with bloody stumps sticking out of them on the floor in front of Zero and as she looked beyond Zero's pain and fear, she could see chunks of flesh, torn clothing and brain matter.

Zero's screams echoed in her head, and distantly she realized they were echoing out of her mouth as well. She fought the onslaught of fear and fury to try to send calming waves into Zero's body. There was the sound of laughter and Raven followed the sound to a window into the room.

She recognized the man behind the glass as Zero's father, the man who had tormented her and tried to turn her into a weapon.

Energy flowed into her, letting her disconnect from the dream and ride out into the clearer space in Zero's head. She inundated Zero's body with warm healing energy and felt the dream melt away. Zero shifted, clinging to her mentally for a moment before pushing her away.

When Raven opened her eyes, Connor was behind her, a hand on her head. Zero's eyes opened and met hers. Connor stepped back and cleared his throat. "I should go check on the boys."

Zero didn't move until he had disappeared down the ladder. She sat up then, rubbing hands up over her face and head as she drew in a deep breath. "I'm okay," she said pre-emptively.

Raven shifted from her knees to a sitting position on the floor. "No, you're not. How could you be?" She tried to make sense of what she had seen, but she only had part of the story, and that part of the story made her not even want to know the rest.

"He…" Zero closed her eyes and Raven could almost see the scene replay behind them. "I killed a man that day." Her voice was soft, nearly a whisper. "I was thirteen. He…the experiments…."

A tear slipped past her lash-less eyelids and she shook her head. "It was after the last of the Shadow treatments. I wasn't manifesting the gifts he wanted me too. So he…provoked them."

Raven frowned. "Provoked them?"

Zero stood. The t-shirt and underwear she was wearing to sleep in were soaked through, with both sweat and urine. "That machine…he used it to flood me with...I don't know, but they stripped control of my emotions and then he poured rage into my brain until..." She swallowed and shook her head again, as if she could clear it of the memory. "He sent a man in to hurt me."

Her hand fell to a thick scar on her thigh, tracing over the four inches of raised tissue. She blinked, but her eyes were still distant. "I fought it. I didn't want..." She exhaled slowly. "The blood was all that was left."

They were silent then. Raven couldn't begin to know what to say. She stood slowly and took Zero's hand in hers. She squeezed it, letting some comfort warm her hand and feed into Zero.

"I'm sorry." Raven offered. "I wish there was some way I could take those memories away."

Zero stiffened. "No. I just got them back." She pulled her hand away and paced over to the ladder and then back. "As awful as they are, I need them. I need to know who I am, what he did to me. What he turned me into."

"Zero, you don't have to become whatever it was he was trying to make you."

"No? I did that day. That man *exploded* because my brain reached inside of him and pulled him apart. I didn't have a choice then."

"He was hurting you." Raven tried to reach for her, but she pulled away.

"And that makes it okay?" Zero pulled her shirt off and turned her back to Raven. "What about all of the men who did this? Should I have exploded all of them too?"

Raven stepped closer, turning Zero's back toward the light coming from the overhead bulb. Scars from some kind of blade marked her shoulders, and there were one-inch squares of flesh that were discolored, their centers pierced, probably from that machine she'd seen in Raven's dream.

She lifted a hand to Zero's skin, reading the lingering effects of trauma, and stepping back as she realized that the squares of skin weren't her own. "What...what did he do?"

Zero moved away, dropping her shirt. "I don't know. I was usually asleep when he did that."

"It was part of his treatments? Experiments?" Raven asked.

Zero shrugged. She was clearly done with the conversation. "I need a shower." She stripped out of her wet underwear and grabbed a towel that was hanging from a nail, wrapping it around her as she shoved her feet into her shoes. At the top of the ladder, she paused, looking at Raven again. "By the way, Parker's mother died. And so did the others who got out with Alaric."

"Did he contact you?" Raven asked.

Zero shook her head. "No, he's... I don't know really. But all the stuff I got from him before he went dark is unpacking slowly. Only he and two of his Keepers survived."

She descended the ladder then and Raven followed, emerging from the barn as Maddie came into view, dragging a deer with her. She stopped just inside the light cast from the lamp over the barn door, licking the blood from her whiskers.

Leaving the deer in the dirt, Maddie met Raven's eyes before she padded past her into the barn. A few minutes later, she emerged in her human form, buttoning up her shirt. "Figured I should help feed us." Maddie said as she came to a stop beside Raven. "I did a sweep of the village. The 8th Battalion is gone. They didn't leave much. No signs they left anyone behind to watch for people coming back."

'That's good at least." Raven replied with a sigh. "We can't go back there, of course. But, if anyone new comes along, they won't get grabbed. That's something."

"Is it?" Maddie asked. "I should go get Lonan to help me with this deer."

Raven nodded to herself as Maddie headed toward the house. She couldn't begrudge the girl her attitude. She'd lost a lot. But then, so had they all at this point. With another sigh, Raven headed back to the gathered Shades. There were decisions to be made, and for whatever reason, they were all looking to her to make them.

* * *

Raven watched Connor tuck the boys in to sleep in the small spare bedroom. The sun wasn't quite up, and the house had gone quiet when the rest of the Shades had scattered to the other homes offering them shelter.

Lonan touched her shoulder, nodding to her. She followed him to the small kitchen. "What is it?"

"It would seem the 8th Battalion isn't content with raids on towns of Shades." Lonan said, pouring himself a cup of coffee.

"What do you mean?" Raven asked. She sank into one of the chairs around the table, her eyes tracing his movements as he added milk and stirred his cup before he too sat.

"There are troops massing along the Arizona border, and it looks like they'll be invading soon. There's talk of a militia defending the border and the tribe will be sending men and women to join them."

Raven scrubbed her fingers through her scalp, loosening the tightly braided hair. "I can't believe this is happening," she muttered to herself. The whole thing seemed like some prolonged nightmare she couldn't wake up from. "When?" she asked, looking up at her childhood friend.

"Few hours. I'm leaving the truck and Tusa's old Chevy, catching a ride with Joe."

She nodded. "Okay. I understand. If you want us to move on—"

He held up a hand to stop her. "I told you that you'd be safe here. You don't have to go anywhere."

"What happens if they get by you and they find us here? Do you know what they'll do to your people?" Raven asked. She sighed wished she could find a deep dark forest pond to sink into, so she could block all of the insanity out for a while.

"Whether they find you here or not, the 8th Battalion will not be kind to my people." Lonan said softly. "You should stay. Rest. When you are ready to rejoin the fight, you will know."

She sighed, wondering if she'd ever be ready to rejoin a fight she never wanted to be part of. All of her work with Darvin had been aimed at preventing this very thing, and it had amounted to nothing.

"I'm going to try to get some sleep." Raven said after a long silence. She pushed her chair back and stood, offering Lonan a tight smile before she made her way to the living room. Connor was already stretched out under a blanket on the floor.

"Everything okay?" Connor asked as she spread out her blanket on the low sofa.

"Yeah. I'm just...tired I guess." Raven settled in, hoping her brain would settle as well. She'd feel better if she could reach Darvin. He might know how to get them out of Arizona safely. Or at least a place they could go.

No matter what Lonan said, they couldn't stay here.

Chapter Five

"Damn it!" Bryan exclaimed, falling back from the barrier around the orb. Whatever Alaric had done had left the orb drained and its barrier at near lock down levels. He pulled a hand through hair that was more gray than it had been even a year ago and turned to head back to the house.

It had been nearly three days since they'd woken to find Alaric gone, not just physically. He'd left no trace of himself, no psychic trail to follow. Emily was beside herself with worry.

It was his fault. As Alaric's first Keeper, it was his job to know the mental state of his leader, to keep tabs on his emotions. He should have known that Alaric was never going to let go of Mason's loss.

"Stop blaming yourself." Sahara said, suddenly beside him.

He didn't even bother to deny it. She could see the truth. "Who else should I blame?" Bryan asked irritably.

"Alaric, for starters." Sahara responded, one eyebrow lifting. "He's the leader here, not you. He's the one who is supposed to be managing the clan, not you. He's the one who ran off in the middle of the night, not you."

"Yeah, okay, I get it." Bryan growled. "Not sure Emily sees it that way."

Sahara chuckled lightly. "You should know better than assuming you know what a woman is thinking. Emily doesn't blame you either. She knows that her son is being driven by emotion. She says that's one of the downfalls of being an empath. Emotion can overtake all the rest."

"Maybe, but we should have seen it coming."

"He blocked us out, Bryan. Accept it. He was wrong." Her hand on his arm stopped him. "Let go of it and let's move forward."

"How?"

She smiled, but it wasn't a reassuring smile. "There are other ways to track him."

"After three days?" Bryan asked, assuming she meant her cat.

She shrugged. "Depends. If we combine our efforts, I'm sure we could find his trail."

His eyes narrowed at her. "What are you saying?"

"I've been talking with Emily. We think we have an idea. Come inside."

He followed as she led him to the porch, trying to read her intentions, but she just held the door for him. He stepped into the house, blinking a little to clear his eyes as the light shifted from the bright sunshine to artificial light. "Victoria." He was surprised to see her, surprised he hadn't felt her approach.

"Bryan," she acknowledged with a nod. "I hear our fearless leader has flown the coop." There was no malice or blame in her words, just a calm tone that belied the seriousness of the situation. "You think he's gone to find the men who killed the Shade?"

Bryan nodded, moving to help Emily as she appeared from the kitchen with a tray. She thanked him with a touch, following him as he set the tray on the coffee table and reaching to pour a cup of tea from the pot. She handed the tea to Victoria, then poured one for herself, settling into the arm chair to Victoria's left.

"I can't imagine any other reason he'd disappear like that." Emily said softly. "*I can't even find him.*"

"Well, love mucks with the senses, that's for certain. Quadruple that for empaths, and with the power of his gift..." Victoria said. She set her tea down after sipping at it and gestured at the other chair. "Sit down, you're making me nervous."

Bryan sat, Sahara taking the arm of his chair as her spot, her eyes on Victoria. Bryan rubbed a hand over Sahara's back, though he wasn't sure if he was comforting her or himself, before looking back at Victoria. "So, what is it you have in mind?"

Victoria smiled, one hand toying with the end of one long, silver braid. "For starters, we're going to need to get past that barrier."

Bryan snorted. "I've been trying for three days."

Victoria sipped at her tea and sat back on the couch. "Maybe you try too hard. When we're done talking, I'll go see what can be done."

"Not sure what you think you can do that I haven't, but yeah, sure."

She smiled at him. "I'm not meaning any slight, Bryan. My touch is lighter perhaps, less threatening. And it has known me longer. Now then, once we get access to the orb, we should be able to understand what Alaric has done, and then we can begin to locate him."

"Just like that?" Bryan asked, the skepticism clear in his voice.

"Of course not." Victoria responded. "We'll have to get creative."

"I'm not sure I like the sound of that." Bryan admitted, shifting in the chair. "Creative how?"

"It's a very old trick." Victoria said. "We help you and Sahara here combine your own gifts, and maybe loan you a few of ours."

Bryan frowned at her. He had, of course, heard of such things, but no one had tried them in recent memory. Not that he knew of anyway.

Victoria actually laughed. "I guess I can still surprise you, even after all these years."

"You know how to do that?" Sahara asked, glancing down at Bryan before looking back at Victoria.

"I've even seen it done. Of course, I was just a girl, and it was a demonstration, not something done for a need as important as this one, but yes.

"It's related to true Shadowing." Emily said, meeting his eyes and holding the gaze. "My mother's people called it stitching. There was a family legend where a Shade, a Shadow, a Sage and a Shifter were all successfully stitched into a single person for a time."

"Legends are one thing." Sahara said. "How do we know this will work?"

"We don't." Victoria said. "But, what other options are we left with? We find him, or we leave him out there alone until he comes to his senses and comes home."

"You know Alaric." Emily said. "Do you think that's going to happen before he does something he'll regret?"

Bryan shook his head. "No, I don't."

"All right then, I suggest we get started." Victoria pushed herself to her feet. "Emily, you get these two prepped. I'll go see if I can get that damn globe to open up."

Bryan watched her go, still not sure exactly what was about to happen, but Victoria was right. They had to try. Somewhere out in the world Alaric was stalking the men who had killed Mason Jerah, and when he caught up with them…he didn't want to think about what exactly Alaric would do to them…what he *could* do to them with all the power at his command.

* * *

Bryan and Sahara watched as Emily and Victoria set up a ritual circle outside the chapel of the orb, and he could feel Sahara tracking their movements. The idea of what they were going to try made her uncomfortable, but at least part of that was a reflection of his own discomfort. Even though no one had said it out loud, Sahara had gathered that what they were about to try leaned a little into the darker aspect of Shadow work.

Emily had done her best to prepare them for what would happen, but Bryan's skepticism was affecting Sahara as they waited. He lifted a hand to touch her back lightly. "You okay with this?" he asked.

She shrugged. "In theory, but I'll admit I'm not completely comfortable with…" She waved her hand toward the two women and the space they were preparing. "How about you?"

He sighed, his eyes lifting to the path that led to the orb. "Victoria managed to get the orb to open up, so we might have a chance."

"How reassuring." Sahara said dryly. "Did she say what it was Alaric did to it?"

Bryan's face tightened and he crossed his arms. "Yeah. It isn't good. With what he took from the orb, he could kill someone with little more than the desire to do so. We're not sure where he got the idea, and it's something no one has done in…a very long time."

"Like what we're about to do?" Sahara asked.

"Kind of." Bryan affirmed.

"We're ready." Emily said, gesturing for Bryan and Sahara to join them in the circle.

Bryan's hand slipped into Sahara's and together they walked the perimeter of the circle before stepping inside. The air was cooler somehow inside. Bryan kissed her hand and let go of it, taking a step away.

Emily smiled softly and moved to Bryan's side, guiding him a few steps to the right. Victoria approached Sahara, her steps deliberate. "Now, I know you've got a good mind, or you couldn't be a Keeper. Do you know how to control those shields?"

Sahara nodded. "Somewhat. Bryan's taught me a lot."

Victoria nodded. "Good. I want you to try to resist me."

Sahara frowned at her, but when Bryan felt the *push* Victoria made against her shields, and Sahara's response as she understood and used the techniques Bryan had taught her to shore them up, and then to *push* back.

Victoria chuckled and nodded. "Yes, that will do. Emily, are you set with Bryan?"

"Yes, we're set."

Victoria guided Sahara to stand across from Bryan, then took her position in the circle, between them. Emily stood across from Victoria and together the two women raised their arms.

Sahara could feel the power they raised around them, making the circle a place separate from the world around it. Once the barrier was up, Victoria moved to stand behind Sahara, while Emily went to stand behind Bryan.

"We begin." Victoria said, her hands coming down on Sahara's shoulders. "Open your shields to us, let us become one."

Bryan let his shields down for Emily, watching Sahara as she inhaled and let her shields down. Emily held them back while they watched Victoria fill Sahara's mind, gentle, but insistent. Sahara shifted her weight and fought the urge to fight as Victoria delved into the corners of her very being.

Judging by the look on Sahara's face, the shift took her by surprise, but some part of her recognized that Victoria had triggered it. It was the cat that had what they wanted after all.

Sahara dropped to all fours, Victoria following her down, kneeling in the grass beside her. Bryan sank to his knees in front of her, Emily still holding his shoulder. Emily guided Bryan more fully into the connection, readying him for what came next.

It had been decided that Sahara would be the one to carry the gifts they would combine, leaving Bryan able to interact with Alaric once they found him. Bryan was nearly an outsider in his own mind as Emily *pulled* at spots in

Bryan's mind, passing long tendrils to Victoria who *stitched* them into the center of Sahara's brain that he knew held the instincts of the cat.

Emily released Bryan, letting him remain in the connection, but no longer controlling him, and moved to offer her own mind up to Victoria, who similarly pulled threads from Emily and *stitched* them in. When she was done, Emily fell moved back, and that left only Sahara and Victoria.

"We're almost done. You can shift back now."

At first, Sahara wasn't sure she could, Bryan could feel her testing out her control, and after a deep breath and taking back most of the control Victoria had, Sahara shifted, then eased back so that she was sitting.

"Good. Now, pay attention." Victoria strummed over a tendril that had come from Emily. Bryan eased himself back further from the connection, watching as Victoria gave Sahara a brief lesson in how to use the gifts they'd given her.

Victoria nudged him, and he nodded, pulling a glamor over his face, giving Sahara a chance to understand how to see through it. Victoria and Emily withdrew completely, leaving just Bryan and Sahara. She pulled him in strumming over the lines that had been stitched into her while Victoria and Emily started to dismantle the circle.

The feeling of *Alaric* filled them as she stroked the line from Emily, like a psychic scent. Sahara touched another, and they could *see* the auras of everything around her. It would take some getting used to, for both of them.

Sahara shivered as the barrier was undone and the cool air touched her skin. The shirt and pants she'd been wearing when they began were torn from the shifting, but not enough to fall off her.

Bryan took her hand and helped her stand, an arm wrapping around her waist to steady her before they moved toward the pull of the orb. She felt it more strongly than she ever had.

Emily had warned them that it might take time to adjust, and that the open connections could be draining. She hadn't been wrong. They weren't even sure she'd have the ability to verbalize anything. They could end up having to rely on the psychic connection between them.

The orb pulsed warmly as they entered the chapel, it welcomed them and pulled them closer, offering warmth and strength. They would bask in that strength until they were ready, and then, Sahara and Bryan would set out in search of Alaric, hopefully finding him before he stepped over the line that he could never come back from.

* * *

It was an odd sensation, using Emily's sense of her son's psychic signature, Sahara's hunting instincts, Bryan's ability to see through a Shadow's tricks, but after the first twenty-four hours, it was coming easier to Sahara, even if it was exhausting for her.

The rest stop was all but deserted. The general population was too scared to venture long distances they didn't have to, leaving only truckers using the interstates for the most part.

With the day half over, those who had stopped to spend the night had moved on, and those who would come to spend the night hadn't yet arrived. That left one truck parked near the bathrooms, and one down near the exit, the driver stretching out road weary muscles.

69

Bryan guided their rented car to a spot near the bathrooms, glancing at Sahara before he opened his door. He left her there, knowing their connection would alert him if there was any trouble.

They had collectively decided that Alaric's first step would have to be Washington D.C. That was where they had headed. Of course, the capitol was under lockdown, as they recovered from the murders of the president, and the riots that followed. Alaric had gotten as far as Springfield. It was there that Sahara had picked up his scent, for lack of a better word.

He had taken a hotel room and spent a day scanning the area, into D.C. and must have found something to go on, because he turned west then. They had followed the trail to Morgantown, where the trail went cold.

It had taken Sahara the better part of a day to pick up the scent again, and it was evident that Alaric had found someone to question. The man had turned up in a local ER just the day before, suffering from amnesia and claiming some shining angel had taken his memories.

That led them to another motel, outside of Pittsburgh. The anti-Shade movement was large in Pittsburgh, with rallies and marches and protests aimed at getting the city government to ban Shades from the city. It had distracted Alaric for a short time.

It had been a fitful night with little sleep, at least for him. The exhaustion pulled at them both and they had set out that morning without a real idea of where they were going, only that Alaric had started west again.

Sahara was circling the bathroom building, Bryan's head was buzzing with all the psychic input she was sending him, impressions of people who had been here, where they were going. It was as she approached the men's room door that she found it; Alaric had let his mantle of invisibility slip, he'd needed to be seen.

Sahara stood, a hand on the warm stone of the building, letting her borrowed senses read what had happened as Bryan emerged. "He was here." Sahara said, her voice deep and resonant in her chest. "Got a ride with a trucker headed for Chicago."

Bryan nodded. "Chicago it is then. Do you know where?"

Sahara shook her head. "Once he had a ride, he buttoned back up. Truck for Allied Pharmaceuticals."

Together, they got back in the car and started out. Sahara slumped a little in her seat as they pulled out onto the freeway. Bryan's hand brushed her thigh and she lifted her head to smile at him. "*I'm okay. Just tired.*"

He nodded. "Get some rest. I'll get us to Chicago."

Chapter Six

Alaric stood in front of the building for a long time. It was much like any other office building in Chicago, a gleaming façade of glass and steel filled with people working diligently. The understated sign above the address said "Bellington Tower," a twenty-one-story office building that was home to exactly one business, "Keller Science."

His research told him that Keller Science was in the business of bettering human existence through science. They had brought several technologies to market in the last ten years, most in the medical field. But that was not what brought him to Bellington Tower.

Under the exterior of a highly secured business building, Alaric knew another kind of business lurked. The kind he had been looking for, and in that building, his target waited, even if he didn't know it yet. Alaric opened the door and entered the lobby, smiling at the guards sitting behind the lobby desk.

"Good morning, I'm Alaric Lambrecht. I'm here to see Adam Darvin."

The bigger of the two guards looked him over, then picked up the phone. He spoke quietly for a moment, then hung up. "Someone will be down to see you shortly."

Alaric nodded and moved away from the desk to peruse the lobby and the people moving through it. Most of them had no idea the darker uses of the building, or the sublevels below them hiding former government agents.

"Mr. Lambrecht?"

Alaric turned from the painting and raked his eyes over the approaching man in a suit, his brown hair slicked back, his dark eyes taking stock of their surroundings before lifting to meet Alaric's. He might have appeared to nearly anyone to be just another businessman, but Alaric could see his shoes were well worn and built for stability and movement, his hands were calloused and accustomed to handling weapons, and he knew the placement of every single person and possible exit in the lobby where they stood.

"Mr. Darvin, thank you for seeing me." Alaric reached out to shake his hand, gleaning knowledge he needed as they shook hands, assuring himself that this was the man who could help him.

"I was uncertain what this is about?"

Alaric met his eyes, the cold fire of his pain leaching out into his veins. "This is about revenge, Mr. Darvin. Revenge and putting an end to the 8th Battalion."

Darvin responded by raising an eyebrow. "While I appreciate the delivery, I'm not sure why you've come to me for this?"

"Please, let's not waste each other's time. I know who you are and what you do. I know more about you than you might think anyone could." Alaric's hand strayed to the pendants around his neck, his thumb rubbing over them, drawing the man's eyes to them.

Darvin reacted predictably, his eyes narrowing, his breathing tightening. "Where did you get that?"

Alaric dropped his hand. "Mason was…" His throat closed, and he had to cough to clear it. "We were lovers."

Darvin glanced around them, then back at Alaric. "Were? Is he…?"

Alaric's jaw clenched, and he nodded. "He was killed by the 8th Battalion."

He could sense the recoil, the scrambling thoughts, the slow burning anger. "I see you cared for him." Alaric said. "Help me put the men who did it in the ground."

Darvin looked him over. "You're not a Shade."

"No, I'm a whole different kind of animal, Mr. Darvin. I can do things you have never seen." Alaric searched the man's unprotected mind. "For example, give me five minutes with the spy you caught yesterday, and I'll tell you exactly where he's been, who he's seen and talked to and what his mission is."

Darvin's mouth dropped open. "How did you… you're a Shadow." He shook his head. "You know I can't just…"

Alaric smiled because he knew he had the man. He held out a card with the phone number to the burner phone in his pocket. "No, but you can reach me here. Feel free to check my background. Let me know when you're ready. Just remember that every day you wait is a day they get closer."

He put on his sunglasses and turned on his heel, walking out the front door of the building, not surprised to find Bryan waiting for him. Alaric had felt him when he and Sahara had arrived in Chicago. It was only a matter of time before Bryan found him. "Not now."

"Yes now." Bryan countered, grabbing Alaric's shoulder. "You can't keep shutting us out."

Alaric glared at him. "Last I checked, I was in charge, not you." He didn't have time for distractions. If he wanted to, he could make it so Bryan would never distract him again. Alaric pushed the temptation away. He swore to himself he wouldn't get lost in the rage and power.

"Except you're not, are you?" Bryan responded. "You haven't been in charge since Riley and Mason—"

Alaric pulled himself out of Bryan's grasp and stalked away. Bryan was not going to be easily dissuaded though. "Don't you walk away from me, Alaric!"

Alaric whirled on him. "Who do you think you are?" He shoved Bryan, but Bryan didn't budge.

"Your fucking Keeper." Bryan responded, shoving back. "But you make that pretty damn difficult when you disappear in the middle of the night." Bryan grabbed him psychically and held on when Alaric started to pull away. "You have an obligation to your clan, Alaric."

Alaric stopped pulling away and Bryan loosened up on him. "Besides, your mother is worried sick."

"I can't be the leader they need me to be. Not now." Alaric said when the silence had grown long between them.

"No, you can't. Not when you've got your head so far twisted around someone who wasn't even a part of the clan." Bryan sighed and let go of him completely. "I knew the minute I laid eyes on him, Alaric. He was never going to be more than pain and misery."

Alaric bristled and took a step back. Bryan held up both hands. "Look, I get it. He saved my life. I owe him…and if he were alive, I'd be right beside you, fighting to save him. But he's dead, Alaric." Bryan's guilt was palpable, but Alaric wasn't going to be swayed and Bryan knew it. "What you're doing…what you plan to do…"

Bryan looked at him, his eyes dark with disapproval. "That is not what your gifts are meant for."

"Maybe not." Alaric said, already preparing to pull the psychic mantle around him again to hide himself from Bryan and the others. "But if it ends with the men who killed Mason dead, I don't care."

He shoved Bryan physically and psychically, laying a mental mine of confusion and disorientation before pulling his mantle around himself and running away into the bustling noonday crowd, disappearing from eyes both physical and psychic.

* * *

Finding Darvin had been work. He'd nearly killed the first man he'd found with the information. He'd nearly *wanted* to kill him. After that first one, he'd figured out how to get what he needed without stripping his subject so completely.

It hadn't helped that Darvin was damn good at hiding, not just himself, but his entire shadow agency. They had been disavowed by the government, but that hadn't stopped them. Darvin had been prepared for years. The facility under Bellington tower had been functional for a long time.

Alaric knew that Darvin would call. Just as he knew that if he took the next step on this road there would be no turning back. He told himself it didn't matter. Nothing mattered but finding Shallon.

He wanted to tear the entire 8th Battalion into pieces, leave them incapable of waging their ideological war against anyone different than them. He wanted to find the Colonel who had held them both prisoner and rip his mind into shreds.

In the dark of his motel room, Alaric sat and waited, his mind scanning the city around him. He skipped from mind to mind, dismissing those just going about their mundane lives. He was convinced that the 8th Battalion had operatives in the city, in the military still, in the government. Just like the spy Darvin had in custody. One of them would give Alaric the information he wanted.

All he had to do was find the one.

He inhaled and pulled himself slowly back inside himself as the phone rang. He lifted it, a slow smile creeping across his face. "Hello Mr. Darvin. I can be there in less than an hour."

Alaric slipped his feet into shoes and gathered his belongings. He would not be returning to this place. He stepped out into a cool evening and hailed a cab to take him to the building that he knew was but a façade for the facility below.

Darvin met him at the door with a visitor's badge and a tight smile. "Prove to me that you can do what you said, and there may be a place for you."

"I won't disappoint you. Just show me to him."

Darvin escorted him to an elevator and down three levels. "You can leave your things in my office." They dropped his bag off and then Darvin took Alaric into a room with a window looking into a small interrogation room. "They're bringing him up from his cell. So far we can get nothing more from him than his name and a spew of religious dogma."

Alaric watched through the window as two big guards dragged a smaller man into the room. He was in an orange jumpsuit and chains and he didn't fight as they pushed him into a chair and fastened his cuffs to the table.

"What is his name?" Alaric asked as he observed the guards leaving the room.

"I thought you were a mind reader." Darvin said dryly.

Alaric glanced aside at him. "I was being polite."

"Duffy." Darvin responded, looking in on the man. "Clifford Duffy."

Alaric nodded and waited another beat or two. "I should warn you, if I have to dig too deeply, it could damage him."

When the man began to fidget, Alaric went to the door beside the window.

He took a deep breath and opened the door, not looking directly at the man at first. He explored his aura, the vile psychic stench that wafted off him. Vitriol and hatred permeated the aura. His foremost thoughts nearly screamed across the room at him, thoughts of abomination, desire to convert others to believe as he did. There was fear... lots of fear. Alaric latched onto that and followed it deeper.

Fear of contamination, of being disgraced, fear of the evil his superiors railed about, fear that he would die... fear that he wouldn't die... fear that it was all wrong. Alaric smiled coldly. "Clifford Duffy, you and I are going to have a conversation, and you will tell me everything I need to know."

"You're wasting your time. I have nothing to say."

"On the contrary Clifford. You have already told me so much about you, and we haven't even started." He gathered the easy information as he stepped closer. "You have a sister in California, and she has two children. You don't get along, but you love her fiercely."

Duffy looked up at him, clearly confused. "You believe the bullshit you spiel, mostly, but you doubt your leaders in the 8th Battalion, not for what they do or do not believe, but because you aren't told everything. You like to wear your underwear a size too small because you think it makes you look like you have a bigger dick than you do. Now, shall we dig deeper?"

Alaric put a hand on his shoulder, stepping behind him. He lifted his eyes to the mirror, knowing that Darvin was on the other side watching him. Alaric pulled Duffy back, so that his head was against Alaric's chest.

"I hope you're recording." Alaric said to the mirror before he closed his eyes and sank himself into the very panic soaked brain before him. It wasn't so much like he was reading Duffy, it was as if he *became* Duffy. The knowledge came to him with little effort and he sent it out through a voice that sounded like the man under his hand as if he were giving a report. Alaric exhausted everything Duffy knew about the 8th Battalion and its leadership, which in the grand scheme of things was less than Alaric had hoped for, but he knew it was enough to secure his place with Darvin.

He pulled up and out, letting go of Duffy and stepping back. He braced against the wall as he fell back into himself, the room spinning. His skin felt tight and strange and he was soaked through with sweat. That was as close to the shadowing talent his tribe had been named for than he'd ever been or seen.

Duffy was slumped in his seat, nearly slipping off his chair. The door opened, Darvin pointing at him and gesturing for Alaric to follow him.

When they were back in his office, Alaric sat while Darvin paced. "Can I get you something?"

"I'm going to need to eat, something with protein." Alaric said, rubbing at the low throb beginning in his temples. "And sleep for a few hours."

Darvin nodded, stopping mid circuit from desk to door and squinted at Alaric. "You going to explain what kind of Shadow you are?"

Alaric smirked. "Let's just say that there are no other Shadows like me, Mr. Darvin."

"I'm still investigating you, I will find out. I was under the impression that all that was left of the Shadows were the scattered and unpredictable skill with mind reading."

Alaric sighed and dropped his hand. "The gifts are waning, but some of us still possess them."

Darvin stepped closer. "What I saw in there didn't look like waning gifts. And that doesn't tell me what you are."

Alaric shrugged. "I carry the cumulative gifts of my tribe, Mr. Darvin. I am not your average mind reader." He inhaled and let it out slowly. "I can help you stop them. You just have to give me the chance."

"The cumulative gifts of your clan?" Darvin asked, crossing his arms and looking Alaric over. "What exactly does that mean?"

Alaric shrugged and exhaled slowly. "The gifts vary, from the simple ability to read and interpret body language instantly, to mind reading, empathic ability, to precognition, mind manipulation, memory tampering, even complete reprogramming...though to be honest, no one's demonstrated that ability in decades."

"So you can do all of that then?"

"In theory. I haven't tested all of it, and the flashes of precognition are nearly impossible to predict or access on demand...but yeah."

"Well, that sounds like a handy bag of tricks." Darvin crossed his arms. "So, tell me about you and Mason."

Alaric's hand stole to the talisman, holding it tight as Bryan's memory flashed through him. His voice was less steady when he finally found it. "We...I was in the detention camp when he was first captured by the 8th Battalion."

Darvin nodded slowly. "You're the one he said helped him escape."

"Yes, our escape was already planned. I couldn't leave him there. We...became close."

"You loved him." Darvin said softly.

Alaric nodded, blinking against the tears suddenly filling his eyes. "I still do." He sniffed and pushed the pain away. He needed the anger, he needed the fire. The pain would only cripple him. "And when I find the men who took him from me, Mr. Darvin, they will die in the most horrible way a human being can die."

"Well, Mr. Lambrecht, if that display was any indication, you'd be quite an asset."

Alaric stifled the yawn, but Darvin still saw it and stood. "Come with me and I'll get you taken care of."

He followed Darvin back to the elevators, then out into a hall. He took two steps and stopped. Mason. Alaric could all but smell him. His hand closed around the talisman and he focused himself. He hadn't anticipated the psychic residue. He turned toward the feeling, stopping at a door. "What is this?"

"Library." Darvin answered, looking at him quizzically.

"You have something of Mason's." It wasn't a question.

"Yes, his Book of Line. Do you want to see it?"

Alaric shook his head. "No, I just… I wasn't expecting it."

"Come with me, I'll get you into a room."

Alaric followed him, knowing this was just the next step in a long journey. At the end of that journey, he would have his vengeance.

Chapter Seven

Zero had hiked away from the house and barn while the Shades slept, up to a pile of sandstone boulders that she climbed up. She hid herself in a cranny between them, giving her the illusion of being alone. She needed space. Her ability to keep her thoughts and feelings to herself was frayed and she knew that she was intruding on at least Maddie and Raven's heads.

She needed to get control again. She didn't let herself think about the fact that she'd only been in control before because her father had hidden her memories and abilities behind walls that she had asked Alaric to destroy.

Her father had succeeded, more than she ever imagined. It was his blocks that had kept her from realizing it. The memory of killing that man showed her how very well his experiments had succeeded. The combination of the Shadows he had harvested to empower her had given her access to gifts she had never even known existed.

She couldn't control any of them, but she could feel them, just out of sight…just out of reach…and she itched to let them loose like she'd done in that room.

Zero exhaled and pulled her thoughts back, focusing herself inward. She had to believe that they weren't all destructive, that she could learn to use them. She walled off all of the gifts that could manipulate the physical. She didn't want to accidentally kill someone.

Not that the mental gifts couldn't do their own damage. She knew that far too intimately, but they were a little more familiar. She'd always been a decent reader and she'd learned glamors early. So, she started with what she knew. Once she'd stilled her mind, she opened herself up, rolling back her shields to take in information from her surroundings.

The air was hot and still. There were small desert animals scurrying along the ground not far away. A roadrunner was off to her right. There was a storm gathering to the west, it would arrive near nightfall.

Stretching a little further, Zero found the nest of sleeping Shades that was the home of Lonan and his wife. Beyond them was the heart of the reservation, a school and a small store, a handful of ramshackle buildings.

Zero inhaled slowly and stretched further, though the reservation town was close to what she knew to be her limits. It was a struggle at first, until she realized that she was strangling the new-found ability and she cautiously opened the wall to allow it out. There was a rush of power that was nearly physical, and her awareness swooshed away from the reservation, out to the west, past the barren landscape and into a military camp.

The American flag flew from a flagpole in its center, under another flag that was navy blue, with a white cross wrapped in red flames emblazoned on its center. The men wore 8th Battalion blue. There were cages around that flagpole, three of which held prisoners. They had open lesions on their faces and were trying to hide their skin from the sun. Shades.

There was a man who seemed to be in charge. He was saluted as he moved through the camp, and aides followed him, taking notes as he spoke. He was gaunt, his cheeks narrow, his eyes dark.

He wasn't in uniform however, he wore a dark navy suit. He paused near the cages, and gestured toward a truck. They would be moved. She couldn't tell to where.

Zero let her attention move, north now toward the Canadian border. There were people moving back and forth, taking refugees across the border. She got the sense that there was a system in place to relocate them quietly.

There was a flare of something that pulled her east, toward Chicago. Alaric. It was a brief flash, brilliant with cold fury that disappeared almost as soon as it appeared. There was another familiar mind there though, and it took her a moment to recognize it. Alaric's Keeper, Bryan. He acknowledged her touch, offered her information. She took it gladly and returned what she knew.

Closer to her physical body, she felt someone approach and pulled herself back. It took a bit to get herself fully settled, and when she opened her eyes, she was not surprised to find Maddie watching her from the desert floor.

"I didn't mean to interrupt."

"You're not." Zero said, stretching slowly. "Just…practicing."

"Practicing what?" Maddie climbed up the rocks with the grace of her cat and sat lightly beside her.

Zero shrugged. "Seeing, I guess. Since Alaric broke the walls my father put in my head, I can do more. Just trying to figure it all out.

"What did you see?" Maddie asked.

"The 8th Battalion. They have prisoners. Shades." She lifted a hand and pointed west. "Out there."

"From the village?"

Again, Zero shrugged. "I'm not sure." She stretched her legs out in front of her and leaned back against the rock behind her.

After a long silence, Maddie licked her lips, looking out across the desert. "I was their prisoner once. The 8th Battalion."

Zero had known that on some level...something she'd picked up from Alaric along the way. Maddie and her sister had both been held in some lab in California.

"Mila and I...it was my fault we got caught. I wasn't in control of my shifts yet. Sahara told me it was normal, that we all go through it, but Mila's dead now...and that's my fault too."

Misery dripped off Maddie, mixed with guilt and fear. Zero wasn't accustomed to giving comfort, but she put a hand on Maddie's knee. She got a blast of images when she did, from cages in a dark room to a bear to shifting into the cat.

Everything was more intense as the cat took over and for a moment, Zero couldn't disengage, feeling the power as she struck out at those closest and the van careened off the road, the roar of grief as she tried to escape into the trees...then came the guilt as she realized what she had done.

Zero's hand shook a little as she pulled it away. "Sorry...I didn't mean to..."

Maddie shook her head. "It's okay. I'm kind of getting used to being a freak."

Zero snorted. "Well, if you're a freak, I'm worse. At least you come by yours honestly. Mine is all.... Frankenstein."

"We make a pair, don't we?" Maddie said, wiping at a tear. "Can't help but wonder if I shouldn't just..."

"What? Run away?" Zero asked. "I tried that. Raven found me."

"I doubt she'd come looking for me." Maddie said.

Zero moved to stand up. "She wasn't looking for me either." She stretched her arms up over her head, scanning the horizon. "Where would you go, anyway?"

Maddie stood too. "Out into the woods. I could let the cat out and no one would know."

"You talk like you and the cat are different beings. You now that isn't true."

"Do I?" Her face showed her distaste. "It does things I would never do."

"It is still you." Zero countered.

"If it was, I wouldn't have hurt those people."

"That's not what I saw." Zero put a hand on her shoulder and reached into her mind, pulling out the memory of her shift in the van, rewinding it back to the moment before it happened. She slowed it down, showed Maddie how she was already hitting Riley as he told her that Mila was dead, how she was striking out in her grief and anger even before she shifted.

"It was instinct."

"If I wasn't a freak, instinct wouldn't have let me try to kill people." Maddie said miserably.

"If you weren't a freak, you wouldn't have been able to defend those same people from a deranged bear Shifter either." Zero responded. "If you're going to blame the cat for one, you have to accept the cat for the other."

"Easy for you to say, your gifts don't kill people."

Zero pulled away from her and started to climb down the rocks. "You don't know that." Her head filled with the memory of pulling a man apart from the inside out and her stomach twisted. She could almost smell the blood as the rage bubbled up inside her.

She forced it down, locked it up behind a wall in the back of her mind. She wouldn't show that to Maddie. She started walking and Maddie fell into step behind her. "I saw a place up north, in Canada. People helping Shades get over the border and finding them places to live. Maybe they'd help you too."

Their shoulders rubbed a little as they walked. "I don't know if I'd be welcome."

Zero nodded. "Do you know any others like you?"

"There's Sahara, but I don't even know where she is right now."

"Chicago." Zero answered reflexively. She felt Maddie's stare and shrugged. "She's with Bryan, trying to talk Alaric out of... whatever it is Alaric is doing."

"And you know this... how exactly?"

Zero rolled her eyes. "I... found them. Bryan at least. He relayed a bunch of information, but I don't feel like saying it twice. We should wait until Raven's awake."

They fell quiet then and Zero let the silence numb her, let her thoughts go slack and wander. The restlessness that filled her made her think that maybe Maddie wasn't wrong about running away... somewhere she didn't have to worry about hurting people, where she was sure she couldn't be used.

The problem was, she had no idea where that would be, so she just kept walking back to the Shades that had accepted her when she had nowhere else to go.

* * *

"D.C. is still under martial law, according to Bryan." Zero said. "Lock down at sundown, permits needed to be out after dark. The South-

97

ern states have declared their intent to withdraw from the US... Tennessee, North and South Carolina, Georgia, Alabama, Mississippi, Arkansas, Texas."

"Florida?" Connor asked.

Zero shrugged. "I'm not sure. The military is a mess. Congress is divided and aside from passing emergency legislation to force Shades into custody, they can't agree on anything."

"Nothing unusual there," one of the Shades said.

Zero didn't know his name and looked to Raven who nodded. "That's not helping Roger."

"I'm just saying, the divide between Democrats and Republicans has been growing for decades. We might as well admit it."

"He's not wrong." Connor said.

"I know he isn't." Raven sighed. "Can we let her finish?"

"I'm still not sure how it is we're trusting what she says." The woman speaking was short, her hair prematurely gray. Zero only knew her as Charlotte's mother.

"She's a Shadow, Mom." Charlotte said, her tone telling the whole room her mother was an embarrassment. "She can talk to people with her mind."

Zero licked her lips to hide her smile. Charlotte was only thirteen, but had a well-developed sense of teenage attitude.

"From what I understand, the new President is deeply in the pockets of the religious right that has been screaming for our heads." Roger said. "None of this is good for us."

Zero nodded. "You're right, but he isn't the person you need to worry about. He won't hold office long." The former speaker of the house was nearly seventy years old, and in poor health. "He's just named his vice president. Norman Douglas." At least now she understood why her father and Douglas had been in the capital. She was certain the whole thing had been her father's plan. "He gets sworn in tomorrow. Don't expect Hardin to live for long. Douglas will be our president before the month is over, and then..." She shook her head. She had no idea what came after that.

"So, what are we going to do?" Charlotte's mother asked.

"The way I see it, you all have two choices." Raven said, her voice quiet. "You can try to get north. Zero tells me there are people willing to help you get into Canada where you can try to start over. Or you can give yourself up to the government and hope they treat you better than the 8th Battalion will."

"Either way, we need to get out of Arizona." Zero added quietly, looking up at Raven. "There have already been skirmishes and we're losing ground every day. The 8th Battalion is pushing this way. It won't take long for them to take the state, not with prevailing attitudes toward Shades." She didn't comment on the fact that no matter which government held the land, none of the Shades were safe.

No one spoke for a long time. Neither option was great. "What about you?" Connor asked after the silence had dragged on.

Raven didn't look up. Zero already knew her mind. "I have an obligation. The 8th Battalion has Shade prisoners. I'm going after them."

"By yourself?" Roger asked.

"No." Zero responded for her. "I'm going with her."

Beside her on the floor, Maddie stirred, lifting her head. "I am too."

"No, you're not." Raven said, standing. "Neither one of you are ready for this."

"Ready or not doesn't seem to matter." Zero countered. "You're going to need help."

"No, I'm not going to risk your lives—"

"Every moment we're alive our lives are at risk." Maddie said, taking Zero by surprise. "At least let us do something with them."

"Now isn't the time to talk about it." Raven rubbed her forehead. "We need to focus on getting everyone to safety."

"There is no safety." Zero said. "Not anymore." She stood. "I'm going with you, or I'm going after my father. You decide which is safer." She walked away, heading for the loft and sleep. Raven wouldn't leave yet, the night was too far gone. She'd wait for sundown the next day, and Zero was determined to be ready to go with her, whether the Shade wanted company or not.

Chapter Eight

"You understand we are no longer a government agency." Darvin said as he handed Alaric a stack of paperwork. "We don't actually exist in any official capacity, not that we ever did. Our history is complicated, but when my partner and I started out, we always knew our relationship with the government was tentative. We prepared to have to go underground right from the start."

Alaric already knew that. It wasn't a government job he was after. "But you have resources."

Darvin grinned at him and leaned back against his desk. "Like I said, we anticipated. We're not as connected as we were before the president died, but we can still function."

Alaric nodded. "You have people no one would suspect to be Shade sympathizers." He scanned around him and was surprised to find that there were a few Shadows, not from his clan, but Shadows, and at least one Sage nearby. "I see you're branching out from Shades."

"We've worked with a number of Shadows over the years, mostly in our intelligence gathering unit. And we have a few Sages, but most of them are out in the field."

Alaric glanced at the paperwork in his hands and snorted. "Really? A full physical?"

To his surprise, Darvin was quite serious. "No one goes into the field unless we know he's fully fit. Keep reading. There's more."

Alaric turned his attention to the stack of agreements he would have to sign before they could move beyond this. The physical was just the beginning. They wanted a psych evaluation, plus assessments of his ability to manage himself in combat situations, weapons testing, hand to hand.

"You don't play around." Alaric said, letting a little bit of his respect color his voice. "Mason never really talked about much of this part of his life."

Darvin smiled and went back to sit behind his desk. "He was green in every way when he came here. We did the best we could to enhance his skills and teach him how to handle himself so that he could do the job we wanted him to do."

"He was your spy." Alaric said. "You sent him in places you couldn't get your other spies."

Darvin nodded. "You knew that before you came here."

Alaric held out his hand for a pen. "I did. I like that you aren't hiding anything."

"I got the impression it wouldn't matter if I did." Darvin responded, handing him a pen.

Alaric started with the non-disclosure document and worked his way through the stack. "It wouldn't." Alaric met and held his gaze, pushing his determination across the light connection he'd established. "Where do we start?"

Darvin stood and gestured to the door. "I'll take you to our clinic. I've asked our doctor to do the honors."

Alaric followed him and let Darvin introduce him to the doctor. He was not as easy to read as most of the others Alaric had met since arriving the day before. He was middle-aged, but fit, his dark red hair kept neatly trimmed. His mind was well shielded and felt familiar somehow. The doctor was looking at him with a raised eyebrow and a smirk. "Are you quite finished, Mr. Lambrecht?"

Alaric held up a hand in apology. "Sorry, I'm a little…I like to know who I'm spending time with."

"Well, you're going to have to figure that out the old-fashioned way with me."

"You're Dr. Anthony. You treated Mason Jerah." Alaric said as Darvin left them.

"I am and I did. Mr. Darvin tells me that he met an unfortunate end."

Alaric nodded. "Yes."

"And that's what brings you to us."

"I'm here to find the men who did it, and with luck, put a dent in the 8th Battalion while I'm at it."

Dr. Anthony's face was drawn and tight. "It's about time someone does. We've lost far too many good people to those bastards." He closed his eyes and exhaled carefully. "Now then, let's get down to business. There are gowns in the changing room, just over there. Go ahead and get undressed and gowned and we'll begin."

Alaric wanted to be out hunting, but he knew he was going to need the resources Darvin could give him, so he submitted to the blood work, the physical, even sat with a psychologist who looked like she was barely old enough for college.

After that came physical drills, runs, weapons assessments.

He shook his head as he put down the hand gun. "I did tell you I'm no good at guns," he said to the instructor. "But I make up for it with other skills."

"A spy who can't shoot is a spy who gets dead."

Alaric raised an eyebrow, reaching into the man's mind. He lifted the gun Alaric had just put down and brought it up to his temple. "I don't need to shoot. I can make you do it." He released his control and the man dropped his hand.

"Point taken."

"Good. Are we done?"

"Mr. Darvin would like to see you in his office," the instructor said, crossing to a cabinet to lock the gun away.

Alaric put down his ear protection and goggles and left the firing range, headed for Darvin's office. Darvin was seated at his desk, on his phone when Alaric looked in. Darvin waved him in.

"Thank you. Yes, that will have to do."

He hung up the phone, looking up at Alaric. "You do know how to make an impression."

Alaric shrugged and sat. "I'm tired of playing along."

Darvin nodded. "Well, you passed almost everything with flying colors. Dr. Landon doesn't think you're completely fit for field duty. She's worried that your need for vengeance will get in the way of following orders."

Alaric knew he'd abandon orders if he got an opportunity to get Shallon, but he kept that to himself. "Like I told her, as long as orders are getting me closer to the 8th Battalion and involve hurting them, I'll follow them."

Darvin's eyes narrowed and for a long moment, he just looked at Alaric. "I'm ready to test that theory."

Alaric sat forward eagerly. He'd half expected more foot dragging. "Yeah?"

"You ready to get a little dirty?" Darvin asked, standing up.

Alaric smirked and stood too, rubbing his hands down his jeans. "Oh, I've been ready."

Darvin led Alaric through a maze of corridors and into a conference room, though a war room might have been the better descriptor.

One wall was filled with a map, not unlike the one they had once kept themselves, with boundaries drawn in pins and colored thread. The blue that marked the 8th Battalion's border had moved east into Montana since he'd last marked it himself, and they had pushed further in the southern territories, controlling most of Arizona and New Mexico now. Black dots marked several places still within the US boundaries. Alaric lifted a hand, already understanding before touching the nearest pin. "They aren't playing by the rules."

Darvin was grim beside him. "What appears to be random attacks. Bomb, in a Kansas City mosque, a gay nightclub in Chicago, and a night clinic rumored to be run by Shades in Pittsburgh. Shooting spree in Cincinnati at a vigil for five suspected Shades killed in a single weekend. Riots in Virginia, Alabama, Texas. All in the last three days. 213 dead, 194 injured."

"And this?" Alaric touched the line of pins and red thread that ran down the western edges of the Dakotas, down into Nebraska, taking the eastern edges of Colorado and New Mexico before slicing off the western tip of Texas.

"That is the line President Hardin has drawn and is right now attempting to secure. He's withdrawn all troops worldwide and is busy deploying them there, as a measure against the 8th Battalion pushing any further east."

Which meant getting into 8th Battalion territory could prove difficult. Alaric turned his attention to another wall covered in high tech displays and as they approached it filled with faces.

"These are the ones we know." Darvin said.

Alaric glanced across faces, comparing them to the information he'd gleaned from the globe, from Duffy and others he'd managed to read while he'd been secreted away in the facility. He found one he recognized, barely containing the cold rage that filled his stomach. "That's Colonel Shallon," he said coldly. "He fixated on Mason. I believe he sent the strike force that killed him in Arizona." His mind flooded with Bryan's memory of that moment, followed by the sound of Mason's screams in that cell in California and he had to push them away.

"According to our intelligence, he's in charge of all Shade operations now."

Darvin's voice pulled him back to the moment and Alaric nodded slightly. That made sense. Shallon had gotten a lot of information from Mason. "He's probably the one who was running whoever betrayed us in Arizona. He learned a lot about Shades when he had Mason." Alaric crossed his arms. "He's a true believer too. He believes he's doing god's work."

He scanned the other faces, pointing to one he knew. "This is James Flanders, politician." He made a face. "I knew his wife in Sacramento. He was a State Senator. Smooth talker. Not a true believer in their rhetoric though. He supported Norman Douglas and others like him, but he only believes in himself, and what will get him to the next level of power." His eyes caught another familiar face. "Reverend Thomas Roth."

Alaric moved to stand in front of the picture. "He was on the city council with my father. Nasty little man."

"He's running a detention camp in Utah." Darvin added, taking a folder someone handed him. "We believe that it is where they are holding the 'undesirables' for interrogation and eventual execution."

"How very third Reich of them." Alaric murmured. "Any idea how many of these 'undesirables' are being held?"

"Nothing accurate. We believe they include Shades and more than a few Sages. As well as a number of political dissenters and other people that don't fit into their plans."

Alaric moved his attention back to the map. The detention camp was well placed, deep into 8th Battalion territory. "I could read Duffy again, see if I missed anything the first time." Alaric offered.

Darvin shook his head. "By now anything he gave us would be outdated." His hand tapped the map in two places. "We picked up chatter about a hand off of a high value target that was captured."

Alaric took the knowledge before he voiced his annoyance. "You mean the Shadow you've got embedded in military intelligence told you?"

Darvin lifted an eyebrow. "There isn't going to be any kind of hiding information with you is there?"

Alaric didn't answer. Instead he narrowed his eyes at the map and extended his senses toward the locations, scanning minds in the areas to get a feel for what was around them. "The Arizona location is compromised, pull your men out. This though…" He tapped the spot in Wyoming. "There's activity there." He shook his head to clear it and inhaled. "They are waiting for a strike team with a prisoner."

Darvin raised an eyebrow. "Who?"

Alaric shrugged. "Hard to tell at this distance and third hand. I would have to be there to figure it out."

"So, ever been to Wyoming?" Darvin asked. "Chopper's on the roof." Darvin headed for the door and Alaric followed.

"Just like that?" Alaric asked as they stepped into the elevator.

"I was under the impression that you wanted to get out there and get started."

"No time like the present." Alaric agreed.

"Let me introduce you to your new handler." Darvin gestured as the elevator doors opened and Alaric stepped out into a spacious hallway.

"Handler?"

Darvin led the way to a door at the far end. "I've lost enough people, Mr. Lambrecht. None of my operatives leave this facility without a handler. Evan is one of my best." They stepped out onto the roof and a man in fatigues and flak jacket stepped into place beside Darvin. "Lt. Evan Chayton, Alaric Lambrecht."

"Pleasure." Chayton said with a nod of his head, but Alaric could tell it was a mere pleasantry without trying to read the man. "We're ready and the team is already on the ground at the target site."

"Your mission is to determine who they've captured and effect a rescue if at all possible. You are not to follow deeper into enemy held territory, is that clear?"

"Crystal, sir." Evan responded.

Darvin looked at Alaric. "Clear?"

"Search and rescue, but no heroics, I get you loud and clear." Alaric responded.

"Good luck."

Evan led Alaric to the helicopter waiting for them. It was disguised as a hospital transport. Alaric stepped up and sat, adding a little extra camouflage mentally, similar to the wards they'd used to hide the camp in California. It would just discourage average people from noticing them.

Evan put on a set of headphones as he sat beside the pilot and pointed at another pair on the seat next to Alaric. He put them on and could hear Evan giving the pilot instructions. "We're on a plane out of a private airport that will put us near our target in a few hours. From there we chopper in closer, and one of our team will pick us up."

"Just get me close." Alaric said, sitting back. He watched Evan turn back to the front, trying to place what was different about him. He was a soldier, that much was easy to read. A career soldier too. But his mind was inordinately shielded, nothing leaking or broadcasting from him.

As if sensing Alaric's assessment, Evan turned to look at him, his eyes flecked with gold, sharp and appraising. Before either of them could say anything, they were setting down and Evan's attention turned to getting them on the small plane. It wasn't until they were in the air again that Evan pinned him with that stare once more.

"I think you will find I'm not an easy read." Evan said, looking him over. "There's a reason Adam put me with you."

"Adam, huh?" Alaric was a little off balance. Since taking on the combined power of his people and the globe, he hadn't met a person he couldn't at least surface read until now.

Evan smiled a small, tight smile. "I'm not most people."

Alaric narrowed his eyes and buttoned up his own defenses. "You aren't a Shade or a Shadow."

Evan shook his head. "No, I'm not."

Alaric couldn't put his finger on it. Evan turned to look out the window, his expression softening. His eyes traced over the clouds, then closed, as if savoring a memory.

Curiosity got the better of him and Alaric spent the next half hour carefully setting up a series of blinds and shields while casually observing Evan from behind half closed eyelids. The lieutenant was clearly of Native American descent, his dark hair cut close to his head in military style, his skin a deep tan. He couldn't place what tribe though.

With his shields in place, he let a tendril of thought drift out, casual and nonchalant. It encountered shields he'd never seen in anyone not of his own people, but Evan certainly was not. He was—Alaric pulled back and shifted himself in his seat.

He was like Sahara. Only not exactly. It wasn't a feline hunter he sensed. A hunter though, that was obvious.

Mason had told him that Shades were not the only types of people Darvin's organization worked with, but Alaric had never encountered Shifters, other than Sahara and her girls and had started to think them gone. He didn't know if he could trust the man, but then, he hadn't trusted anyone since the betrayal without reading them deeply.

The lieutenant busied himself with paperwork, pointedly ignoring Alaric. That was just as well. He tried to ground himself and center. He was going to need to be focused once they were on the ground.

It was one thing to use the skills at his command in the relative safety of Darvin's facility. It was another thing entirely to rely on them in the field. A flicker of prescience told him that this mission was just the beginning, and that before it was over, blood would be spilled.

He was remarkably okay with that.

Chapter Nine

Zero was already sitting behind the wheel of the beat up old Chevy that Tusa had loaned them when Raven exited the house, her hands filled with supplies. Maddie was in the back seat.

Raven sighed and opened the passenger side door. "Do you even know where we're going?" Raven asked as she handed the bag of supplies back to Maddie.

"North." Zero replied. "If we hurry, we might catch up with the prisoners."

Raven wasn't going to talk them out of going with her, they'd talked about it before they'd helped Tusa load blankets and a first aid kit into the car. Raven climbed in beside Zero and pulled the door shut. "This is going to be dangerous."

Zero just looked at her and she sighed again. "I take it you know where they're headed?"

"I have an idea." Zero affirmed. "Utah."

"Great, more desert." Raven muttered as Zero started driving.

"Either that or we can head east, go after my father." Zero said with a shrug. She had more reason than ever to go after him, and with his attention on Douglas, she doubted he would even see her coming.

"I think those prisoners are going to be a challenge enough." Raven countered.

"We wouldn't get near him anyway." Zero said. "He's glued to Douglas, and with his swearing in as VP he's buried under so much security a fly doesn't land on him without half the government knowing."

"And we have no idea what your father's end game is." Raven added.

Zero didn't respond, just kept her eyes on the road out of reservation lands. The strike team had days ahead of them. The truth was they could already be at their final destination, and the whole mission was futile.

Zero hadn't tried to read that far ahead, so she wasn't exactly sure what they would find on the other end of the drive. Beside her, Raven was stewing over the lack of plan, over taking the two girls at all. Zero rubbed at her head and tried to block out Raven's negative thoughts. She was doing this out of duty, but she was pretty sure that the mission was probably at least ill-advised and probably worse than that, suicidal. She just couldn't continue to sit around with all of the expectations piled on her.

"Hey," Zero said when Raven's thoughts kept spiraling down into darker places. "We're all feeling it."

Raven blinked at her. "I'm sorry."

"I know. I don't mean to be eavesdropping, but..." Zero gestured at her head. "It's not all under control just yet."

Raven nodded and inhaled deeply. "I'll try to keep a lid on it."

"We may be young, Maddie and I." Zero said softly, addressing at least one of the concerns she could speak to. "But we won't let you down."

Raven nodded. "I know that. But you're just children. and here I am taking you into a war."

* * *

"*Pretend you're asleep.*" Zero pressed into Raven's head with an image of a roadblock. Raven didn't respond. She'd been zoned out for the better part of the last hour, her eyes closed as the numbing monotony of the drive lulled her into a half-asleep state.

The car slowed and behind her, Zero could feel Maddie stirring sleepily. Zero put her window down, her heart pounding loud enough to alert half the world. Her voice seemed loud and out of place as she greeted the man in uniform. "Evening, officer."

A light flashed into the car, and Zero could feel the heat of it on the skin of her hands. Raven kept her face averted, forehead against the window, her hair protecting her skin. The light was designed to make Shades uncomfortable.

"Where are you three headed?" The man's voice was deep.

"Into Utah, my grandmother lives near Salt Lake." Zero responded. She sounded nervous to herself, even as she started trying to get a hold of the man's thoughts.

"Is that right?"

"Yes, sir. Our mother died a few weeks ago. Grandma's the only relative we have left."

"Do you have travel papers?"

"I'm sorry, I didn't know we needed any?" Zero said. They hadn't even considered it, which was stupid on their part. Zero kicked herself mentally, scrambling to get enough of a grip on the man to force the thought on him that they were free to go. It wasn't that he had any shields to speak of, her mind was just occupied with all of the other things she could sense.

"New requirement, just came through today. Let me see your ID at least."

Zero leaned over Raven for the glovebox. She had no idea what she would find in there, but she used the cover of looking to push out all of the input and focus on the officer at the window. With a *push,* Zero bridged the gap, handing him three random pieces of paper from the glovebox and making sure he saw them as ID. He examined them, then waved to his men to open the barricade. "You ladies drive safe, and make sure you stop up ahead for the proper permits."

Zero was still clutching a handful of papers, her eyes darting to the rearview mirror before checking in on Raven who lifted her head. "I wasn't sure I was going to be able to get him."

She thrust the collection of papers at Raven. They included the car's Arizona registration, and old insurance card and a receipt from a gas station.

Raven shifted in her seat, sitting up and pushing her hair out of her face. "Where are we?"

"Not far into Utah." Zero replied. "You should know that the 8th Battalion has just claimed majority control of Arizona. They crushed their way through the militia."

"Then we got out just in time." Raven said dryly.

It wasn't lost on any of them that Utah was where the 8th Battalion got its start and they hadn't won anything getting out of one 8th Battalion state into another.

"Anything else I should know?" Raven asked.

Zero shrugged and glanced at her. "I think the feds are finally realizing they need to address the 8th Battalion's constant push east. Our friend back there was thinking about rumors of troop movement."

"I thought you were having trouble getting into his head?"

Zero gestured at her head. "It's like a radio I can't turn off at this point. The information was flowing one way, I was having trouble turning it around."

"Is that good or bad?" Raven asked, though she suspected it was a little bit of both.

"When it starts to be a problem, I'll let you know." They drove in silence for a while before Zero looked at her again. "How are we going to handle daylight?"

Raven sighed and looked around at the untinted windows. They were going to need to get off the road or find some way to protect her. "How far are we from where you saw that camp?"

Zero shook her head. "Not far. We don't want to get close though."

Raven looked at her watch. They had about an hour before the sun was going to be a problem. If all else failed, she could crawl into the trunk, but that wasn't the most appealing idea.

Zero guided the car off the road and closed her eyes, casting about for anything that might provide them some shelter. After a moment, she opened them again. "There's an abandoned motel ahead of us. I think I can get us into one of the rooms."

Raven nodded. It wasn't ideal, but it beat the trunk. It looked like Zero needed the rest too. "Yeah, okay."

They were quiet then as Zero got them moving again. The motel lurked in the pre-dawn darkness, sitting just off the road in an L-shape. The windows were all boarded up, and the whole place looked like a strong wind would knock it down.

Zero pulled off the road, circling the building and pulling the car up into the elbow of the L-shape, where it couldn't easily be seen from the road in either direction, and as the morning progressed, the building's shadow would work to help conceal it as well.

Once they were parked, Zero got out from behind the wheel and approached the closest door, putting her hand on the handle. The motel was old enough that it had never changed to electric locks. Zero exhaled and closed her eyes, squatting down so that she was eye level with the lock.

It took her a few moments to quiet her mind and reach into the lock, then suddenly it popped, and the door opened under her hand. Zero was the first one in the room, calling back to let them know it was safe. The place had the musty smell that came with being closed up for so long. There was no furniture, but she'd slept on floors before.

"I'll get our stuff." Zero said, stepping back out.

Zero returned with an armful of blankets and the bag of food. Together they set up a spot to sleep. Maddie paced around the room, nervous energy spilling off of her.

"You okay?" Raven asked.

Maddie shrugged and then rolled her eyes. "Don't worry about me. I'll sit guard."

"You should sleep too." Raven countered, a hand touching Maddie's as she started to undress to shift.

"I slept in the car. Someone should keep an eye on you."

Maddie shifted and padded around the room sniffing at things before crossing back to the door where she lay down so that she was blocking the entry.

Raven took her shoes off and shed her jeans before sliding under the blanket. Zero followed suit, her eyes and senses sweeping the room several times before she was sure they would be okay.

Raven settled beside her, even if sleep didn't come right away. Zero was almost afraid to sleep, but the tired burned inside her bones and even if she'd wanted to, she couldn't hold sleep at bay for long.

* * *

Maddie lifted her head and sniffed the air. The room was stifling in the afternoon heat. The smell of old dust and stale air covered all but the scent of the two she was with.

Outside the room she could hear wind blowing through the barren landscape. Other than the wind, nothing seemed to be moving.

Stretching, she stood and moved around the room, stopping as she came to the corner where Zero had curled up to sleep. Zero's face was slicked with sweat, her hands fisted in the blanket that covered her.

Maddie was familiar with the nightmares that plagued Zero's sleep, they'd shared the same sleeping space since escaping the town. Maddie sniffed her, nuzzling her face before laying down beside her, between Zero and the door, and resting her head on Zero's arm.

In only a few moments, Zero seemed to calm, rolling toward Maddie and spooning against her. Maddie let her, even though it would impair her ability to defend them if she needed to. It seemed Zero needed the warmth of a solid body to hold on to and to be fair, Maddie found it comforting as well.

She would let them both sleep another few hours before she woke them. The sun would be down, and they could get back on the road.

Not that she really knew where they were going or what they would do when they got there. She wasn't even entirely certain why she had insisted on coming with them, other than the fact that she couldn't bear the idea of being alone.

It had always been her greatest fear, especially after her parents had been killed. Mila had never been afraid of anything. She had been fierce, like Sahara was. She'd embraced her cat, loved the freedom, the power. Mila had breezed through the change while Maddie was still too young to fully understand it.

Maddie, however, had fought it. Right from the very first. She'd never wanted it. She wanted to be normal, to be safe. It was a laughable idea now. She'd never be safe or normal.

None of which helped her understand what she was doing with Zero and Raven, traveling deeper into territory filled with men who wanted her dead. With a sigh, Maddie tried to put those thoughts out of her head. She needed to be more like Mila, fierce. No matter what happened, she would defend her new friends, the same way Mila had always defended her.

"Hey, you okay?" Zero whispered in her ear, making Maddie turn her head. In the dark room, Zero looked younger, her eyes half open. Maddie rubbed her face on Zero's hand to say she was fine. "Let me up."

Zero sat up, stretching before she stood and disappeared into the bathroom. A few minutes later she was back, rummaging in the bag of food and coming back with a jar of peanut butter and some bread. Maddie took it to mean she was done sleeping and shifted back to human form, dressing in the dark while Zero made sandwiches.

Maddie came back to the blanket where Zero had been sleeping and sat, nodding her thanks as Zero handed her a sandwich. "Nightmare?" Maddie asked as softly as she could.

Zero shrugged. "No more than usual." She swallowed and looked up at her. "But thanks, it helped."

"All I did was—"

"I know. But it was grounding. Helped me find my way back. I appreciate it."

"So, do you know where we go from here?" Maddie asked when she had finished her sandwich.

Zero nodded. "North. There's a place near Salt Lake City. I think…" She bit her lip and looked like she was considering how to say something. "There's this guy that my father used, a Shadow with some other talents. He helped create the hysteria that led to the 8th Battalion. In fact, it was his idea to use that stupid book. He and my father had a…falling out, I guess." She shook her head and leaned back against the wall. "Anyway, he's there. Or will be. It isn't exactly clear."

"What does that mean?"

Zero shrugged. "I don't know exactly. My father thought he'd bought into his own bullshit though, started to believe the religious crap. It's one of the dangers of that kind of Shadow work."

"Can he…does he know…" Maddie wasn't really sure how to ask the question.

"About me?" Zero asked. Maddie nodded. "I don't know. He's pretty well shielded. If he were looking, maybe. But I don't think he is."

"So, what exactly are we going to do when we get there?" Maddie asked.

"With any luck, we're going to free the prisoners." Raven replied, rolling toward them.

"Without getting caught ourselves." Zero added.

"How?" Maddie asked, though she had a sneaking suspicion neither of them actually knew.

"We'll figure something out." Raven responded. "First we have to get there."

Chapter Ten

"Get me closer." Alaric murmured to Evan as they crouched behind a stack of crates at an abandoned railroad station. His hand was on Evan's shoulder, his eyes closed.

"Not much closer we can get without being seen." Evan responded.

"Three men." Alaric breathed. "Waiting for convoy with a prisoner…someone…woman." He shifted and tried to stretch over the distance. He focused on just the man nearest them. "Low level, bored…would rather be up north on the Canadian front…wounded left knee. Stuck on transport duty since getting out of the hospital. Thinks his captain is a tool." Alaric licked his lips. The man wasn't worth much to him. He exhaled and stretched a little more. "Captain Joe Milman, his father was a marine, died before the split."

He shifted and shook his head. "I can't read much deeper from this distance."

Evan looked around for other cover, then looked at him. "How about we get one of them to come to us?"

Alaric nodded slowly. "How you going to do that?"

Evan grinned. "Already on his way, walking perimeter I'm guessing."

He slung his gun around his back and readied himself. As the man cleared the boxes, Evan sprang forward, one hand instantly over his nose and mouth, the other on his neck as he pulled him back behind the crates.

Alaric monitored the others for a sign they'd seen, but they kept their attention on the dirt road leading up to the station on the opposite side. The man Evan brought down was unconscious as Alaric knelt beside him.

"Okay, I'm going to go pretty deep."

"I've got your back." Evan said.

Alaric centered and put a hand on the man's head, and he had to work to keep from dropping into him the way he had done with Duffy. He needed to contain the information and there was no one to record it. He sorted through the immediate memories and thoughts, sifting through until he found what he wanted. Memos and orders and files the man had been privy to. "Woman is someone named Nancy Dawson?" Alaric flipped through the virtual file in the man's head. "Shade, caught in a raid in North Dakota, transporting her to the detention camp for interrogation."

He scanned under the current mission. "He's been to the facility. I can get an imprint of the layout, personnel."

"Do it, and be quick. Vehicles approaching."

Alaric grabbed as much information as he could quickly, not analyzing anything, just tucking it away for them to review later. He erased the remnants of his presence as he pulled out, replacing the last few minutes with the constructed memory of taking a piss.

"What's the plan?" Alaric asked as Evan pulled him back away to rejoin the small team.

"You and I fall back to the truck. The boys will see about liberating the prisoner."

"We could help—" Evan's glare was hard and Alaric nodded. "Fine, the truck it is."

Evan nodded. "Gentlemen, you have your orders."

Evan pulled on his arm, forcing him to focus on moving and not trying to read the tight tone of Evan's words. "What orders?" Alaric asked as they got to the truck.

"Save the prisoner from the 8th Battalion." Evan responded, his tone still tight and clipped. "One way or another." He tapped a finger against Alaric's head. "You dig through that information you grabbed."

"What are they going to do?" Alaric asked, squinting at him and trying to read him.

Evan snapped his fingers. "Focus. You have a job to do."

Alaric glared, but it was clear Evan wasn't telling him, consciously or not. He turned his attention to the virtual box he'd thrown the information into and started sorting it into categories. "I think I've got most of the layout of the detention center. This guy was assigned there for the last three months. It's not really a camp. It looks like it used to be a hospital or something."

He set that information aside, knowing it would mean sitting with someone to recreate a computer model. "Information on staff is likely dated. Wait. This might be something." He slowed down and replayed a memory from the briefing for this operation. "They're supposed to be meeting with another team with Shade prisoners, and get them to the facility by Tuesday." He could feel Evan frowning at him.

"Why Tuesday?"

Alaric's throat constricted and he had to clear it to speak the words. "Colonel Shallon is due to arrive next Tuesday, from Southern California." Alaric shook his head. "He didn't know why."

"Why isn't important." Evan said. He started the engine on the truck and Alaric looked up. The team was piling into the back and Evan started them back toward the safe house they had left a few hours before, moving quickly. The woman wasn't with them. Alaric knew instantly she was dead. One way or another. Evan's face was hard. "Trust me, it's better than waking up in the hands of someone like Shallon."

"I see we have a mutual dislike of the man." Alaric said quietly.

"When we get back, you sit with Jones to dump as much of that information as you can. I'll report back, get our next set of orders."

Alaric nodded, already going back to sorting through the data. It could take them days to go through it all and verify what they could. He was flipping through a bunch of random images. They were all jumbled, out of order and he couldn't get any sense of when the man had seen them, then Alaric's blood turned to ice, and he stopped, holding a specific moment in place.

The details were fuzzy, and the man's focus had clearly been on the person he was speaking to at the time, not the others around them, but there, in the background, within the detention center was a face...a familiar face.

It was bruised and bloody, but it was a face Alaric knew.

His hand grabbed Evan's arm. "I don't care what our orders are. I'm going to that detention center."

The last thing Alaric wanted to do was sit and talk through the information he'd gathered. It was all he could do not to waste valuable resources scanning minds that were too far out of reach. He was already feeling the fatigue of the work he'd done so far, despite the fever of anger still burning through him.

"Which one is Jones?" Alaric asked as he walked into the house they were squatting in.

"That'd be me, sir," a young man with dark skin and a shaved head said.

"You ever worked with a psychic before, Jones?"

He grinned. "Only if you consider my black grandmother knowing before we did it that we done something wrong."

Alaric snorted and shook his head. "Let's get to it then. There's a lot of stuff to give you."

"Give me a few minutes to get set up."

Alaric let him get set up at the kitchen table. The house was sparse on furniture. Most of the men would be leaving in the next few hours, back to less contested ground. The chatter he was picking up from them told him a lot about just how secret this mission actually was. Adam may have called it, but the only one in the group who seemed to know that was Evan. The rest all thought it had come through normal military channels.

Alaric looked up when he felt eyes on him. Evan was watching him, his eyes sharp. "Need something?" Alaric asked.

"I'm trying to decide how likely it is that you'll disappear on me in the next twenty-four hours."

He held up both hands in a surrendering motion. "I'm not going anywhere. Not right this minute anyway."

Evan held his gaze for a long moment, then nodded. "Okay. I'm going to call Adam. Get on with the data dump."

Jones looked up expectantly from the kitchen table and Alaric proceeded to sit beside him. "Okay, where do you want to start?"

"I don't know what you have, so I can't say."

Alaric nodded. "I want to try something, if you're okay with it?"

Jones looked at him with a funny face, something that expressed interest, and a healthy skepticism. "Try what?"

Alaric licked his lips and held out a hand. "I want to try passing some information to you. It might speed this up."

"You're going to...what? Put thoughts in my head?"

"Something like that. I promise, only what you can manage and I'm not going to be reading you at all. Just something to facilitate getting this information out of my head."

Jones nodded guardedly and lifted a hand. Alaric took it and exhaled, reaching out for the untrained mind. Like most soldiers, Jones had a particular order to his mind, but he had no shields and he couldn't feel Alaric's touch.

"Relax." Alaric said softly in his mind. "It isn't going to hurt."

"Easy for you to say."

Alaric opened his eyes and smiled. "True. Let's start simple. I'm going to show you an image of the facility. Okay?"

He nodded, and Alaric closed his eyes again, pulling up the image and passing it into the other mind. "Whoa." Alaric followed with another image from a different angle, one that included 8th Battalion soldiers guarding a door.

He released Jones' hand and let him assimilate the information. "Okay. I think I…" Jones put his hands on the keyboard and started typing. Alaric watched for a minute to see how he was interpreting the memories from another mind.

"I have a sort of map." Alaric said when his typing slowed. "Built out of his movements and memories. It isn't complete, and I'm not perfectly clear on all of it."

Jones offered his hand. "Show me."

Alaric took his hand, though he probably didn't need the physical link, and passed the information through. Jones pulled up a different program and started a diagram. One of the other men appeared and set a cup of coffee down beside Jones, then looked at Alaric. "Black, a little sugar."

The man nodded and withdrew, coming back a few minutes later with another cup of coffee for him. He sat back in the chair and brought the cup to his face, letting the smell fill him for a moment. Jones asked a question and pulled his attention back.

Even working like this, it was going to take a long time to download the important information. Jones worked diligently, his eyes glued to his screen, his fingers moving between the keyboard and mouse. He didn't speak but to ask clarifying questions. When he was ready for more input, he would wordlessly hold up a hand.

Hours passed like that, countless cups of coffee. The rest of the house had gone quiet when Alaric looked up, the sun long since gone down.

Alaric rubbed at his forehead, his ability to focus shot from exhaustion and pushing himself too far for too long. He shook his head as Jones asked him another question, holding up his hands. "Stop. I'm cooked. I need sleep."

"Yeah, okay. We've been at this a long time."

Alaric pulled himself out of the chair and shuffled down the hall and into a room with a bed, dropping onto the bed. He pulled his boots off and unbuttoned his pants, but he didn't get as far as pulling them down before he laid back, fatigue pulling at every fiber of his being. He was nearly asleep when Evan came and stood at the end of the bed.

"He wants to know if you're sure."

"About which part?" Alaric asked, looking up at him.

"All of it. Shallon, the Shades…"

Alaric closed his eyes, the image of that face immediately popping up. He nodded. "I'm sure."

"You know we can't go in there." Evan was frowning, his face hard. "Not officially."

"You think I give two shits about official any-thing?" Alaric asked. He would sit up if he could, but he was so wiped out that it was taking everything he had not to just fall into sleep.

"I told him you'd say that." He shook his head and inhaled. "Shallon will be there?"

Again, Alaric nodded. "Tuesday."

"Get some sleep. I'll have some answers by morning."

Alaric felt him walk away. Morning seemed a long way off, but he couldn't fight off the darkness anymore and sleep pulled him under.

* * *

"You know I love you?" Mason asks him softly, one hand gliding over Alaric's skin as they lay together on the sun-warmed rocks.

Alaric smiles and lifts up to kiss him, tongues dancing as Mason lays under him, guiding him closer. "I know I love you." Alaric whispers, kissing along his collarbone and up to his ear.

Mason makes a noise that is breathy moan and guttural need all at once. "Want you so much, Alaric... want to be with you forever."

His mouth tastes like salt though when Alaric kisses him again. He opens his eyes and Mason is stiff, cold...his eyes start to glaze over. "No. No. Mason!"

Bryan is pulling him away, but Alaric doesn't want to leave him. "No!"

Alaric sat up, his skin slicked with a cold sweat, his breath coming in gasps. Evan was standing in the doorway. "You okay?"

He nodded slowly and swung his feet to the floor. "What time is it?"

"Nearly nine. There's coffee."

Alaric inhaled and pulled a hand through his hair. "When do we leave?"

"Tomorrow. I need some time to get some stuff together." Evan replied.

"Darvin?"

Evan crossed his arms. "We're on our own. He'll fund us, give us weapons, but no more men, and no sanction. We get caught, there won't be a rescue."

"He know we'll kill him if we get the chance?"

Evan let out a hard, cold laugh. "Know? Why the fuck you think he put us together?"

"I'll be down in a minute. I need to shower."

"I got breakfast started. You're a protein kind of guy, right?"

Alaric nodded. "Yeah. Eggs and bacon."

"Screw bacon, I've got steaks on."

Alaric's stomach rumbled, and he lurched upward, aiming for the bathroom as Evan headed back to the kitchen. He was hard under his clothes, the dream hanging with him as he stripped and turned on the water...the touch of Mason's hands and thoughts so real...his hand circled the talisman and moonstone pendants, the feeling of Mason so real he half expected he could reach out and find him.

Instead, he inhaled and stepped into the shower, letting the water wash away the memory and the dream. When he stepped out a few minutes later, he could smell the breakfast Evan was cooking. He took a few minutes to pull his clothes back on before heading out to the kitchen.

There was coffee already on the table and a plate onto which Evan was putting a decent sized steak next to the eggs already there. "So, what stuff?" Alaric asked as he sat.

Evan sat at his own plate and cut into his barely cooked steak. "We're going to need supplies and an untraceable vehicle, and I'm going to need…well, let's just say I have a few basic needs your average soldier doesn't."

Alaric snorted and ate a forkful of eggs. "I ran across a desert with a Shade and no provisions once. This can't be worse than that."

"Well, at least we don't have to hide from the sun. That can really muck up an operation." Evan said. "I should have us ready by tomorrow. I'll run out and get us some provisions later today. In the meantime, we need to go over our route, and find the fastest, cleanest way to get there."

They ate in silence for a few minutes. Alaric was nearly finished with his steak when Evan sat back in his chair, cradling his coffee cup. "I figure if we're working together, you should know a few things." He pressed his lips together and looked anywhere but at Alaric. "Shallon killed my brother. He was undercover, working security for Douglas. We don't know how they found out, but they did. Shallon…" He cleared his throat. "Shallon captured, tortured and ultimately, killed him."

For the first time since meeting Evan, Alaric could feel emotion bubbling behind his shielding. He narrowed his eyes at Evan. "And you know this, how?"

Evan's eyes lifted. "We were twins. Our mother was…powerfully telepathic. My brother and I always knew what was going on with each other, especially when…" He licked his lips and stood, taking his plate to the sink. "…when in our animal form."

Alaric turned to look at him. Evan's brown eyes were once again flecked with gold and he could feel the other in him very strongly…not unlike Sahara, though Evan was no cat.

"Falcon." Evan said just as Alaric opened his mouth to ask. "And yes, it comes in handy. And no, no one knows. Aside from Adam."

Alaric's hand circled Mason's pendants. "Your secret is safe."

"Good. I don't want it to be a problem."

Alaric smiled. "I've worked with Shifters before."

That made Evan look at him. "Aren't many of us left."

Alaric nodded. "We found them in California. Three women that were being transported from a lab to a research facility run by the 8th Battalion. One of them has become a very trusted advisor."

Not that Alaric had heeded any of her recent advice. He pushed that thought away. Now wasn't the time to dwell on that. He needed to move forward.

"Now it's your turn." Evan said, coming back to the table with a full cup of coffee. "If I'm going to trust you to have my back, I need to know why you're so gung ho to hit this detention camp. It isn't just Shallon."

Alaric nodded. "You're right. It isn't." He lifted his coffee cup and sipped at it. "After we abandoned our camp in the mountains and headed south, we were living with some Shades. I should have seen it coming." He closed his eyes. Once again, he'd gotten so wrapped up in Mason, and then helping the girl, he hadn't seen.

It had been arrogant on his part, to assume that no one would get close enough to attack them without Alaric and his guardians knowing. His stomach twisted around the memory, the feeling inside him as Mason's distress reached him, the panic pulling him from Zero's bed. "Salt in the water". The sight of Mason's salt burned body when he finally got to him made Alaric's blood run cold.

"One of the Shades, someone betrayed the town. It was hard to know who. The only people who weren't Shades there were my people, and a couple of normals married to Shades."

"Hard to believe someone would betray their own people." Evan said, lifting his coffee cup.

Alaric nodded, clutching at the pendants, at the memory of their final moments together. He could almost taste Mason on his tongue.

"You ever figure out who betrayed you?" Evan asked.

Alaric looked at him. "Not until yesterday. He's there. At the detention center. Or he was at some point." Alaric could see that face in the memory he stole.

"Doesn't mean he betrayed you, he might have just been caught." Evan offered.

Alaric knew that, and he sighed, pulling up the stolen memory again. He knew that the it was at least remotely possible that no one had betrayed them and Shallon had caught their scent another way.

Alaric shook his head. He needed the anger. "He was with them. And when I find him, I'm going to kill him."

Chapter Eleven

Bryan turned away from the chaos that filled the streets around him, his hand firmly in Sahara's. Her eyes watched everything, and she was bristling with anger, not all of it her own. Her amped up senses were being fed by the crowd's heightened emotions and even though Bryan was trying to shield her, the input was nearly overwhelming.

They had left Chicago when it was clear that Alaric wasn't going to listen to reason and had disappeared behind an impenetrable shield. They'd only gotten as far as Indianapolis, which was where they were when the news came that the President had signed the bill requiring all Shades to be registered, effective immediately.

The penalty for not registering was prison. There was a second bill on its way that would require them to live in a segregated area, gated and guarded camps. Sahara had no delusions that the congress might come to their senses and realize what they were heading for.

The protests in front of them were loud and more than a few scuffles had broken out between the two sides; those who supported the registration act and those shouting about Nazis. Armed men were holding a corridor up to the city hall doors, ostensibly for Shades to use to come register. So far though, only politicians and city workers had used it.

So far there had been no public acknowledgement of any of the other tribes, just the Shades and while at one time that might have been a comfort to the two of them, they both knew now that this was only a first step. It wouldn't be long before they included Shifters, Bryan had overheard enough thought about capturing one to prove they exist earlier in the day.

Sahara wanted to shift and tear a hole in the crowd, she could almost taste the blood. Bryan tugged on her hand, pulling her back into the shadows and turning her away from the crowd. "Keep it together."

"Easy for you to say, it's my people they'll turn on next." Memory filled her of the last time she'd been caught, the cages, the torture.

"I know." Bryan soothed, leaning in to kiss her forehead. "I say we get back to Virginia and Emily. Let them know what little we know, and figure out where we go next."

She nodded, though she was still bristling. "Fine, but I'm going to need to hunt."

"Once we're out of the city. We'll find someplace," Bryan promised, keeping his hand in hers and moving them along the edges of the crowd, next to a building. They were nearly clear of the building when the sound level surrounding them doubled and he turned. Sahara could smell the fear and anger on the air, and almost without realizing it, her hand started to shift in Bryan's. "What?"

"There." She pointed more with her mind than her hand. They couldn't quite make out what was happening before shots rang out and the crowds erupted.

Bryan grabbed Sahara and turned them out of the direct line of fire, bouncing off the building behind them and inadvertently into the rush of people running for safety. The fury and fear reverberated around them. He tried to wall them off from it, pushing through the bodies physically and psychically to try to reach a safer space. Sahara hung onto him, let him lead, her arms around his neck.

More gunfire whipped up the growing fear, and she got the sense that this was what they wanted, whoever they were. As they moved, Bryan shoved Sahara into an alley and pressed her up against the wall of the building, his body shielding hers, someone nearby was thinking about a bomb and the thought ran from Bryan's brain into hers.

The people with guns were herding the crowds into a contained space, the single street open for leaving the site. Protestors from both sides, a mass of people that she figured to be five thousand or more, would die all at the same time, only moments away. "We need to get out of here." Bryan growled into Sahara's ear. "Before—"

The ground under their feet seemed to swell upward before it suddenly erupted and then began to sink. Bryan pushed Sahara toward more solid ground, scrambling after her as the bottom floor of several buildings blew inward toward each other. The world turned inside out as every mind, gifted or not, in that crowd screamed out in agony. Bryan stumbled and lost Sahara's hand as he went down in a rain of debris.

"*Keep going, get out of here.*" Bryan responded to the alarm he felt from her as she turned to see where he'd gone. He was trying to get to his feet, but there was too much input in his head to remember how to make his legs work. She grabbed his arms and hefted him up, pulling him a few more steps through acrid smoke and falling debris and flames.

The amount of noise in his head was deafening her, making it harder to move, but she fought to keep them in motion. It was like finding their way through a battlefield, inching forward, nearly blinded. Sirens were starting to sound, adding to the cacophony in his head and the connection between them was crippling her.

Something hard hit Bryan's back and he went down again, taking Sahara with him. She crawled forward, but more debris kept coming and an increasing amount of it was striking at them. The additional input was too much and Sahara passed out.

* * *

Sahara's first conscious thought was that she couldn't feel Bryan. It took a moment to filter anything past the panic that raised. She recognized the pounding in her head next.

That could be interfering with the connection. She wasn't skilled enough to tell if the connection was severed or just suppressed.

She opened her eyes, and found herself in what looked like a hospital emergency room. Her head hurt, and there was pain in her left hip that radiated up into her abdomen.

"Good, you're awake."

She blinked and looked up at young nurse. "What happened?' she asked.

"You took a chunk of brick to the head. Some people pulled you out of the debris field. You were one of the lucky ones."

She tried to sit up, but his hand on her shoulder held her in place. "I was with someone. He was behind me." Sahara said, remembering Bryan trying to push her away.

"Dark hair, scar?" he asked.

"Yes. Did they find him?"

"He got it a little worse than you. He's in surgery. Now that you're awake, I'll get the doctor back in here."

He left the room and Sahara sat up, lifting one hand to her hairline where her fingers found bandages. She lifted her shirt to look at her hip. The bruising was pretty fantastic, deep black that disappeared beneath the waistband of her pants, with reds and yellows and purples and blues that spread upward toward her ribs.

Sahara was about to ease herself up onto her feet, when the nurse was back, with a woman in a lab coat who smiled at her. "You weren't trying to sneak out of here were you?"

"Not a fan of hospitals," Sahara said, her voice low.

"I understand that, but I'd like to get a look at that hip, and run a few tests now that we've slowed down some. You were out for quite a while."

Sahara frowned, but that hurt, so she forced herself to relax her face. "How long is a while?"

The doctor glanced up at a clock, then shook her head. "Long enough that the worst of our share of the victims have all been moved to surgery or otherwise out of the ER."

"Your share..." Sahara frowned. "What happened?"

"We haven't gotten a lot of details. A bomb of some kind. Or bombs. Hundreds dead, thousands injured. All of the local hospitals, and urgent care clinics, and pretty much any other place we could get the wounded got slammed." The doctor stepped closer. "Could you lay back down please? Let me look at that hip."

Sahara laid back, moving her arm up over her head as the doctor started to slowly feel over the bruised area, her fingers moving under the loose waistband of Sahara's pants. "Okay, I'm sending you up to imaging for an MRI and some X-Rays."

Sahara touched her hand as she started to turn away. She had gotten this far in her life without getting either X-rays or an MRI, except for while she was a prisoner of the 8th Battalion. She didn't know if they would show anything unusual. "I—can I talk to you in private?"

The doctor looked slightly alarmed and nodded to the nurse, who smiled and left the room.

"Okay, just us girls," she said as the door closed and she sat on the rolling stool.

Sahara exhaled. "Okay, so…I've never actually had an MRI."

She smiled softly. "Are you claustrophobic?"

Sahara licked her lips. "No, that isn't it. I'm—well, not a fan of small spaces necessarily, but not claustrophobic." She was just terrified that the images would tell a story that would land her in a federal hospital getting poked and prodded the same way she had been as a prisoner. "I'm not…sure how to say this."

The doctor inhaled and nodded. "Oh." She glanced behind her at the door, then scooted closer on the rolling stool. "Which clan?"

"What?" Sahara's heart sped up and she could feel the desire to shift in response to the adrenal flood.

"My grandfather was Ruma."

Sahara's eyes widened. "There are Ruma left?"

The doctor shrugged. "Not anymore that I know of. My grandfather was the last of us who could shift."

Sahara nodded. "I know of a few Aveks, and I recently had reason to tangle with a Semisa, grizzly. Other than that, I thought the few Feles I knew were like the last of us."

"You'd be surprised. I've treated a number of Canis clan recently." Her hand touched Sahara's knee. "So, you tell me then. Are these something that will heal better with a shift, some protein and some sleep? Or is there deeper bone damage?"

Sahara sat up again, swinging her legs down to the floor and standing slowly. There didn't seem to be anything broken. She shifted her weight and pressed her hand along the bruise. "I'm good," she said, looking up. "A shift, some sleep, it should heal."

The doctor nodded and stood. "Okay, I trust you to know yourself. Here's my card," she pulled a business card from the top pocket of her lab coat and handed it to Sahara. "Call me if you change your mind."

Sahara nodded and pocketed the card. "When can I see my friend?"

"I'll have Dave take you up to the surgical waiting room and left the staff know you're there."

The doctor opened the door of the room and beckoned an intern with one hand. "Dave, show her to the surgical waiting area and let the duty nurse know that she's there for..."

"Bryan Wagner." Sahara supplied.

"Sure, follow me."

Sahara nodded her thanks to the doctor and followed the intern to the elevators. "I take it you were at the rally?"

"Not on purpose." Sahara said dryly. "We kind of got stuck in the crowd."

"My brother was there too. He got out un-harmed though."

"Good for him."

The elevator stopped, and Dave lead her down a hall and up to a nurses station. "Hey, Darlene, this lady is here for Bryan Wagner. He came in with the rally bombing victims?"

Darlene nodded. "He's just coming out of surgery now. I'll let the doctor know you're here. You can wait just over there."

She pointed to a small room lined with chairs. Sahara thanked her and headed for the room. She paced for a few minutes, until the pain in her hip got to be more than she wanted to deal with, then she sat, her eyes scanning the room, then through the window out to the nurse's station. She needed to shift, hunt, but she knew it would be hours before that was possible.

She needed to make sure Bryan was going to be alright, then she needed to get ahold of Emily and Victoria to let them know what happened.

Sahara got up to pace again. She never was good at waiting. Out of the corner of her eye, she saw movement and turned to a doctor coming toward her.

"Family of Mr. Wagner?"

"Yes, I'm his partner."

"I'm Doctor Lyle, I was one of the surgeons operating on Mr. Wagner."

"And?"

"I expect him to make a full recovery, though it may take some time. The damage was quite extensive. Our biggest concern was the damage to his lung, but he also sustained injuries to his extremities. There may need to be more surgery to restore function to his left hand, but we saved it."

"Can I see him?" Sahara asked, relief flooding through her.

"Soon. He's in recovery right now, and we'll get him moved down to a room shortly. I'll have someone come get you."

Sahara nodded. "Thank you, Doctor. I have a few phone calls I need to make." She wasn't sure how she was going to do that, since she'd left her phone in the car and she had no idea what had become of Bryan's.

Of course, there could be another way.

She rubbed at her forehead, wishing her head didn't hurt so much. She still had no sense of her connection to Bryan, but way back in her mind, where Victoria had stitched in Emily's sense of her son, Sahara could sort of sense Emily.

Licking her lips, she sat in the chair furthest from the door and closed her eyes. Slowly, she narrowed her attention down to just that sense of Alaric that was all Emily. It was easier said than it was to accomplish. All of the noises of a hospital interfered with her focus. Her own body kept demanding her attention. And between her and Alaric's mother lay a city in chaos and several hundred miles.

Eventually she quieted herself enough, all but drifting outside of herself as she meditated on Emily's touch inside her mind.

"*Sahara?*"

The connection was tenuous, and she wasn't sure she could verbalize her need, so instead she sent flashes of images, culminating with a rush of her fears and her need to find a safe place to shift, hunt and feed.

"*Sit tight and stay safe. Help is on the way.*"

Emily pulled back and Sahara slumped in the chair, drained. She would need to sleep soon, and not in a chair while keeping vigil. Stretching slowly and favoring her wounded side, she stood, hoping movement would help keep her from dozing off in the chair. She was still pacing when a nurse came to take her to Bryan's room.

Sahara stopped at the doorway, her breath short in her lungs at the sight of Bryan's pale face under the dark of his facial hair. His left hand and arm were heavily bandaged from his elbow down, leaving his fingertips barely visible. There were more bandages around his head and several different machines beeped and flashed. On the other side of the room was a couch. She assumed the bag on that couch held whatever personal items they had taken from him.

With a sigh, Sahara crossed to the bed, sliding her fingers under his right hand. "You better not die, you bastard."

After a few minutes, she pulled the chair over to the bed and sat. She contemplated the couch, but she could rest once she assured herself he was going to be okay.

* * *

There was a tingle, somewhere in the back of her mind, pulling her up from her doze, not fully aware of the reason. Then there was a burst of static and like a sudden door was thrown open, Sahara got a head full of *Bryan*.

It was unfiltered and unfocused, the pain, confusion, his heart beat filled her chest and she hurt in so many ways. She tried to sort through the input but there was too much of it as Bryan came awake, unable to control the flow.

She lifted her head as his eyes opened, squeezing his uninjured hand. "It's okay," she murmured softly. "You're okay."

His eyes darted around the room and came back to her. "Where?"

"Still in Indianapolis. You were pretty banged up."

He nodded, though his eyes still held a measure of confusion. "You okay?"

"Yeah, nothing a good hunt won't cure."

"How bad was it?"

"Bad." She stood, pacing over to the couch. "Hundreds dead. The 8th Battalion claimed responsibility." She'd spent hours watching the news coverage while he was out. Video footage from both sides of the protest, from news cameras and cell phones had played on endless loop. It was fairly clear in many of them that the crowd was being whipped into a frenzy by agitators long before the first gunshots went off.

Bryan was already fading, she could feel his attention drifting. She turned back to the bed. "You should sleep. I'll be here."

He reached for her hand. "You should go find a place to hunt, and a way to contact Emily."

"I already did. She should be here soon, provided she can get into the city. It looks like they were closing off all the roads in."

"It's Emily." Bryan said. "She'll find a way."

Sahara smiled. "I imagine so. I'm staying until she gets here though. Then I'll take care of my needs."

Chapter Twelve

The sun seemed to take forever to go down. Zero and Maddie got the car loaded up while Raven paced inside the room. There was a sense of urgency driving them and Zero couldn't shake the nervous energy. The sleep had helped her control, at least to a degree, but the dreams had done nothing to calm her nerves.

She scanned the area around them for maybe the fourteenth time in as many minutes, freezing as a convoy entered the perimeter of her awareness. She grabbed Maddie's hand, put a finger to her mouth. Very carefully, she laid a glamor over them, over the motel to hide any suggestion that anyone was inhabiting the dilapidated building. She held her breath as they came close, watching them until well after they had passed.

Raven emerged from the room as Zero dropped the glamor. "What was that?"

Zero frowned at her. "You felt that?"

Raven nodded. "A very strong urge to be still and silent, followed by.... a blanket of some kind?"

"Sorry. There was a convoy of military trucks moving past on the highway. I wanted to make sure that we weren't seen."

"Were we?" Maddie asked, fear evident in her voice.

"No, I think we're good. We should wait a few more minutes before we go though."

"We've got about a four-hour drive into Salt Lake, barring any complications." Raven said, sighing. "And then we have to figure out where this prison camp is and find somewhere we can plan...without money."

Zero shook her head. "Don't worry about money. I'll take care of it."

It was clear Raven didn't like that idea. Zero met her eyes. "We have nothing but this car. I'm pretty sure camping out in this junk heap is going to draw attention."

"No, you're right. I know that." Raven agreed. "But you need to be careful."

"I will be." Zero tossed the keys to Raven. "You drive. I need to be able to throw a glamor if we come across anyone, especially that convoy." She circled around to the passenger side and got in. She wanted to be able to scout around them too, so she would know if anyone suspected them of anything. Or if there was someone she could *ask* for money, or better yet, credit cards, maybe even ID.

Raven took them back out onto the interstate. As far as Zero could tell, they wouldn't meet anyone on the road until they caught up to the convoy.

In the backseat, Maddie was settling in to sleep. She stretched out across the street as much as she could. Zero could feel her thinking, her mind clouded with doubt and there was a strong sense of grief. Zero couldn't begin to know how to comfort her.

She looked up as Raven glanced at her. "I'm fine." Zero said reflexively. "Just keeping an eye on things."

"Did you sleep?"

Zero nodded. "Yeah, better than I have in a while. Maddie helped." She wasn't really ready to analyze why Maddie had been helpful. All she knew was that when Maddie had come to lay with her, the dreams had eased out of nightmares and into something that might not have been hers at all. Alaric had featured heavily in it, still closed off to his friends, and working with what she thought was a military group of some variety. It was just images, vague and shadowy and there wasn't enough detail to figure out where he was.

Nearly two hours passed without much to mark them, then she felt the kind of person she wanted if she was going to get them what they needed. "Next rest stop." Zero said softly to Raven.

Raven nodded and steered them off the road into a small rest stop. There were a few trucks parked there as they pulled in. There was light on in the cab of one. Zero opened the car door, leaning back in to look at Raven. "Stay here. This should only take a minute." She pulled a glamor over her face, giving herself short black hair and making her face less memorable.

She jogged over to the truck and climbed up, so she could see in the window. The woman in the truck was working on a laptop. She looked up as Zero knocked on the door. Putting the laptop down, she leaned across the passenger seat and opened the door. "Can I help you?"

Zero smiled her best smile. "We're just a little lost. It feels like we've been driving forever. I saw your light and thought maybe you could help?" She swung herself up and into the passenger seat. The proximity was enough to let Zero assess the woman's mind, but she wanted to have a physical connection before she tried to read her any deeper.

"Where are you trying to get?"

"We were hoping to get into Salt Lake for tonight, then west into Nevada," Zero said, inching across the seat. "I mean, I know this freeway goes into Salt Lake, but we've been driving forever, and I was hoping you knew of a motel or something nearby?"

"Yeah, sure, give me a sec." She reached across to the floor beneath Zero's feet, her arm brushing Zero's leg.

That was all the opening she needed. Zero grabbed the unguarded mind, delving deeper as the woman sat up with a road atlas. Some part of Zero's mind dug through for details, information about the state of Salt Lake City and any news they needed to have. The rest of her *pushed* her to hand over her wallet. It was easier than it was with the officer at the roadblock because she blocked the two tasks off as separate things, rather than trying to accomplish all of it at once.

There was no resistance, and in under five minutes, Zero had erased her presence from the woman's mind and pressed on the controls that would knock her out, the way she'd knocked Evan out back when she and Raven had only just met. It seemed like a lifetime ago. She paused to look through the wallet. She had an ID and several credit cards, and to their good luck, there was nearly $100 in cash.

She shoved the wallet in her back pocket and nodded to Raven. "We're good. Go."

* * *

Zero was nearing her limit when they finally reached Salt Lake City. She'd bluffed them past two check points and she still had to get them into a room before she could rest.

Raven pulled up to a rundown motel and looked at Zero. "You're up."

Recalling an old spell of her mother's, Zero pulled a hand over her face, murmuring the words to make the fatigue wash away, at least for a while. "Okay, stay here." She climbed out of the car and went into the office, ringing the bell on the counter.

A man shuffled out of the back office, yawning.

"Checking in?"

Zero nodded, pulling the wallet from her back pocket. "I need two beds." She handed across the ID, making contact with his fingers, and pressing the thought into his head that she was the woman on the card. Keeping that thought prominent, she handed him the credit card as well. "Two nights for now, we may stay longer."

He nodded, ran the card and handed both cards back to her. "How many keys?"

"Three please." She spared a glance over her shoulder while he programmed the key cards. All in all, she was done inside ten minutes and directing Raven back toward the far back corner of the motel. She was yawning as they all climbed out of the car and carried their things inside.

174

"You okay?" Raven asked as they shut the door.

Zero nodded. "Just wiped out."

"You two get some sleep." Raven pointed toward the bathroom. "I'm going to soak for a while."

Maddie locked the door and threw the safety lock before she stripped down to underwear and t-shirt and crawled into the bed. Zero followed suit, climbing into the same bed. Maddie rolled toward her. "I can shift if you want."

"No, it's okay." She closed her eyes and pushed at her rambling thoughts, telling herself to settle and sleep. Her mind rolled through memories of dreams, of Alaric and into warnings of impending danger.

Alaric was close, she could feel him near. He wasn't alone. There was still some kind of barrier between them, she could tell he didn't want to be bothered.

Zero moved onto her back and reached out to a different mind. Bryan's response was sluggish, and she got the sense of drugs impairing his control. He was hurt. She pushed across the impression she got from Alaric. He responded with images and feelings about how he'd been hurt and where he was.

Someone was with him. Someone who felt like Alaric in a way. That someone injected herself between Zero and Bryan. "*I'm Emily. You must be Zero.*"

Zero almost pulled away. Emily, Alaric's mother. "*I don't want to intrude.*" She hesitated, then relayed the same thing she'd given to Bryan. "*I know Bryan's been looking for him. He's close by.*"

"*He won't be found unless he wants to be,*" Emily responded.

"*Unless we're both here for the same thing,*" Zero flashed the only image she had of where they were going, a vague idea gleaned from a mind far too far away to even know if it was accurate. "*He wants revenge.*"

Emily agreed, even if she didn't articulate it. "*I'll find him.*" Zero said with more confidence than she felt.

"*I'll send Sahara your way in the morning.*"

Zero's control was slipping, and Emily pushed her away softly, sending a wave of comfort and stillness behind her, easing Zero into sleep.

* * *

"President Norman Douglas today signed two new bills into law. The first designates land and facilities to be used as residential camps for Shades and unspecified others deemed to be a national threat. The second makes it mandatory that all Shades be relocated into these camps before the first of September. The U.S. Military is ramping up to begin operations to round up all registered or otherwise known Shades starting next week."

Raven had kept the volume low, but the words echoed around in Zero's head anyway. She squinted at the TV in the early morning gloom. "And so it begins."

Raven turned to look at her. She seemed dazed. Zero sat up. "Raven?"

She shook her head, inhaling deeply. "I don't know why, but some part of me didn't believe we'd actually get to this point."

Zero could understand that. No one wanted to believe that their country would turn on them. "What I don't understand is what my father gets out of this." Zero said as she spotted her father in the group of people around the new president.

Douglas had only just been sworn in, and he was already signing laws that would tear what was left of his country in two.

"Well, the experts are saying it will reunite the Southern Coalition with the northern states, so it keeps at least part of the country together." Raven offered.

Zero shrugged. "I guess. Maybe I just don't understand his end game. I thought I did. I thought all he cared about was his experiments."

"Power is seductive." Raven observed, her eyes back on the television. "Maybe he saw the opportunity to put Douglas in the presidency and let the rest of it fall to the wayside. He essentially controls the country now."

Something still felt off about the whole thing. There had to be more to it. Zero got up out of bed and padded on bare feet to the bathroom. After relieving herself, she leaned out. "I thought Maddie and I could go out and do some recon. Figure out where this camp is. But first, I'm going to shower.

Raven nodded. "I'm going to try Adam again."

They had called the fed at least three times since leaving the reservation, and all of the calls just dumped to voice mail. Zero thought maybe he'd gotten caught, maybe they hadn't hidden their tracks as well as they should have. She didn't know the man well. She had no idea how much reach he'd had.

What she did know was that the American government had named Shades and any who associated with them as enemies of the state. That couldn't bode well for a government agency that had employed them.

She stripped down and started the shower, stepping in when it was hot. It bothered her that her father seemed to have dropped his drive to combine the tribes, but she wasn't sure why it bugged her. Maybe because of the trauma of the experiments? At least if he learned how by hurting her, the pain wasn't empty? She shook her head and ducked it under the weak spray of water.

It should be a relief that he had given it up. The last thing this world needed was a supernatural megalomaniac with the combined powers of the tribes, especially not one who was controlling the President.

She sighed and turned her thoughts away from her father. Her immediate problems were closer to hand. She closed her eyes and turned her face into the spray. She needed to find this prison camp, and then they had to figure out a way to get the prisoners out. And she had to worry about the man who her father had sent to the west coast to whip up the 8th Battalion, a man who was a powerful Shadow. If he was close by, he could be a problem.

Zero turned off the water and stepped out of the tub, rubbing a towel over her wet skin before wrapping it around her. She retrieved her underwear and shirt from the floor and emerged from the bathroom.

Maddie was awake, sitting in bed and eating a sandwich. Raven had climbed into bed, but she was still watching the television. "So, I need to find some hair." Zero said, rubbing a hand over her bald head. And we all need clothes. Anything else you want while we're out?"

Raven shook her head. "Just be careful, okay? Don't overuse that credit card."

"I won't. Maddie, you want a shower before we go?"

Maddie nodded, sliding out of bed. Zero got the impression that Maddie was doubting herself, certain she was in over her head.

Zero touched her shoulder as she passed, but Maddie just kept moving. Raven sighed as the water came on in the bathroom. "She's afraid," Raven said.

"I know. So am I. This whole idea is nuts."

"You could have stayed on the reservation. You would have been safe."

"Yeah. Sure. Until the government finally found us or someone turned us in." She shook her head and started getting dressed. "You reach Adam?"

"Voicemail again."

"Maybe—"

"No." Raven stopped her. "Don't."

"Raven, we have to consider that we're out here alone. There is no back up."

Zero finished getting dressed and waited for Maddie to be ready. "We won't be long. Get some sleep." She grabbed the car keys and made sure the stolen wallet was still in her back pocket before heading out.

"Is Raven okay?" Maddie asked as they pulled out of the motel parking lot.

"Yeah, I think so," Zero responded. "She's tired and stressed, and the country she has been working to protect just declared her a non-person, but other than that..."

Maddie nodded and was quiet for a few minutes. "So, do we have a plan, or are we just winging it?"

"I sort of have a plan," Zero said. "First we find some clothes and someplace for me to get a wig or two. Then, we find this camp."

"And how exactly are we going to do that?"

Zero exhaled slowly. "We find someone who knows about it and I read them."

"Just like that?"

"I hope so." Because beyond that lay the way of exposing herself to any sensitives in the area, including her father's former partner.

Chapter Thirteen

The rest of the team had vanished, probably back across the border into Nebraska and on to their next assignment. Alaric buckled his seat belt, but said nothing.

"This isn't going to be easy." Evan started the jeep and eased them out of the driveway. The day was barely started, and the street was still sleeping, better for them to move about unnoticed. "Any little thing could blow our cover."

"Better not do anything wrong then." Alaric countered. His senses were stretched out around them, ready to squelch any sign that someone was on to them. "You watch the road. I'll worry about the rest."

"Right." He could feel Evan looking at him and turned his head. "Don't wear yourself out."

"I got this."

"Okay, if you say so. I'm going to take back roads. It'll take us longer, but it might keep us off the radar better."

They were quiet for a long time as they left the town and moved out onto two lane roads. With his senses extended, Alaric was even more aware of Evan's presence beside him. He was a solid wall, strong, impenetrable.

"You said your mother was telepathic." Alaric said into the silence.

"Yes, she was."

"But you're not related to any of my people, that I can tell."

Evan sighed and rubbed a hand on his chin. "No. She was...different."

"She was a shifter too?" Alaric asked.

"Yes, why?"

He was sensing some annoyance, so he pulled back a little. "Just curious. Making small talk."

"Well, let's not talk about her."

"She trained you well. Best set of shields I've ever encountered on anyone who wasn't one of us."

Evan's face was tight. "Stop."

"Sorry."

After another long stretch of silence, Evan sighed again. "Look, I'm a private person. You

already know more about me than I'm comfortable with."

Alaric shifted in his seat. "I don't want to make
you uncomfortable. I'm not used to working with
someone who doesn't use their gifts."

"Get used to it." Evan responded. "Focus on the
intel. I'm counting on you to get us where we're
going."

"I'll do my part." Alaric said. "You get us to
Salt Lake City, I'll get us the rest of the way." He
went back to his surveillance of the world around
them and shut Evan out of his attention.

They were less likely to run into troops and
law enforcement on the back roads, but much
more likely to arouse the suspicions of regular
people who bought into the 8th Battalion's particular brand of religious moral judgement.

He focused on them, smoothing over any re-
actions to their passing. As they passed out of
towns, he'd relax and pull his senses back to con-
serve his energy.

That was when he could go back to the information he'd pulled from that soldier, building his
own map to the facility that was more detailed

than the one Jones had provided from the computer, built from the same information.

"Heads up." Evan said suddenly, pulling him out of his thoughts. In the distance he could see a vehicle coming their way. It looked like a military transport.

"Just act natural." Alaric said softly, extending his thoughts over the barren terrain. "Yeah, 8th Battalion. Headed to the border. There are three vehicles." He wasn't sure he could control that many minds at once. He exhaled and turned his attention to a different tactic. He focused on the jeep, on making it appear to be an average family sedan. "No sudden moves. I can only hold this for a few minutes."

"Hold what?" Evan asked.

"Just drive. I'll explain later."

The jeep kept moving, and so did the 8th Battalion vehicles. Alaric held the glamor for a while after they'd past, then released it, along with the breath he'd been holding. He was a little dizzy and light headed, and he leaned forward in his seat.

"Going to tell me what that was?" Evan asked.

"Something I've never tried on that scale before." Alaric said, sitting up. "Most of us with active gifts can affect how we're seen, to some degree anyway. It's called a glamor. I just glamored the whole jeep. Made it look like an average sedan to anyone who was looking."

"Little risky, don't you think?"

He shrugged. "It worked. Three troop transports. I couldn't fool that many minds directly. With a glamor, I'm only extending effort on a single object, and whoever looks at it sees what I want them to see, instead of what's there."

"We'll probably see more of them, the closer we get to cities."

Alaric reached behind them for the bag of food they'd packed, pulling a protein bar out. He needed to keep his energy up. "How far?"

"Hours." Evan responded. "Back roads, remember?"

"Right." It made him restless. He settled back into surveillance mode and tried to quell the churning need to be doing something more active.

* * *

"I don't like this." Evan said in a voice just above a whisper.

Alaric didn't either. "You have another suggestion?"

Evan was quiet, and Alaric stepped out of the jeep. They had gotten into the city just as the sun was setting. "We need more information." Alaric said, gesturing at the diner. There were clearly 8th Battalion men inside eating dinner.

"There are other ways–"

"All of which take time." Alaric countered. He stepped up to Evan's side of the jeep. "We go in, we have some food. I'll read what I can."

"And if we get caught?"

Alaric smiled. "We won't."

Evan rolled his eyes. "I'm going to regret this."

Alaric headed for the door, knowing that Evan would follow. Four sets of eyes tracked their entrance, but the men all turned back to their drinks and conversation as a waitress in a blue uniform dress and an apron told Alaric and Evan to take whatever seat they wanted.

Alaric chose a booth not far from the soldiers' table, but not too close either. Evan joined him just as the waitress dropped two menus on the table. "What can I get you boys to drink?"

"Just water for me." Alaric said, turning his eyes to the menu. He felt for the soldiers, getting a first impression. Evan was watching him closely. They were assigned to the local police department, serving as liaisons with the 8th Battalion government.

"I think this will be all right." Alaric said aloud. "Told you I wanted a burger." He lifted an eyebrow, watching Evan struggle to find a way to ask a question without resorting to telepathy.

"Did you find something you like?" he finally said.

Alaric nodded. "I think so."

When the waitress came with their drinks, they both ordered a burger off the menu. Alaric glanced at the men. They were talking quietly among themselves and it took little effort to listen in on the conversation. There wasn't much to glean from their spoken words. It was all everyday procedure talk.

But the more he listened, the better he could decide which of them was the best target for the information he wanted. The waitress served the soldiers and Alaric pulled himself back to nod at Evan.

They were quiet then until their food came. Alaric thanked the waitress and started to eat, glancing up at the soldiers from time to time. As the men ate, Alaric started to push the idea that they needed to use the bathroom. The one closest him seemed to respond better than the others, pushing his chair back and excusing himself. Alaric waited until he had opened the door to the men's room, then stood himself, wiping his face.

"Be right back."

Evan gave him a look that said he really wasn't liking this plan, but Alaric ignored him, striding into the bathroom with an unhurried gait. The soldier was washing his hands as Alaric entered.

He looked up, nodding hello as Alaric stepped into the stall behind him. When his attention was diverted back to his business, Alaric grabbed him, mind first, then hands, pulling him back into the stall and kicking the door shut. He knew he didn't have a lot of time.

Alaric got both hands on the man's head and dove into his mind. He struggled at first, but as Alaric got better control he settled, then slumped.

There was a time when he would have been much gentler in taking what he needed, but he didn't have time to be kind. He took everything he could about the local facilities, units, troop placements, superiors.

He tucked the information away and cleaned up behind himself, creating a memory of being sick, pushing at various buttons in the brain to stimulate a fever and upset stomach. It wasn't permanent and would fade quickly, but it would hide the attack and keep them safe.

Alaric knocked the poor man unconscious, then arranged him so that he was kneeling at the commode, as if he'd thrown up. He stepped out of the stall and checked his work. Nodding to himself, he stepped out of the bathroom. Evan was watching for him, lifting take out boxes to let Alaric know they were ready to leave.

Alaric paused by the soldiers' table. "Sorry for interrupting, guys. I think your friend is sick. I heard him throwing up and he didn't look good."

One of them stood. "I'll check on him, thank you."

Evan led the way back out to the jeep, getting behind the wheel and handing Alaric the boxes. "Well?"

"Head west. The facility is outside the city."

* * *

The night was nearly absolute darkness. The only light came from distant stars that were often obscured by dark clouds. They were pulled off any semblance of road, out in the desert to the west and south of Salt Lake City.

They couldn't risk a hotel, or a fire, so they were laid out beside the jeep in sleeping bags. Alaric stared up at the stars, but he was trying to read the landscape, determine the distance they needed to cover and what resistance they might find.

It was clear they couldn't use the roads. They needed to stay off them and journey through the desert. It wasn't ideal, but they'd keep themselves off of the local radar.

"Stop." Evan said beside him.

Alaric turned his head, frowning. "Stop, what?"

Evan sighed. "Everything. You need to sleep. I need you to handle yourself tomorrow. You can't be frayed and exhausted."

"I'm just trying to–"

"I know. Believe me, I know." He turned in his sleeping bag, lifting up on his elbows. "We're safe enough for the moment. We're far enough out we can't be seen from the nearest road. We're miles from anywhere. And you said you've put up defenses. We'll know if someone comes snooping."

He lowered himself back down, pillowing his head on his arms. "In the morning, I'll get an aerial view and we can work on a plan."

Alaric tried to relax enough to sleep, but he wasn't sure sleep would happen. Not when they were so close. He did eventually drift off, not waking until the sun began to warm the air.

Evan was already up, his sleeping bag rolled up and stowed back in the jeep. Alaric sat up, looking around and finding Evan standing behind the jeep, clearly undressing.

"Do you mind?" Evan asked.

"Uh, sorry." Alaric said, pushing his sleeping bag down so he could get out.

"I don't like to be watched."

Alaric made show of turning his back.

"I'm going to take a look around. I'll be back soon."

There was a strange rustling noise, then a squawk that made Alaric turn. Perched on the roll bar of the jeep was the largest falcon he'd ever seen. He spread his wings and took flight, circling over Alaric before heading toward where the facility was.

Alaric busied himself with rolling up his sleeping bag and digging out breakfast. He hiked up to the top of the rise they'd parked behind, shading his eyes to try to spot Evan in the air.

After a long time, he turned his attention the road that led out to the facility. It sat outside the city proper, a former home for the criminally insane that no one had wanted built near schools or homes. He closed his eyes and extended his senses over the miles.

All that met him was a wall of misery, grief, pain. It was so strong it knocked him back, blocking all other input. For a moment he could barely hold it at bay, his stomach churning until he managed to pull back. He hiked back down to the jeep with only the vaguest idea whose pain he was reading. There was at least one of his clan there, his or her own suffering magnified and radiating out the pain of all of those around them.

It was frustrating. He didn't like waiting with nothing to do to get him closer to his goal. As he sat, he felt something, a vaguely familiar touch pushing against the wall he'd put up to keep Bryan and the others out.

Alaric pushed back, strengthening the wall. He didn't have time for arguments. It wasn't Bryan this time though. The touch was stronger, closer and it distracted him. Zero.

The girl was somehow nearby. She was looking for the same thing he was, and she'd found him instead. She pushed against the wall again and he opened it just enough that he could feel her out, see if she had information he didn't.

She latched onto him almost immediately, pulling herself to him so strongly it was almost like she was standing beside him. "*Your mother is worried about you.*" Zero said, floating information to him that included his mother, Bryan and Sahara, the news from Washington. He accepted it and thanked her.

"*Don't interfere,*" Alaric told her. "*I don't want to hurt you.*"

"*We're looking for the same thing.*" Zero said.

"*Oh, you want revenge too?*"

"*No, but there are prisoners in that building. We aim to get them out.*"

Alaric shook his head. Of course the girl was going after the prisoners. He should have seen it coming. She couldn't go after the man she really wanted, so she would chase after the idea of saving others. And she wasn't alone. She had the Shade who had worked with Mason and the Shifter who had nearly killed them.

"*Stay out of it.*" He shoved her away, but she held on.

"*We should work together.*"

"*No.*" He pushed her harder and got the wall back up before she could come back at him.

No, it was better that it was just him and Evan. They would kill Shallon, and anyone who got between them and their target.

Chapter Fourteen

"Bryan?" Sahara sat up from the couch where she'd drifted toward sleep. Bryan was sitting up on the bed, his eyes closed as he swayed from the effort. She could *feel* him extending himself westward.

She crossed to the bed and touched his back, effectively drawing his attention back to his body. "God damn that fucking asshole." Bryan grumbled.

"You should be resting. You do remember that you had a building fall on you just two days ago?" Sahara asked. "If Emily was here—"

"She isn't. I sent her back to the hotel to sleep."

Sahara frowned, she must have been deeper asleep than she thought, she hadn't even heard Emily come in. She was feeling better, the bruising all but gone from her hip. Victoria and Emily had shown up and given her the chance to go somewhere private to shift and heal. There was no hunting, not in the city and not with the recent changes in the government. It wasn't safe.

Still, she was stronger. Strong enough to head west, toward Alaric. Hopefully to find Maddie and the two with her, then Alaric. Which is what Bryan had just been doing. "I take it he's still blocking you?" Sahara asked gently, handing him a bottle of water.

Bryan took the water and rubbed his bandaged hand over his face. "I have an idea where he is, but yeah, still blocking me."

She caressed his back, settling in beside him. He was tense and tight, his muscles bunched up and bound in his worry. Her fingers kneaded at his shoulders, pressing against muscles tight and knotted. "Obviously, he doesn't want to be found."

He sipped at the water and shook his head. "He has responsibilities."

"I'm not arguing that," she said in his ear, her voice deep and soft. "But you beating your head against that brick wall he put up is only going to hurt your head, not get him back."

Bryan's thoughts invaded her head, flooding into her. He knew she was right, but he wasn't sure they would ever really get him back anyway. Of all of them, Alaric had always been the pacifist, the one who would argue for the peaceful solution in any conflict, but the Alaric that Bryan had seen outside that office building in DC was out for blood.

Alaric wanted revenge. Bloody, violent, horrific revenge. And even Sahara knew that if Alaric found the men he held responsible for the death of his lover, without Sahara and Bryan there to help him, temper him, he would use all of the power at his disposal to exact that revenge.

If that happened, the Alaric they knew, the Alaric that Bryan would willingly sacrifice himself for, would be gone...and Bryan wasn't sure that they'd ever get him back.

Sahara pulled away from him physically and nudged the overflow back toward him, so he could realize what he was doing.

"I'm sorry." Bryan offered, his voice scratchy.

"You're tired. You need to rest."

"I know. I can't...." His voice trailed off and memory overwhelmed him, flooding into her, replaying the whole thing again.

The sound of the incoming missile, the explosion, the fire, the smell of burning flesh...then Mason was at his side and they were trying to escape...*the gunshots and the look on Mason's face...the garish look of the blood across his lips...the way he went limp against Bryan's body.*

Alaric had never blamed him, Sahara knew that Bryan understood that...but that didn't mean that Bryan didn't blame himself. He should have gotten out before Mason had to come looking for him. Should have put himself between Mason and the bullet that took his life. Should have moved faster.

Sahara covered her ears as if it would help block out his thoughts. "*Bryan, stop.*"

"Can't." Bryan said tightly, his eyes glazing over.

Sahara climbed up on the bed, sitting behind him and wrapping her legs around his waist, pulling him back to rest against her. She breathed in deep and could feel the shift inside her, the rise of the cat within and when her hands moved against his skin, it was her claws, pressing in, breaking skin. It was grounding, focusing. He breathed in and stilled, the replay slowing.

"Let go of it," she whispered, her words curling in his ear. "Be here, with me."

"I'm here." Bryan murmured, and she *watched* him focus on the sharp pricks of pain. The loop of memory slowed and finally stopped. She rubbed against him, purring somewhere deep inside her as he opened up even more, and they came together, slipping past a need for words or even images, a contact far more intimate than any sexual act she could imagine.

All feeling faded except for the ten bright spots of sharp pain where her claws penetrated his skin, all sound withdrew but his heartbeat against her chest and the sound of their breath, coming as one.

He drifted in that comfort and she held him there until the drifting took him into sleep, and then for a while longer. She hadn't told him yet that she was leaving, probably before he woke.

Sahara was still sitting there when Victoria appeared in the door. Her hands were no longer claws, but they still held Bryan's arms. Victoria raised an eyebrow at her and Sahara slowly untangled herself from Bryan and eased him down to lay against the bed.

"He was having trouble controlling…" she gestured at her head. "He's replaying Mason's death over and over. I couldn't take it."

Victoria nodded knowingly. "As he heals, he'll have better control. Won't make the memory stop, but it will keep him from ambushing you with it over that connection. Distance will help too."

Sahara nodded. She already knew that. "I'm ready. I just need to know where I'm going and how I'm getting there."

"Emily is working on it."

That wasn't as reassuring as she was sure Victoria meant it to be. At least there would be a number of places where she could shift and hunt. It should be enough to finish the healing process.

All she knew from Emily was that she was headed to Salt Lake City, which was heavily guarded and locked down. She would have to cross the border into 8th Battalion territory, which meant getting past the US troops holding the border and the 8th Battalion troops on the other side, before she could even begin to get into Salt Lake.

Emily kept telling her not to worry. Sahara figured that was easy for her to say, she wasn't the one who was about to go into enemy territory.

* * *

"No." Sahara shook her head to emphasize her disagreement. "Alaric would never forgive me."

"It's the only way you're getting past those blockades." Emily said calmly. "Bryan can't go, not like he is, and even if he could, he wouldn't have the strength to hold the illusion."

Bryan snorted. "Bryan is sitting right here." He was starting to sound more like himself, and his color was much improved. "And he's going. Sahara is right, Emily. If Alaric were here—"

"But he isn't here." Emily cut in. "He's off trying to get himself killed. And I'm his mother. I'm going with you."

The room was quiet for a minute before Victoria stood. "Don't look at me, I'm not going. I know my limits." She looked squarely at Bryan. "You should stay here and finish healing."

"If we catch up with Zero, she's got a Shade with her."

Sahara looked at him sharply. "You, actually wanting a Shade?"

He sighed and shrugged. "If it will stop the daggers in my gut, yes."

This was not how Sahara had expected this whole thing to go. She'd expected another rental car, or a stolen car and some fake documents or something. To be fair, she'd never done anything like this. To think, only a year before she'd been hunting, free and without anyone depending on her. Now she had all of these people looking to her, expecting her to go in search of the man who had saved her and Mila and Maddie after the three of them had been captured.

"You need someone who can use glamors and push people to go against their own minds." Emily said softly. "Consistently, and not compromised."

"I don't know why both of you are expecting me to make a decision between you." Sahara said finally. "You're both adults. I'm on record for saying you should both stay here, but if you're coming, let's get moving. I have the feeling Alaric is already in position. We need to catch up."

Bryan stood, already dressed as though he'd known she was going, which she supposed wasn't surprising with as much as he'd been in her head. Victoria shook her head wearily. "Stay in touch. And don't get dead."

* * *

Sahara ran with abandon through the trees, though she was mindful of the precarious position of her companions waiting in the car and their need to keep moving. They had done the hard part, Emily bluffed them past the two border stops, convincing the guard on the US side that they were a military vehicle headed out on patrol, and the guard on the opposite side that they were refugees, fleeing the US.

Still, the last thing they needed was to be found waiting on some back woods road through the forest, waiting for a shape shifter to return. It was hard to judge time in her animal form, but the sun was rising, so she slowed her run, licking her whiskers to taste the free air. She missed this. Before any of this had happened, she'd stayed in her cat form for days, weeks even.

She turned to head back to the car, pausing at the downed tree where she had undressed. Sahara shifted and dressed before heading back to the car. Emily was pacing.

"What's wrong?" Sahara asked.

Emily gestured at the backseat. "He's running a fever. We should not have let him come with us."

Sahara chuckled. "Like you were going to stop him?"

Emily shook her head. "I'll feel better once we reach Zero and the others."

"You heard from her." It wasn't a question, somehow Emily's tone told her it was true.

Emily slid in behind the driver's wheel and started the car that she said she had "borrowed" from someone. "I did. We're close enough now I could reach out to her. The Shade knows we're coming and is ready to help. I have an address."

"And?"

Emily rolled her eyes. "And, my son is a stupid, stubborn horse's ass."

"You sound like Bryan."

Emily didn't respond, just turned them around on the barely two-lane road they had found running off the highway and into the trees. Sahara turned to look at Bryan who seemed to be asleep, then she settled into her seat. The sooner they got into Salt Lake City, the sooner she could stop worrying about him.

It wasn't long before they were approaching yet another check point. Emily slowed the car and held her hand out to Sahara for their paperwork. It was a fair approximation of the 8th Battalion's travel papers, made all the more authentic with Emily's mind game.

The man in the blue uniform of the 8th Battalion took the papers and Emily's hand lingered on his. A few seconds later he was waving them through.

The city was quiet, despite the fact that it was the middle of a weekday. Emily drove through nearly deserted streets until they reached the address Zero had given her. The girl was waiting for them, leaning back against the soda machine in a blond wig and waving them toward the back.

"You made good time." Zero said as Sahara got out to the car.

"Roads were clear." Emily said. "You're Zero?"

"The one and only." Her voice was dry, her eye dancing over Emily before coming back to Sahara. "Bryan?"

Sahara reached for the door to the back seat, feeling Bryan stir. She leaned in and stroked his face. "We're here."

He grunted and moved toward the door, his feet hitting pavement as his hand reached for her to steady him. He was burning up and the pain in his stomach reverberated through him.

"Raven's waiting." Zero opened the door to a room and held it while Emily and Sahara helped Bryan into the room. Maddie stood as they entered, and the Shade was just coming from the bathroom with a glass of water.

"Here." She patted the bed and Sahara and Emily guided Bryan to it, easing him down.

"Get off me." Bryan groused, pushing their hands away. "Let her do what she does."

Raven nodded, and the two older women backed off. Maddie rushed at her and Sahara submitted to the needy hug. "Are you okay?"

Maddie nodded when she'd pulled back. "I'm good. You?"

Sahara smiled softly for her. "Yeah, I'm good."

Zero joined them. "We should talk." She gestured to the door and they followed her out to the car. "I've been tracking Alaric's movements since I found out he was here. He's with someone, a Shifter I think. They're planning on hitting the facility tomorrow."

"So soon?" Emily asked, squinting as if she might somehow see him if she just looked hard enough.

"He's trying to block me and he won't talk to me, but it has something to do with someone named Shallon."

That made sense. "Shallon is the man who is responsible for Mason's death."

Zero nodded. "Yeah, I gathered that. Thing is the guy he's with has no love for the man either."

"They're going to kill him." Emily breathed the words, the horror of it clear on her face.

"Yeah, and they won't be dissuaded. Believe me, not even telling them that we were tracking Shade prisoners made him more reasonable."

"Do you have any idea how they're planning to do this?" Emily asked.

Zero shook her head. "Only vague ideas. The last time I was able to get anywhere near him, they were still hashing it out. But whatever they're doing, it will be tomorrow."

"Then I suggest we get started with a plan of our own." Emily said.

"Oh, sure. We'll just infiltrate a secure facility, rescue the prisoners, save Alaric from doing something he'll regret, and escape back over the border without any of us getting killed." Zero said sarcastically. "Why didn't I think of that?"

"Canada." Maddie said, grabbing Sahara's arm. "We don't have to try to get all the way to the eastern border. We can go to Canada."

Emily shook her head. "They're about the same distance. And both are a litany of bad news, especially in more than one vehicle, which...if we're talking about the six of us, and Alaric and his friend and however many prisoners..." She sighed. "You're right Zero. I don't know *if* we can pull this off."

Chapter Fifteen

"This would be a lot easier if you would let me—"

Evan cut him off with a nip, his beak stopping before drawing blood, but just barely.

"Fine." Alaric pulled his hand away. "I'm just saying it would be easier." He turned away, reaching into the jeep for his pack. Evan was possibly more sensitive about being seen shifting than he was about the telepathy.

"Easier isn't always better." Evan replied when he was once more in his human form. Alaric could hear him dressing and kept his gaze averted.

Alaric pulled out the map they had picked up. He'd been drawing information onto it from what he'd learned either from soldiers he'd read or Evan's feedback when he'd come back from flying runs. They'd had two days to work out a plan and execute it. He smoothed the map on the hood of the jeep while Evan got a bottle of water out of the back.

Alaric wasn't going to stop trying to get Evan to let him try communicating telepathically. It was clear the man was gifted, but closed off to the idea. It would save them time and in some situations, their lives. "Show me." Alaric said as Evan joined him.

Evan pointed out five spots along the southern wall. "Guard posts with heavy guns." He dragged a line down the road leading in to the compound. "Checkpoints here and here." He drank half the bottle, then sighed. "I got a pretty good look. There isn't much cover around there. Our only way in or out is through the front gate and that is heavily guarded."

"Which means we're back to needing a cover." Alaric said. "And uniforms wouldn't hurt."

Evan bristled. "Where are we going to get our hands on uniforms?"

Alaric sighed. "We'll have to head back to town and get creative. If we try taking them off anyone out here, they'll connect the dots and we won't get in."

"I do not want to put on that uniform." Evan countered.

"Neither do I." Alaric agreed. "Can you think of another way?"

"We could just ambush Shallon." Evan offered, but even his tone said that it wouldn't work.

"If we wanted to cleverly disguise ourselves as prisoners." Alaric said, shaking his head. "If we can get uniforms we can slip in with Shallon's escort."

Evan looked at him like he was crazy. "That's your plan?"

"It's the simplest way. We join the back of the group."

"Can't you use that glamor thing? Make everyone think we belong there?"

Theoretically, he could. "It is possible, but would hold up better if we had actual uniforms." Alaric said.

"How about clothes the right color, but not actually 8th Battalion uniforms?"

Alaric nodded slowly. "Could work."

"Get in. I think I have an idea."

Alaric folded up the map and got into the jeep. Evan stepped on the accelerator and they sped back toward the road. It didn't take long to reach a small industrial park on the outskirts of the city. Evan pulled the jeep to a stop and pointed to an Industrial uniform supply place.

"Wait here, I'll be right back." Evan slipped out of the jeep and headed for the door. In less than ten minutes he was back with a bag in his hands. "We're going to have to do something about that hair."

Alaric frowned at him. Evan grinned. "That won't pass as military."

Alaric pulled a hand through the shoulder length hair and sighed. He wasn't wrong and the closer he could look to the real thing, the less effort the glamor would take.

It took nearly an hour to get his hair cut into something resembling a military cut, and get back out to a place where they could see the main road out to the camp. Off in the distance they could see Shallon's approach. They had maybe a half hour.

"I'm going to do a quick flyby."

"We don't have time." Alaric said, already pulling off his clothes to don the dark blue clothing they'd picked up.

"Tell me again why we aren't just hitting them and taking Shallon out." Evan said suddenly, crossing his arms.

"We've been over this." Alaric fought taking out his frustration physically, his hands fisting at his sides. He wanted to shake the man out of whatever was holding him back. "Inside we can do more. We can gather information, maybe take out more than Shallon." He turned to look at Evan, trying to read whatever it was he wasn't saying.

"Our orders are just for Shallon." Evan countered.

Alaric snorted. "Yeah, our orders that don't exist. You said yourself this mission is off the books. We have no orders." He pushed against Evan's shielding.

Evan lifted his head, his eyes flecked with gold. "Don't play games with me. My job is to keep you alive, and I will pull the plug on this entire mission if I think for a minute that you're going to get reckless on me." Evan started pulling his clothes off, but kept his back to Alaric. "And stop trying to get inside my head."

Alaric pressed his lips together and breathed in through his nose, counting to ten before exhaling. "There are men and women in that facility suffering right now. I can't read how many, not from here, but I can feel their pain. They're being tortured slowly like your brother was." He couldn't get a full sense of the place, too many people, too much distance and he was running on days with very little sleep, but the pain, the anguish washed over him anytime he tried to see into the facility.

"Stop." Evan's face was ashen, and Alaric felt a shift in his control of his emotions. Grief, dismay, horror all washed over his shielding at Alaric.

"Evan?"

He took a step away, but it did little to mitigate the overflow. "They have…they're…shit…Fuck, Alaric. They're burning people. They have…"

Alaric took a step closer and suddenly Evan looked at him, his shields falling away. Alaric was assaulted full on with the image of three stakes with writhing figures covered in flames, the smell of flesh melting and the sound of the fire and the screams slamming into him. He had a bird's eye view as Evan flew around the open yard, avoiding the smoke, but circling before lifting up and away over the walls of the yard.

His instinct was to pull away, but it was the first time Evan had given him even a glimpse inside him. Alaric held the image, horrific as it was, and reached beyond it. "*We can stop them.*"

Evan pushed him out and buttoned up his shields. "Or join them." He moved away, and moved to finish getting dressed "We don't have a lot of time."

Evan remained closed off as they dressed and got into the jeep, easing themselves toward the main road, doing their best not to raise a dust trail.

The convoy was only three vehicles, instead of the nine or ten they'd expected based on the intel. Alaric scanned them with a growing sense of unease. They were coming fast, and he was getting the sense that Shallon had chosen to surround himself with far more competent men than the ones he and Evan had been dealing with up until now.

"Stop." He put a hand on Evan's arm and the jeep came to a stop. "We can't do it that way."

217

He stood and lifted the binoculars to get a look as the convoy approached the checkpoint. There was a flurry of activity and further up the road, the second checkpoint was already opening the massive front gates of the facility.

"What then?" Evan asked.

Alaric brought his attention back to the soldiers left manning the first checkpoint as the vehicles moved through. He scanned them and nodded. He could get in that way, he was fairly sure.

"You are not going in there alone." Evan said, grabbing the binoculars from him and looking for himself.

"I wasn't-"

"Don't lie to me." He turned to look at Alaric. "Okay, let's get you dirty."

Alaric frowned at him. "What?"

Evan grinned at him and shoved him out of the jeep, onto his ass in the dirt. "I'm the one with the military background. I know my way around a checkpoint."

"What are you going to do, drag me through it?"

Evan jumped down off the jeep and shook his head. "No, but I'll carry your sorry ass." Evan reached for him and Alaric pulled away involuntarily. "Look, we make it look like you're hurt. I carry you in and straight to the infirmary."

"And then what?" Alaric got what he was going for though and nodded when Evan reached for him again.

"Then we find this traitor of yours and figure out how the hell we're going to shut that fucking prison down. Sorry."

Alaric almost had time to ask what for before Evan's fist slammed into his face, knocking him back to the ground. His cheek was going to be a massive bruise before long and he could taste blood.

A few minutes later, Alaric had dirt and engine grease on his face and hands, his clothing was torn and a few shallow, but bloody cuts on his arm gave the illusion of a more serious injury.

"Okay, so just…play dead." Evan said as he approached. He bent at the knee and put his shoulder against Alaric's hip, hefting him up and over his shoulder.

"You're stronger than you look." Alaric said as his head bobbed down near Evan's ass.

"Dead men don't talk." Evan chided, shifting and adjusting until he had Alaric where he wanted him. One arm braced Alaric along the back of his thighs, the other hand held Alaric's wrist over Evan's other shoulder. "You set?"

Alaric exhaled and pulled the glamor over them that would make their blue janitors uniforms look like 8th Battalion uniforms. "Yeah, we're good. Just, no sudden moves."

"Hold on." Evan set off at a brisk pace in the heat of a dry afternoon.

It didn't take long for Alaric to feel the sweat seep through Evan's clothes, and the rhythm of his gait was actually soothing. Alaric tried to relax against him, go with the movement of his body, rather than fight to establish his own.

The rhythm changed as his feet found pavement and he turned them to move up the road. Eventually, Evan slowed. Alaric could hear voices. He reached out for them, offering up a cloud of confusion and urging them to accept whatever lie Evan was going to offer them.

"He's hurt. Our jeep…we ran off the road a few miles back."

Alaric could hear the gate opening and footsteps approaching.

"And you are?"

"Lieutenant Stanley, this is Lieutenant Thomas, we're relocating from San Diego." Evan made a show of reaching for his pocket. "Damn it. I left my orders in the jeep with our gear. Please, he's hurt pretty badly."

Alaric groaned weakly and pushed a little harder on the suggestion that they let them pass.

"I'll take you up to the compound. Put him in the back."

Evan's body conveyed his relief as they moved toward whatever vehicle the man had. Evan lowered him into the back seat of what Alaric assumed was an SUV. The engine roared to life and they moved out, stopping once at the inner checkpoint, then peeling away to the east. "The front entrance is probably still a mess from Shallon's arrival, I'll take you to the east door, closer to the infirmary anyway."

Alaric sat up slowly, reaching over the back seat to grab the man by the throat as the SUV

221

came to a stop. He reached inside him and set up a false memory of seeing them into the infirmary and getting confirmation that they belonged there.

He nodded to Evan and they both climbed out, heading inside. They saluted their way past the guards and Alaric gestured to a hall off the main corridor. He exhaled slowly and nodded, pulling up the map of the facility he'd built in his head. "Okay, this is where it gets tricky."

"What do you call what we just did?" Evan asked, checking to make sure they hadn't aroused suspicion.

Alaric shook his head. He didn't have time to discuss the levels of work involved in the things he had done and would need to do. "We need to get the lay of the land, and find a safe place to meet up so we can set up."

Evan nodded. Suddenly, Alaric could feel him. "*Hear me?*" Alaric nodded. "*Nothing more than this. I feel you prying, I'll snap you in two, got it?*"

"Yeah, okay." Alaric breathed out loud.

Evan nodded too. "Okay. You figure out how we're going to do this. I'm going to get us a room and some real uniforms. Shallon's here for two

days. We need to blend in and look like we belong."

Alaric didn't ask how he was planning to get them a room, he was too busy planning out his route for finding Shallon.

* * *

Alaric slipped into the room, lightly touching Evan's mind first so that he wouldn't get shot. As military quarters went, it was a step up from open barracks, though not by a lot.

A set of bunk beds, a small table and two chairs and a small closet. Evan nodded at him. He was in a real uniform and there was another laid out on one of the beds.

Alaric pulled a map of the compound out of his pocket. He'd spent his time trying to build on what they'd had before getting there. He spread it out on the table. "I filled in some de-tails." He pointed to a wing that had the fewest markings and notes. "Near as I can tell, this is where they're keeping the prisoners. Heavy guards, tight security. No one goes in or out with-out approval."

Evan nodded. "That makes sense. They want to limit the number of people that actually come in contact with the prisoners." He pointed to the area on the map that corresponded to their location. "We're here. Shallon and the rest of the upper echelon are rooming here." He pointed at the end of a long corridor.

"He's here to witness the execution of some important prisoners, as well as oversee some strategic preparations for their Shade agenda." Alaric added. "I got bits of it from people. I really need to get someone close to the top to deep read."

Evan made a face. "That won't be easy. They're all holed up in command." He dug in a pocket and pulled out two protein bars, passing one to Alaric. "From what I gathered, this operation they're planning is pretty intense."

He put a notebook down beside the map and flipped it open. "These are the names of people with unlimited access to all areas of the compound."

It was a short list. Alaric looked at the names, trying to feel for them. He crossed two off the list immediately, they were far more ordered and in control of their minds than he had time to deal with. He stretched a little further, then pulled back, finding one of them nearby. In the hallway outside their door even.

Alaric stood and moved to the door, cracking it open. He brushed across the mind, looking for a way in. He smiled and glanced back at Evan. "Get ready."

He opened the door and stepped neatly into the man, a young soldier with conflicting ideas of what cause he was serving, a man in his position because he was somebody's nephew, not because he'd earned it. Their bodies collided, and he went sprawling to the floor, the folders in his hands cascading and fanning out around him.

"I'm so sorry." Alaric said instantly, dropping to one knee to help gather the documents. "Are you okay? I really need to watch where I'm going."

"Yeah, fine. I'm fine." He got up to his knees and started pulling papers to him.

Alaric handed him the papers he'd collected, making sure to make contact with the guy's hand. "You're Major Levar, right?"

The guy looked surprised, but nodded. "And you are?"

"Oh, sorry. I'm Lieutenant Thomas." Alaric scanned names and faces from his surface memories. "I served with Commander Dickens in Nevada."

Levar nodded, though he was frowning as he finished gathering his papers. He was confused, scattered, and there was crack Alaric could exploit if he got the chance. He needed physical contact though. "Can I help you get those back in order?"

"No. I should get back to ops with these."

Alaric stuck out his hand. Levar took it slowly as Alaric urged more confusion. Alaric gripped his hand tightly, using the physical contact to gain a little more control. "Now," he sent to Evan.

The door opened, and Alaric guided Levar inside. Evan took the papers to the table, while Alaric guided Levar to the beds. "You should rest, let me make sure you're okay."

"I need to…" Levar trailed off as Alaric exerted a little more control, sitting on the lower bunk in jerky motions.

"That's it, sir. Lay back. This will only take a minute." Alaric knelt beside the bed and closed his eyes, reaching into Levar. He didn't want to waste time being tidy, but he knew they couldn't afford any slips.

Levar was younger than Alaric had guessed, and his devotion to the 8th Battalion's cause was wavering. If they had time they could probably recruit him using more honest methods, but they didn't have time. Alaric sifted through his assigned tasks, his dealings with Shallon, his schedule for the next forty-eight hours.

He left Levar drifting in a light trance and lifted his head. "This is our guy. He's in and out of the command center. His immediate superior is the compound's commander."

Evan nodded. "These are prisoner files. There's at least twenty here. Details of their interrogations, torture, execution dates."

Alaric watched Evan sort through them. "Fuck, this one's only twelve."

"Are there names?"

Evan shook his head. "Shade #4-1, Shade #6-2…Shifter #1-1, wolf." Alaric could sense the turmoil spilling out over Evan's shielding. "We can't just…if we get Shallon and leave, they'll just keep burning the prisoners alive."

"What are you suggesting?" Alaric asked. "You're the one who said we're only here for Shallon."

Evan pressed his lips together and paced the small room. "If we can't get them out, we put them out of their misery," he said quietly.

Alaric shook his head. "I can't think like that."

He felt Evan's eyes. "Have you seen what they do to these people?" He lifted a file. "Shade #1-1. His last interrogation included salt poured into open wounds on his face, stomach and thighs. The wounds were made using a cat o'nine tails. There's more. Weeks of it. Notes that say he wasn't even coherent when they started some-times." Evan was shaking. "And that doesn't even touch how he was captured, shot in the stom-ach with a bullet made to ricochet around in-side, laced with gold and leeching salt and chlo-rine and other chemicals into his body. He's alive because Shade #13-1 has been forced to keep him alive so that they won't do the same with Shade#13-3, a female child."

Alaric turned away. He didn't need to be read the details of how the 8th Battalion tortured Shades. He'd seen it firsthand. "I'm betting that poor bastard would rather we put a bullet in his head on our way out than leaving him for the stake." Evan added. "Which he's apparently scheduled for tomorrow at noon."

Alaric paced between the bed and the door. He had no problem killing Shallon. He had no problem killing the man who had betrayed them. Killing prisoners though...that was a whole different thing. Even if it was merciful.

"Wait." Alaric turned back. "Shade 13-1. Is his file here?"

Evan went to the stack of files on the table and sorted through them. He nodded and lifted it, his eyes scanning quickly. "He's...apparently he was captured the first time with his pregnant daughter and he escaped." His finger trailed down the page. "The daughter was kept alive and gave birth shorty after capture. He was recaptured during a raid...oh."

Alaric felt it click into place. "He's the one I want." He went back to Levar, dropping into his head and digging for what he knew of Shade

#13-1. The image welled up, the familiar face, bruised and dirty as he clung to a small child. Levar had seen him earlier that day, had been the one who brought the girl to her grandfather. Alaric could taste Levar's revulsion of what Shallon had ordered, the girl was set to die alongside her grandfather and another... the image shifted, as Levar's head turned in the memory.

Alaric jumped away from Levar, landing on his ass near the table, shaking.

Mason.

Shade #1-1 was Mason.

Mason was alive.

Alive and within reach.

He was hurt, bloody and bruised and he didn't seem to be fully aware of himself. But he was alive.

Chapter Sixteen

"Alaric?"

He turned his head toward the sound of Evan's voice, but all he could see was Mason's face, his scarred and marked body, the way he shook as he hung there while Shallon pressed his gloved fingers into the open wounds.

"Alaric."

He jerked away from Evan's hand, but Evan grabbed his face, forced him to focus. "What is it?"

Alaric licked his lips and shook his head. "Mason." He closed his eyes and scanned through the memory again. "He's alive. He's here." He shook his head again and looked up at Evan. "He's…" He swallowed and forced himself back to Levar. "We have to get to him."

Evan grabbed his arm. "We have to get to Shallon. That's why we're here."

Alaric looked up at him. "I'm not leaving this place without Mason." He couldn't. He had believed Mason died in the desert in Arizona, believed it because he couldn't feel him, couldn't find him anywhere. That belief had taken him down some very dark roads.

Evan stared at him for a long moment, then relented, letting go of him. "How do you propose we do that?"

Alaric wanted to storm into the prison wing now that he knew. Wanted to blast anyone that got between him and the man he loved. That would be suicide with just the two of them. He knew that.

But it didn't have to be just the two of them. Three if he counted Levar. "I have an idea."

"I'm not going to like it." Evan said. It wasn't even a question.

"No." They didn't have much time. "I need you to keep watch for a minute. I need to connect with some people." Alaric lay on the floor beside the bed. "And then I'm going to have to connect with you."

"See, I knew I wasn't going to like it." Evan responded, though he took up a protective position as Alaric laid his head back and closed his eyes.

He was going to need Bryan and Sahara for this, at a minimum. Of course, he wasn't sure that they would, or even that they could do it. What he was considering was nearly unheard of in modern times. It was the skill that had earned them their name. Memories pushed past the wall he'd been using to prevent them from influencing him, memories of a time before time when their kind were considered witches and sorcerers, when they were closer to the beginning and the gifts flowed powerfully through them all. It was a long shot.

He exhaled and dropped into himself, into the quiet center that hadn't been all that quiet of late. It had been a long time since he'd actively connected with any of his own people, preferring instead to surf the surface of those he needed and keep the truth from those who would try to stop him if they knew.

He reached out across the miles in the general direction of Chicago. That was where he had seen Bryan last. He pulled up well before Chicago though, somewhere close by.

"Bryan."

He felt Bryan's flash of anger, followed by worry and then Bryan was grabbing at him, shoring up the connection. "*Where the fuck are you?*"

Rather than trying to use words, Alaric sent a burst of images, ending with the image of Mason he'd taken from Levar. Bryan recoiled, absorbing the information. "*How?*"

Alaric sidestepped the question, reaching for Sahara now that he had an active connection with Bryan.

"*Hold on.*"

Alaric got the sense that Bryan was talking to someone and a few seconds later, he brought Sahara into the link, but she wasn't alone. They were with his mother. Here, behind enemy lines.

"*Oh no you don't,*" his mother said. "*You don't get to lecture me.*" Her words belied the surge of relief that flowed from her, though it was laced with a good dose of worry. Zero joined the connection a moment later and he could sense a scurry of activity that she was keeping to herself.

This was far more than he had expected. It might even work.

"*What's the plan?*" his mother asked.

Alaric sent the pertinent information in bursts of images and thoughts.

"*You want to try what?*" Bryan asked, scouring through what Alaric had sent through. "*How?*"

"*It's theoretically possible,*" Emily mused.

"*I could do it,*" Zero inserted. "*Energy drain though.*"

Alaric realized there were a lot of risks, and not just for those who would be actively shadowing someone on the inside. "*Bryan, I need you and Mom to build an energy network to support the three of you. But first, Zero, we're going to need transportation.*"

"*I'm on it. Where?*"

Alaric passed her the location. "*As many vans and SUVs as you can safely manage without leaving a trail.*"

Zero dropped out of the link and Sahara shared something with Bryan and dropped out as well.

"*Zero is taking Sahara and Maddie with her. Raven wants to know how she can help.*" Bryan said.

"*We're going to need medical supplies and food and water.*"

"*This would work better if we had the globe.*" Bryan said and thoughts about how to manage that scuttled between them until Emily pulled back a bit from the link, leaving just Alaric and Bryan.

"*This is insane, you know that, right?*" Bryan asked.

"*I'm not leaving here without him.*" Alaric responded.

He could tell Bryan was doubtful, but could feel him consent. "*Give us a few hours to get ready.*"

It would take some time for them to set up a complex network with enough people to draw energy from without killing anyone. It would take Alaric a good deal of time to set up on their end. He disconnected and opened his eyes, pinning Evan in place with his eyes as he sat up.

"We're going to need three people with very little ability to shield themselves from mental intrusion. Can you read strangers enough to find them?"

"Find them? Sure." Evan said cautiously. "Get them to come back here without arousing suspicion? I'm not so sure." He frowned at Alaric. "Are you going to tell me what you're planning?"

Alaric rubbed a hand over his face. "We need more hands. My friends are going to borrow them for us."

Evan frowned harder. "Come again?"

"It's complicated…but we're going to build a bridge that will allow three other Shadows to insert themselves into the minds of the people you pick. They will have access to some basic functions, but the important part will be the work I have to do first, which is even more complicated than that. I'll start on Levar here, while you go recruit us three more."

"And then what?" Evan asked.

"And then you, military man, are going to create us a plan. One that needs six sets of hands to free those prisoners, kill who needs killing, and gets us the fuck out of here."

Evan looked at him like he'd lost his mind. "Just…just like that?"

Alaric offered him a grin. "Just like that. Now, go on. I have work to do, and we need to get Levar back out there before he's missed."

Evan shook his head, but headed for the door. "You want them one at a time, or all together?"

Alaric moved so that he could reach Levar again. "One at a time is easier."

"I'll be back."

The door closed, and Alaric turned his attention back to Levar. He slipped in with no resistance. Carefully, he segmented off a place to store commands that Levar would follow without question when Alaric needed him to. He then implanted a few basic commands, including one to come to Alaric when called and an imperative to obey Alaric's commands above all others.

He pulled back then, covering his tracks with false memories of helping Lieutenant Thomas with reports on prisoner transfers. In a few moments he had Levar on his feet, the files back in his hands.

"Thank you Major. I appreciate your help." Alaric said as he opened the door.

"Of course, Lieutenant." Levar responded, moving into the hallway. "Any time."

"I'll see you soon."

Levar smiled and headed down the corridor.

Alaric exhaled and closed the door. He was starting to feel the drain, but he had a long way yet to go. He went to the table and opened the protein bar, eating it quickly before laying down on the bunk.

Mason was alive.

For months Alaric had been sure he was gone. There had been no glimmer of Mason's presence, no sign that Mason was still alive.

He closed his eyes. He should try to sleep. He was going to need the rest and it had been a while since he'd slept for more than an hour or two at a time. His hand crept up his chest, pulling the tangled cords of the pendants from under his shirt. His hand closed around them and he let his mind caress them, feeling for the memory of Mason's touch, Mason's mind.

* * *

"Alaric."

He woke to Evan's urgent whisper, sitting up swiftly and taking in the slack expression on the young man standing beside Evan.

"I can't hold him much longer."

Alaric nodded and got up, his hand cupping to the soldier's face as his mind slipped along Evan's tether to the other man and took over the control function. "Very good. He's perfect."

Alaric guided him to the bed and laid him down.

The sleep had helped restore him some. Alaric took a deep breath to center himself. "He has access to the prison wing?"

Evan nodded. "Yeah. Got lucky."

Evan was clearly agitated. Alaric pushed the soldier into a deep, restive state and turned to Evan. "Are you okay?"

"Okay? No. No. I am not okay." Evan started pacing, rubbing his forehead. "This is insane. Okay? Insane."

"What happened?" Alaric intersected his pacing and reached for him with his hand and his mind. His mind was racing, adrenaline pumping through him. He scanned the surface of Evan's thoughts and got the gist of it. He'd nearly been caught subduing the man and the corridors had been a mine field of questioning officers as they'd made their way back. "Okay, calm down. You're fine."

"Don't tell me to calm down." He pulled back and turned away. "We can't do this. Not with ten sets of untrained hands. Maybe...maybe if we had a trained team and week to plan..."

"We don't have either of those things." Alaric said quietly. "We have you and me, and a chance…a very small, desperate chance."

"I don't know what I was thinking." Evan exhaled and rubbed his face.

"You were thinking about revenge." Alaric moved back to the soldier. "For your brother."

He stopped pacing and stood with his hands on his hips, watching as Alaric sank to his knees beside the bed. "Now, if you're done with your break down, we need two more." Alaric didn't look up at him, just lifted his hands to the soldier's head so he could start his deep read.

"How long do you need?" Evan asked from near the door.

"Give me a half hour." Alaric said. "If it can't be done by then, it can't be done."

The man was docile. There was no fight for control, no indication he was aware of what was happening. He'd be perfect for his mother. For all her talent, he had rarely seen her use more than very minimal skills to read people. She preferred to influence those around her with her words and actions.

Alaric sat the man down on the floor beside the bunk before moving to sit with the man between his knees. Pushing away thoughts of Mason that hovered, Alaric focused his attention on first reading the man under his hands, then beginning the work of preparing him for what would come.

The man was on rotation for guard duty in the wing where they were keeping prisoners who were awaiting execution. Alaric swept through his memories, trying to catalog how many there were in the prison wing. At least twenty, as near as Alaric could tell from the man's memory of the cells.

There was no way to know what shape any of them were in. It was good that they had Raven to help heal those that needed it. He held no delusions that she would be able to heal them all, but they could deal with that when the time came.

The first step was to get as many of them out as they could. Alaric scanned the soldier's memory for what he knew of the guard rotation and how the prisoners were brought in. There was a loading dock behind the prison wing, accessible through a heavy metal door. In fact, there was a large prison transport sitting out there now, after bringing in the latest prisoners.

Alaric tucked the knowledge away to fill Evan in when he returned and set about the work of making the soldier ready for his mother's control. He was a good candidate, prone to obeying orders without difficulty and not given to asking questions. It wouldn't take much to turn him into a puppet.

"Okay, Private First Class Lyle Orrin, let's get this done." Alaric murmured as he shifted gears and started the work.

In less than a half hour, the man was ready. Alaric set him to sleep until it was time, then turned his attention to himself. He needed to be ready too.

He cleared away clutter that had collected, hiding the evidence of how far away from himself he had traveled, though he doubted any of them would be fooled. He still wanted Shallon to die, but finding Mason had changed his priorities, brought him closer to the man he had been before all of this.

Mason. Alaric closed his eyes and reached out toward the prison wing, searching for the familiar presence.

Chapter Seventeen

He curled around the pain, let it hold him to the moment, to himself. He was more alert now than he'd been in a long time. Pieces were coming together, and he was aware of his situation again.

He was a prisoner of the 8th Battalion. He had been for quite a while.

Ever since Arizona. Ever since the night he should have died.

He remembered the bullet hitting him. Remembered looking at Bryan and seeing the realization spread across his face. He remembered trying to run, but the pain was too much, his body too weak. He remembered feeling Riley die beside him and falling. He remembered telling Bryan to run and killing at least three men in an effort to buy him the time to get away, fully expecting to die.

After that it all went dark. He should have died on the sand. Instead he remembered random moments of pain, of waking in the dark, of the presence of others; sometimes soothing him, helping him, sometimes hurting him more.

There had been transfers from a military camp to a hospital to a caravan moving north...all before they had brought him here. And he had been here a while, in the care of another Shade who was supposed to keep him alive, heal him enough that they could resume torturing him.

They had kept him heavily sedated when they weren't hurting him. Until now. He could still feel the drugs working through him, but the numbness wasn't enough to mask the extent of his injuries now.

He groaned and rolled onto his back. He needed water. He needed to soak in deep, cold pools of water and drink it into him. He needed darkness and time to finish the healing the other Shade had started.

He opened his eyes, his head turning. Damon. He blinked. Damon was in the corner, half asleep with a girl in his lap. She was small, thin and tiny and so fragile looking.

Damon's eyes opened and met his. There was anguish in them, anguish and despair. Mason lifted a hand toward him, but before he could even try to say anything, he felt...something.

He froze, closing his eyes. It was a soft whisper of a thought, unreal and yet it felt as though he could catch it, if he lay still and quiet enough. It breathed over him, into him, almost like it was searching and uncertain.

Mason breathed in and it flooded him, warmth and comfort and *Alaric*.

There were no words exactly, just the flushing of his presence inside him, joyous and relieved and overwhelming. Tears streamed from his eyes as he tried to reciprocate, but it was too much, and he couldn't. Alaric calmed him, caressing against him.

"Soon. I'm coming."

The presence pulled back and emptiness rushed into him. He reached out, trying to chase after the familiar comfort. Pain ripped through him and he fell back against the dirty mattress where he lay, gasping.

Damon touched his face. "What was that?"

Mason swallowed the hard knot of emotion that had risen in his throat. "Help."

Damon shook his head miserably. "No one can help us."

The girl climbed up onto the mattress with Mason, her dirty thumb in her mouth, her head on Mason's chest. It was oddly comforting. He closed his eyes and tried to recapture the feeling of Alaric's presence, but he couldn't lift his senses out of his own skin.

* * *

The dark of the cell was cloying and stank of betrayal and desperation as Mason woke again, memory rushing in. He opened his eyes, searching the dark shadows until he spotted Damon and the girl.

Pain bloomed when he tried to move, deep in his gut and his left hip and right shoulder. He lay back, panting, trying to feel through him for the injuries. The last of the drugs they'd been keeping him under with had burned away. He was dry and wouldn't be healing without water.

There was movement, then a hand on his shoulder. Mason opened his eyes to find Damon leaning over him. "Lay still."

248

"Get off me." Mason said, though he couldn't really pull away.

"They backed off the drugs, but you're still seriously injured." Mason could feel him, the ghost hand of his power feeling through Mason's body. "I guess they want you to feel it before they kill us."

"Stop." Mason grabbed his hand. "You don't get to—"

"No." Damon stopped him and pulled his hand away. "No, you don't."

"You betrayed us." Mason said, scowling at him.

"No, I didn't." Damon sat heavily, scrubbing his face with his hands. "I was still healing from the crash, the head wound damaged a part of my brain that allowed me to heal myself. They found me there."

Mason didn't want to believe him. Anger seemed better suited to keeping himself alive. "How did they find us?"

"They have a lot of us here. Could have been anyone." Damon said. They were quiet a minute, then Damon gathered the girl into his lap. "My granddaughter, Anna. They kept her mother alive until after she'd given birth."

"Is she—"

"Executed." Damon said, his voice dripping with misery. "Burned at the stake a week ago."

Mason tried to do the math to figure out how old the girl was, but it was too much, and he had no idea how much time had transpired between Arizona and here. She was more than a year old, but far less than two. Even so, she was tiny and lethargic.

Without the drugs, Mason could get a better sense of the world around them, and most of what he could sense was *Alaric.* Alaric who was alive and close and coming to save him.

"Well, I don't know about you, but I don't plan on dying here." Mason said, trying again to sit up. It hurt, and he couldn't help but groan with the pain, but he got himself up enough to lean on the wall.

"They don't even need to drag you out to the stake, just leave you here. Without me, you would have been dead weeks ago."

Memories were still filtering through the drug induced haze. He had expected to die there in the sand, but he had passed out after killing at least three men. He woke briefly in a truck, pushed back under by another Shade, someone familiar. There were moments that penetrated the blackness, mostly moments of pain, torture.

"You weren't the one on the truck." Mason ground out, cradling his arm as muscles protested his movement. "When they found me."

Damon shook his head miserably. "No. They put us together when they put us on a train. I could tell there had been someone else, but I don't know who."

Mason nodded. He had memories of the train, the noise of it had pulled him out of his stupor. Before that...he shook his head as the memory slipped away. "The train brought us here?"

Damon nodded. "To die."

"Not today." Mason argued. Not now that Alaric had come for him.

"Maybe that head of yours is more scrambled than I thought." Damon moved back to his dark corner with his granddaughter. "You probably don't remember the visitor we had a few hours ago. He seemed to really hate you. Told me to get you healed up enough to face your execution. In

251

a few hours, Colonel Shallon is going to have us all dragged out into the sun and burned."

Something tickled the back of his mind…a memory of watching three people burn while a mob protested. The smell of it was intense and the heat from the flames and the sun was nauseating. Panting, Mason pushed the memory away.

He turned his thoughts to more pleasant memories, to the time he'd spent with Alaric in the mountains. That's where he had first met Damon. The Shade had come looking for shelter, wounded and telling a story about escaping the 8th Battalion.

Damon hadn't been the one who betrayed the village, he'd been caught in the raid the same as the others. Mason focused on the girl in his lap. His daughter though, she'd been a prisoner a long time. "It was her." Mason said softly after a long time. "Your daughter. She knew about Arizona."

He looked up at him, his brown eyes nearly black with the pain of his loss. Of course a mother would give up a town of strangers to save her child.

His stomach hurt and fever burned through him. Mason slumped back down to the mattress. Damon's assessment of his condition was right. It wouldn't take much to send him hurtling over the edge.

* * *

Bryan paced the small motel room, from door to bathroom and back again. The whole idea was insane. He shouldn't have agreed to it. The door opened, and Sahara slipped inside.

"I thought you were supposed to be resting."

He huffed and shook his head. "I couldn't sleep."

"Well, you shouldn't be wearing yourself out either."

"I don't know what I was thinking." Nothing like this had ever been done, not on this scale, and not with these consequences. At least not in clan memory.

He scrubbed a hand over his face and the stubble that had grown well past stubble. He couldn't remember the last time he'd shaved. Before the hospital at least.

"Emily said she's almost ready." Sahara came to him, setting a hand on his chest to stop him. "If she thinks we can do this, why don't you?"

He inhaled, trying to articulate all of the things that could go wrong. Sahara opened her shields, letting him into the warm comfort of her mind.

The cat was there inside her, nearer the surface than he remembered, reminding him that under the beauty, she was also dangerous, and telling him that for all of her power, she wasn't one of his clan.

"Is that what this is about?" Sahara asked suddenly, moving away. She rubbed her forehead and looked at him.

"What?" Bryan asked, actually not sure what she'd seen.

"You." She shook her head, tossing her hair over her shoulder. "Your damn guilt."

He frowned, trying to follow her, but whatever it was she'd seen in his head, he wasn't aware of it. "My guilt?"

"You told Alaric not to get involved with Mason, because he wasn't one of you." Sahara said, turning to look at him, taking a step closer. "And here you are, with me."

Bryan pulled back physically and shook his head. "No, this...it's not the same thing."

She chuckled. "Right, because it was just a fling, something physical. You weren't going to get emotionally involved."

"Sahara..."

She held up a hand and came toward him, eventually settling that hand on his chest again, over his heart. "I know why I'm here. Do you?"

"I thought I did." Bryan admitted.

They stood quietly for a minute and when Sahara stirred again, there was a feeling that she was putting the moment aside to come back to later.

"For now, we're both here to help Alaric. We should get out the rendezvous point and get set up."

* * *

Bryan and Sahara reached the spot in the desert where the others were gathered. Seven vans and SUVs were lined up beside each other and he could feel Emily setting up inside the dark blue van in the center.

Zero and Maddie were working on changing license plates, but Bryan didn't stop to ask them about how or why they felt the need. He left Sahara to check in with them and see if they needed anything else and he went to the van where Emily was working.

He opened the door and Emily gestured him inside. "We're almost ready." Emily said softly. She held up the phone she had pressed to her ear, before returning it to her ear. "Victoria is setting up a matrix with volunteers. It will let us feed power from the orb and regulate it so no one gets overwhelmed."

Bryan shook his head. "That's an awfully big distance."

She nodded. "Yes, she's got a relay matrix set up in Illinois, eight volunteers there will accept the energy from Virginia, then relay it to us."

"How will we regulate it on this end?" Bryan asked. "If you, me and the girl are shadowing some bastard inside that prison?"

"Let's be honest, Bryan, what we are doing goes far beyond mere shadowing." Emily said before turning away. "Yes, Victoria. Okay good. We'll be ready." Emily lowered the phone. "She's just building the matrix with her volunteers, then she'll connect with the matrix in Illinois. Once that's established, they'll contact me. We need to be ready."

Bryan nodded, "You still haven't indicated how we're going to regulate the energy."

She shrugged. "The distance should do the bulk of it for us. I'll take point, as the senior Shadow among us. You and Zero can connect with me, I should be able to do both the job of feeding you energy and controlling my person on the inside."

"Should be?"

She smiled. "None of us have done this before, Bryan. Not in centuries."

"Yeah, I know. That's part of the problem." He rubbed over his face, scrubbing through his beard. "Can we do this?"

She laid a hand on his arm. "I know I can. I know Alaric can. It's you and Zero I'm worried about. I can show you what to do, but you'll have to do it on your own. Once we're set up, I can't help you and do my part as well."

"Have I mentioned that this is a crazy idea?" Bryan muttered.

Emily sighed and reached out to him with her mind, brushing affectionately along his shields until he opened them enough to let her in. "*He's alone in there, Bryan. He needs us.*"

"*He also needs a swift kick in the ass.*" Bryan responded.

"Which you can give him once he's safe." Emily said aloud. "Can you get Zero in here so I can show the two of you what to do?"

Bryan climbed out of the van. Sahara and Maddie were sorting through a bag of medical supplies in the back of an SUV, filling smaller bags. Sahara looked up. "Almost ready?"

He nodded. "Just about. Need Zero."

Sahara pointed to the black van. "She's in with Raven. Give her a minute."

"You two going to be okay with guardian duty?"

Maddie looked up at him. "We'll be fine. Our jobs are easy."

"When Alaric gets here, we're going to need to move fast. There's a good chance they'll be chasing him."

"We'll be ready." Maddie assured him.

The front door of the van opened and Zero slipped out. "Okay, you two get those kits into the various vans and we should be ready." Zero said, coming to a stop beside Bryan. "Raven says to get the seriously wounded into her van, then if there is a functional Shade among the liberated, to put them with the next most serious. We're getting first aid supplies into all the vehicles."

"Then I guess it's time." Bryan said. "Emily is ready for us."

Zero nodded. She followed Bryan to the van and stepped in, settling to a seat near Emily. In the gloom, she looked younger than her years. They were putting a lot on the girl. She closed her eyes and breathed in slowly. When she opened them again there was a steel in them he hadn't seen before. She nodded to Emily and held out her hand. Emily took it with a smile and reached for Bryan's hand.

It only took a moment to relay the necessary information and he watched Zero absorb it, then relay it back to show her understanding. "Good. Now relax while I get us linked up." Emily said aloud.

Bryan did his best to shove his doubts aside and focus on the task at hand. Alaric was counting on this working, and if it went well, they could deal a blow of epic proportions to the 8th Battalion.

Chapter Eighteen

Alaric finished getting the soldier under his hands set up for Bryan's manipulation, setting up the pathways that he would connect to the bridge to let Bryan take over control of the body. Somehow Evan had found him multiple soldiers with access they needed. The man Bryan would control would be able to take them by the most direct route to the prison wing, through another secured area. After that he would be little more than another pair of hands, helping them get prisoners loaded into the truck.

When it was over, the man wouldn't be worth much, if he survived at all. He pushed away the nagging guilt over that, over how much of the man he'd had to strip away to make this work. Evan wasn't back yet, so Alaric took the moment to reach out to Mason. He was more awake and alert than he had been, annoyed now as well. Damon.

Alaric could see the traitor through Mason, huddled in a corner. "*Soon.*" Alaric sent to Mason as the door opened behind him. Evan led another man into the room. Alaric stood, already reaching for the controls, but he pulled back in surprise. "Evan?"

Evan nodded and exhaled. "I took a chance. I have an idea."

This was no low-level grunt soldier like Private Simon currently laid out on the bed. This was one of three men Shallon trusted without question. Evan gave a mental command and the man sat at the small table.

Evan wasn't releasing the controls, so Alaric stepped back and looked at him. Evan nodded once. "Okay, it's still crazy, or maybe it's even more crazy. But with him, we can get in close. The kind of close we don't get without months of ground work."

"What are you suggesting?" Alaric asked.

Evan met his eyes and lowered his shields. "Give him to me...whatever it is you're doing with the others."

Alaric blinked and stepped back a bit from the intensity of it.

"Do you know what you're asking?" Alaric asked. He put a hand on the man's shoulder, reading past Evan's control of him. His mind was neat, orderly. He was intelligent, committed. Breaking him would not be a simple task, and doing it in a way that no one could tell he'd been compromised would be time consuming. Time they didn't really have to spend.

"I know that this is one sure way of bringing this shit down." Evan said. "With him, I can set this entire place to explode, I can send him in with a needle to kill Shallon…or a machine gun to take out the entire command center."

Alaric crossed his arms and looked at Evan. "So, which is it? I mean, you can't do all three."

Evan looked conflicted for a moment and Alaric could tell something was going on behind his shields. Finally, Evan nodded and leaned over the map of the compound. "I already have improvised explosives in a number of places, including here and here." He pointed at the two access points into the command wing. "The Commander and I are the distraction that buys you time to get into the prison section and get out as many as you can." Evan looked up at him. "The Commander takes me into the Command Center. He and I will clean out anything that moves and when it's done, I'll drop him and meet up with you."

Alaric looked at him, thinking through the possible outcomes. "Are you sure about your explosives?"

Evan nodded. "We set off one here." He pointed to a place near command. That will bring most of the high-ranking officers up to command to see what happened. We blow the other two." He pointed again. "That locks down command completely. It should divert most of the troops attention to rescuing Shallon and the others."

"And we use the cover to liberate the prisoners."

Evan sighed and looked up at Alaric. "It's the only way I can see of meeting our mission objectives and also busting out those prisoners."

Alaric didn't like it. Evan was clearly adept, his mental abilities beyond what even Alaric had guessed them to be, but even so, what he was talking about was suicide. "How are you getting out of there?"

He shrugged. "I'll figure that out when I need to."

Alaric tried to read him, but he was buttoned up other than his control of the officer glaring at them. He was willing to die if it meant killing Shallon. Alaric paced away.

Evan looked at him. "I found a guy for you, he can get you out of the prison wing the same way they bring prisoners in. It has its own entrance, vehicles; covered trucks to protect your Shade."

Alaric pinched the bridge of his nose. Evan just watched him reason through the insanity of the plan. Alaric gestured at the officer. "I'm going to need time to set him up. It isn't going to be easy." Alaric said, giving in. Evan wasn't wrong about this being one sure way of making sure Shallon was dead. "Give me control. Then go get this driver. But understand, this isn't going to be easy, and when I'm done...there won't be much of him left."

Evan met his eyes, his own resolved and hard. "He is dead already. He's seen too much. We do this or I break his neck."

Alaric could feel the commander bristle. Even with Evan's controls, the man was capable of re-acting. He huffed and felt along Evan's controls into the man's brain. He took over the controls and nodded when he had him.

"I'll get the decoy explosive set up, then go for the driver."

When Evan was gone, Alaric paced around the commander, working himself up to what needed to be done. Finally, Alaric nodded to himself and took the man's hand. "I need you to lay down on the floor, Commander."

It took a little push, but he got up out of the chair and lay down. Alaric knelt, straddling over him, both hands on the sides of his face. "Okay, Commander, how about you make this easy on me?"

Alaric pushed past the initial controls that let him keep the commander from throwing him into a wall and raising the alarm and got his first really good look inside. This was a man fully committed to his job. A career soldier and a life-long evangelical, he'd been an easy convert to the 8th Battalion's interpretation of religion and he believed completely that he was doing God's work.

He was disciplined and intelligent, possessing a laser focus that had seen him rise in the ranks quickly. Alaric was going to have to break him thoroughly or Evan wouldn't be able to control him.

He started by cordoning off an area to quarantine things he needed to suppress, like his very violent reaction to what Alaric was doing.

He pulled together specific thoughts, specific inhibitions, like the thoughts that killing his own people was wrong, or that he wanted to kill Evan and Alaric both. Those weren't so hard, but when it came down to actually preparing him to take Evan into the command wing, to actually making it so he would kill, that was far more intricate. It required precision, so that Alaric didn't strip out things that they would actually need.

He weeded methodically through the beautiful mind under his hands, ripping out things that could cause them trouble, knowing that going at it this fast could end with him missing something small that could affect him enough to derail the plan. He spent a lot of time on communication, making it so that the man could talk, could respond appropriately in conversation, while preventing him from asking for help, or telling anyone what they were doing.

When he was fairly sure he'd cut out every-thing he needed to, he sat back and wiped at his sweaty face. He had to hope that his mother had done something that would let her, Bryan and Zero connect with the energy of the globe. He was going to need it to refuel.

Taking things out was only half the battle, he would need to implant suggestions and com-mands as well in the holes he was leaving as he worked. The door opened, but Alaric didn't stir, kept his attention on his task. He was sweat-ing, shaking. He walled up the quarantined area, sealing all of the stripped away pieces behind a solid barrier so that they would never get back out, not without help.

Only then did he look up. Evan had a middle-aged man sitting by the table and he held out his hand with a plate of food. Alaric took the meat-loaf with his fingers, nodding gratefully and re-laxing just a little to wolf it down. "Thanks," he mumbled between bites.

"Thought you might need it."

Alaric nodded, licking his fingers. "I'm almost done here."

"Good, it's nearly two am. We're going to be cutting it close."

"Okay. Just...you got him?" Alaric nodded toward the slack jawed man in the chair.

Evan nodded. "I got a better contact this time. Do what you have to"

Alaric turned back to the commander, taking a deep breath. He closed his eyes and delved back into him, putting in the commands to obey Evan without question, to shield Evan from discovery at all costs, to not stop until Shallon and the others were dead. He paused then and looked at his work. It wasn't the best he could do, but it would get the job done.

That left only one thing. He burrowed in deep and buried a bomb, something set to trigger as soon as the mission was completed. It would destroy everything else and command only one thing, for the commander to die.

Alaric pulled up and out, staggering to his feet and away from the commander. He snagged the plate and sat in the other chair, wolfing down what was left. When this was over he was going to crash hard. He felt Evan's hand on his shoulder, his mind brushing against Alaric's. "I can help."

Alaric frowned up at him, then felt the tendril of energy Evan was offering him. Alaric shook his head and pushed Evan away. "You're going to need it. I'll be fine. When I connect to my people I'll top up and I can pull from Levar once I'm ready."

"If you last that long." Evan rolled his eyes, but backed off.

"Okay, let me set this guy up, then I'll hook you and the commander up." Alaric dragged his chair closer and reached for the man…Michael Sancto, one of the drivers for prisoner transports. It was a good choice, Alaric had to agree.

Like the soldier on the bed, this man was easy to control and it took little time for Alaric to get him ready for the bridge.

"Lay down beside the Commander." Alaric stood as Evan obeyed. "Now, I'm going to need you to really open up for me."

Alaric once again went to his knees, between Evan and the commander. He felt Evan's release, almost like automatic doors opening and Alaric started slowly, just brushing against him for a few seconds before slipping in deeper. "I'm going to bridge you over to him." Alaric settled a hand on the commander's, reaching into him for the command strings and control buttons he'd set up before he opened the bridge and pulled Evan in.

He showed Evan what each string and button did, showed him the kill switch in case anything went wrong, and he had to pull it early, then systematically handed the commander over.

"Take your time. Get comfortable. I'm going to see if Bryan and the others are ready."

Alaric pulled up and out and stumbled as he got up, catching himself against the table. He reached out for Sancto, instructing him to move closer. Alaric sat on the floor beside the bed, where he could touch the two soldiers and Sancto once he was also seated on the floor.

Alaric exhaled and centered, then reached out to his mother, who was clearly waiting and latched on immediately. The connection was far stronger than it had been before. He could feel the surge from the globe as he entered the network and took a moment to savor the familiar warmth, letting it fill up his dwindling stores of energy before he turned his attention to examining the network.

His mother had surprised him. The globe was still in Virginia, but the energy she fed him was only slightly diminished. The network was strong. They would have all the support they needed to draw energy, without worrying about taking too much from any one person.

Bryan joined the connection, followed by Zero, affirming that they as ready as they could be.

He started with Zero, her mind a mix of fire and ice. She followed him easily as he built the bridge to Sancto. He showed her the controls, how to read the stimulus and input as Sancto interacted with others.

"He's going to obey anything you tell him to do, but if you tell him nothing, he'll just do his job. Mostly let him do his job. Ride along. When it's time, we'll let you know. Then, you get doors open and vehicles ready."

She brushed against him to indicate her understanding. "Practice a little, while I set Bryan up."

Zero withdrew a bit and he could feel her testing the bridge. He knew if he opened his eyes, he'd see Sancto moving about. Bryan opened to him easily and he repeated the process with the soldier Alaric had prepared for him. Bryan needed little prompting, and in seconds he was ready. Lastly, he turned to his mother, handing over the private who would help them in the prison wing.

Fatigue washed through him as he opened his eyes. Even with the globe in the loop, he was burning out fast. He closed his eyes once more and took what the network and the globe could offer him. He was going to be hard pressed to get through this without collapsing.

They were as ready as they were going to get.

* * *

Alaric had Levar beside him as he approached the prison wing. The soldier his mother controlled had gone on ahead, reporting for duty as if nothing were wrong. Alaric checked his watch. It was close to four thirty in the morning. They had taken longer than he liked to get started. He had hoped they could get everything in place before they had to worry about the morning shift reporting to duty. The last thing they needed was extra hands.

Levar was fighting him, but he wasn't winning. Alaric still had control. He stopped them just shy of the secured wing they had to pass through, delving a little deeper into the Major's mind. By the time Bryan's man had joined them, Levar was once more compliant.

Bryan's man opened the door and waived them through. They nodded to the man on guard duty and Bryan led them deeper into the wing. The smell of human excrement and blood assaulted them as they moved, and he could see prisoners being questioned in small rooms through small windows in the doors. He recognized the pain and despair that washed toward them.

"*We can't help them,*" Bryan said.

Of course they couldn't, not without betraying themselves. He had known that coming in. In fact, Evan had made sure they would find a different kind of escape.

He nodded and continued following the soldier. At the end of the wing they crossed a corridor. Alaric's attention was drawn to the doors at the far end. He could see men moving in a courtyard. He knew from the minds of the men now under their control that it was where they executed those that they thought could provide no more information.

"*Focus,*" Bryan snapped at him, pulling his attention back to the task at hand. Alaric pushed away his disgust and fear and they continued moving until they came to the gate of the prison wing. His mother's man opened it, nodding to them.

It was now or never.

Chapter Nineteen

The buzz in his head was unsettling, the blur of another person's thoughts under his control, a person who clearly hated him and would kill him in an instant if Alaric's programming slipped in the slightest. It didn't help that he was also connected to Alaric and his three friends and all of the minds that they controlled.

Evan walked beside the commander as if he belonged there, saluting when appropriate as they passed people. Before long the morning shift would be starting, and they needed to be in place before then.

They rounded the corner into the command center. It was four in the morning and it was still fully staffed.

"Commander, I didn't expect to see you so early."

"Well, the Colonel is eager to have today's executions go off without a hitch. I'm here to go over the final details."

The lieutenant colonel who was in charge of the command center at the moment looked put out that the commander would question him. "I assure you, we perform many of these executions. Nothing will go wrong."

"I'm sure. I will still be looking at your plans, sir. As directed by General Shallon." Commander Brown stared at the man. "Or, I could go wake Director Wells and the Colonel, see what they have to say."

"I'm sure that won't be necessary." The Lt. Colonel, gestured at one of the men nearby. "Get the commander anything he needs."

Evan took the files they were handed, flipping through them for the information he needed to relay to Alaric. "*You've got about two hours before they come to move them to the cells outside. Two more until the fires start.*"

He felt Alaric's acknowledgement. He pushed Brown into the next set of steps they needed to accomplish. He had hoped the command center would be light on staff, but supposed that it would make sense that it wouldn't be, not with Shallon there.

From what he'd gathered, Shallon had a personal interest in the planned executions. They were planning on burning several Shades and a Shifter in the first executions of the day.

Alaric and his men were entering the prison wing. Evan fiddled with the detonator in his pocket. They just needed the signal to set the whole thing in motion.

* * *

Alaric could feel Zero's man was already inside, moving toward the prisoner transport as they entered. "Sir?" The man at the desk stood.

Alaric pushed Levar a little.

"We need to secure the prisoners." Levar said, his tone even, his eyes scanning down the list in his hands, then up at the commander of the prison.

"All of them, sir? I thought—"

"Our facility has been compromised, we need to move now. I want all of the prisoners out of their cells, now."

"Compromised?" The man lifted a radio. "I need to check with command."

"Who do you think sent me?" Levar asked.

278

"Now." Alaric sent to Evan. Two seconds later the building rocked with the first of several explosions.

The commander paled and nodded to Levar. "You heard the man, get the prisoners lined up immediately."

Alaric knew the protocol was to execute the prisoners in the case of breach. They would be lined up and gunned down. Except he was there to see that it didn't happen.

The man under Emily's control and the other guard on duty this early in the day moved to start opening doors. Alaric sent the commands to Levar to prepare to kill the guards instead.

"Now, Commander, please call the rest of your men." Levar said.

"Sir?"

"The two on the exit gate? I need them up here."

"Sir, that is not—"

"Now, Commander. I won't ask again."

Bryan's man came in behind them, moving back to the cells to help bring prisoners out. Alaric's hand was on his gun as prisoners started stumbling out and lining up along the wall. He had to keep reminding himself not to give it up too soon. He flicked the switch in Levar' head, setting him up to cover their escape.

Levar moved to the doors and began wiring them with explosives from his bag. Alaric still didn't see Mason, and they had nearly twenty prisoners out now. The radio on the desk was starting to demand attention. The prison commander was reaching for it. Alaric stepped in, grabbing the radio. "I'll deal with this, you go help."

Bryan's man emerged from the hall of cells. He nodded at Alaric as he helped a young girl of maybe seventeen to stand with the others. "I found our boy, but he's in no shape to move."

Alaric told his mother to get her man out to the trucks to meet up with Zero's man and get them moving. "Start getting them out and into transports. I'll take care of things in here," he said to Bryan.

"Alaric—"

Alaric looked him in the eye, felt inside him for Bryan. "Just do it."

After a long, glaring look, he gave in, moving along the line of prisoners and starting them moving out toward the waiting vehicles. There was someone pounding on the gates now. They were out of time. Alaric pulled his gun and called Levar to him. As the commander and two other guards emerged, they both lifted their guns.

Three shots later, they were clear. Alaric climbed over the dead bodies and ran down the length of open cells. He felt Mason before he found him, a weak echo of the familiar touch.

Alaric stopped in the open door of the cell, his eyes meeting Mason's. Movement in the corner drew his attention and he turned to find Damon, a child in his arms, looking at Alaric with fear.

"Alaric." Mason was struggling to sit up. For the moment, Alaric put Damon out of his mind and went to Mason. New scars and still raw wounds covered his skin and he was paler even than usual. His hair was a matted mess and the bruises on his wrists told the tale of restraint and torture.

"It's okay, we're getting out of here. Can you move at all?" Alaric asked.

"You can't—" Damon stopped when Alaric looked at him.

"I should kill you right now." Alaric said. "This is your fault."

"It wasn't him." Mason said weakly.

"We don't have time for this." Alaric said, helping Mason up. He groaned, his body lighter than Alaric remembered.

"You need someone to help him." Damon said. "I've been keeping him alive."

Alaric started for the door, supporting Mason's weight.

"Leave me here, if you want. But my granddaughter doesn't deserve this."

"No one deserves this." Mason whispered, his head rolling against Alaric's shoulder.

Damon shifted, setting the little girl on her feet. "Take her, and I'll do what I can to make sure he lives to get to safety."

Alaric looked her over. The poor thing was frail and thin, barely able to stand. Her dark hair stood out against pale, pale skin.

Damon moved closer cautiously. "The shrapnel inside him is the problem. Specially made rounds...they fracture and spread out inside, leak chemicals and salt into the surrounding tissue. It's an ugly way to die."

He sank to one knee beside them. "I can't take them out, not here. No tools... I can... mask them for a while, give him time to get some place where they can be removed." Damon looked at Alaric. "Just promise me you'll take my grand-daughter out of here, promise me you'll find her some place safe to grow up."

Alaric could feel the urgency from Bryan and Evan. They needed to move fast. "Do it. Do it quickly, we're running out of time."

"At best I can buy him a few days." David bowed his head and went to work. Alaric drew the little girl to him. She was so light and compli-ant. The entire exchange, she hadn't looked up, hadn't changed expression, as if she didn't know what was going on around her.

Damon fell back on his ass as Mason stirred. His eyes opened, and Alaric could see the man he loved in them. He offered a smile. "Can you move?"

Mason nodded. He worked himself up to standing. Alaric looked at Damon briefly, then took a grenade from his pocket. "When they come through that door..."

Damon nodded. "I'll take as many of them with me as I can."

Alaric scooped up the little girl, and took Mason's arm to support him. Together they staggered out of the cell. His mother's man met them, taking the girl so Alaric could concentrate of Mason.

Alaric followed the man his mother conrolled to a truck already full of prisoners who still looked shell shocked. "Almost there." Bryan's man appeared beside Alaric in nothing but his boxers and helped him ease Mason up into the truck. Hands inside helped haul him in.

"We got one truck already out, one of ours was among the prisoners. He was strong enough to drive. I gave him my uniform."

Alaric could feel Bryan's energy fading, his mother too. Zero's man appeared beside them. "Doors open. Can you drive?"

"Go, I've got this." He took the girl from his mother's puppet. Be ready when we get there, we'll need to move fast." Alaric felt Bryan go. Beside him, the man that had been his host slumped to the ground. He passed the girl in to the waiting hands in the truck. "Okay, it's going to be a bumpy ride. Hang on. And keep him safe." He pointed at Mason before he pulled the canvas flap down and tied it.

The two men controlled by his mother and Zero slumped to the ground and he sprinted to the cab and climbed in.

More explosions rocked the building and he sped out into the bright start of the day, hoping Evan was handling his end of things.

* * *

As expected, the first explosion flooded the command center with people, including Shallon. He looked like he'd just thrown his uniform on, and was still buttoning his jacket as he stormed into the room, his eyes scanning around him. "What the hell is happening?"

The officers around the room saluted him and the Lieutenant Commander approached him. "We're still working on that, sir. There have been at least two explosions that we know of."

"How is that possible?" Shallon turned, his eyes scanning the room. He found Brown who stepped forward smartly. "What do we know?"

Evan had to suppress the man's urge to bolt, pushing words into his mouth. "Nothing, sir. I had just arrived in command to go over the plans for today's executions."

Evan set off the next blasts, sealing command off from the rest of the facility. The rest would go off at intervals designed to keep the facility in chaos. The room rocked and Shallon cursed, making for the hall he had just come from only to find it filled with debris.

Evan and his commander began firing as soon as the room stopped rocking, rapidly taking out the men nearest them, before they were even fully aware what was going on. It didn't take long for gunfire to begin coming back at them, though with the smoke and confusion they were mostly wild shots.

Evan split from Brown, circling the room in an effort to set up a crossfire. His gun jammed, and Evan dropped it, grabbing one from one of the men he'd killed.

The screaming of the wounded and dying was punctuated by yelling, as Shallon recognized Brown as one of the shooters. "Stop him!"

Officers were closing in on Brown's position. Evan sent his final command, ducking behind a piece of equipment to protect himself from the coming blast.

"Grenade! He's got a grenade!"

There was a flurry of movement as men tried to get clear, then an explosion that knocked a hole in the wall behind where Brown had been.

In the dusty aftermath, no one was standing. Moaning and the sounds of men dying filled the air. Evan picked his way across the room. The first man he found moving got a bullet in his head. So did the second.

The third was Shallon. Evan stopped. He was trapped under a heavy load of debris, but his eyes were still livid. Evan smiled, standing on the debris and squatting down. "Hello Colonel. Remember me? Or should I say, my brother?"

The man looked at him, but there was no sign of recognition in his eyes. Somehow that only infuriated him more. "I should make this last, torture you the way you tortured him, but I don't really have the time for that. Instead, I'm going to kill you in the most poetic way I can."

He put the gun down and let himself shift. The smells were so much sharper in his bird form and the look of horror on Shallon's face was worth the effort. Evan moved forward, snapping his beak. When his talons found skin, they dug in and Shallon screamed as Evan went for his eyes.

His scream died when Evan's talons tore into his throat and Evan backed off to watch him bleed out. When he was sure the man was dead, he flew through the hole in the wall, though that only put him out into the facility. He needed to find an opening in an outer wall…before someone realized that he was more than just a really big bird.

* * *

Alaric drove them into the rising sun, faster than was probably wise. The other truck was nowhere to be seen. The checkpoint was empty, the men likely recalled to the compound to deal with the chaos. There was evidence that the first truck had been through there. A lone man in an 8th Battalion uniform was dead at his post and the gate arm had been smashed into kindling.

He hit the main road east and set a hard pace, his eyes darting to the gas gauge. Zero had made sure they were full, but a truck this size with a heavy load was going to burn through it fast. At the cut off to the pseudo road that would take him to the rendezvous, he could see signs of the first truck, fresh tracks and lingering dust that would lead to them if anyone had made it out to follow.

He felt a brush that he recognized as Zero, and in his side mirror he could see the dust settling into the tire tracks. It was easy to forget the girl was more than just a Shadow.

He could feel Mason behind him, clinging to life though he should have been dead multiple times over, if Alaric was reading his condition correctly.

His connection to Bryan and his mother was gone and he was too exhausted to try to find them again. He had to focus on driving, until they were safe.

Of course, they were so deep into 8th Battalion territory, he wasn't even sure where that would be. He checked the sun. It was fully up, and the day was going to be a warm one.

Alaric felt something tickling his awareness and reached out for it. Evan was straining a bit, so he did his best to help firm up the connection.

"*You out?*" Evan asked.

"*Out and headed east. Where are you?*"

"*Don't worry. Find you.*"

The connection broke and Alaric glanced in his side mirror. He couldn't see the road anymore and he couldn't tell from the brief contact whether or not Evan had gotten out. Exhaling and hoping the Shifter was okay, he put everything but the drive out of his mind.

Chapter Twenty

They weren't far from the rendezvous when Alaric spotted a dot in the sky moving toward them. He watched it get larger, recognizing Evan's bird form as it approached. Alaric slowed the truck and opened the passenger window.

His trajectory looked shaky, so Alaric slowed a little more. Evan wobbled and missed his first attempt. Alaric could feel the exhaustion rolling off of him and slowed a little more.

Evan all but fell through the window, landing on the seat with a squawk and sliding on the vinyl until his talons found purchase.

Alaric closed the window and looked at him. "You okay?"

Evan held out the wounded wing. "*Shallon's dead.*" He did his best to keep the images from bleeding through, but Alaric saw them anyway. "*Plan?*"

"We get to the rendezvous, change vehicles, keep moving."

"*Not much of a plan.*"

Alaric snorted. "Keep moving and get out of 8th Battalion territory as quickly as we can."

Evan moved into the foot well. He filled it pretty thoroughly, but he wouldn't have to hold on, the tight space would keep him stable for the time being.

"Rest." Alaric said, keeping his eyes on the road. "No telling what comes next."

They hadn't really planned much beyond getting the prisoners out and getting them moving toward the border. Alaric had no idea where they would be safe. The default would be to get back to Adam Darvin in Chicago, but it was hard to tell if even that would be safe.

Up ahead, Alaric could see the vehicles, could sense his mother's presence. There was a flurry of activity around the first of their transport vehicles as Zero and Sahara separated the liberated prisoners between the vehicles.

Alaric pulled to a stop and jumped out, moving toward the back quickly. The Shades all pulled back as he ducked under the flap. Alaric's eyes were only on Mason though.

"Hey."

Alaric climbed into the bed, kneeling beside him, taking his head in both hands before leaning in to kiss him deeply. "You're alive."

"Why did we stop?" one of them asked and Alaric looked up.

"We need to get into other vehicles. So far there is no pursuit, but…"

"Don't mean it ain't coming," one of them said.

Alaric nodded. "I know. We're going to keep going. I need to identify the worst of the wounded. We have a healthy Shade who will do what she can to help all of you."

A woman who sat across from him nodded. "I can help. Mason here is in the worst shape in this truck."

Alaric thanked her with a nod. "We have a couple of vans, and some SUVs with tinted windows. It's daylight outside, so give us a few minutes to sort out some details."

He pressed a kiss to Mason's forehead. "We'll get you moved into the van with Raven as soon as we can." He looked up at the others. "How many of you are Shades?"

Six of them raised their hands. "Okay, sit tight. I'll be back in a few minutes."

Alaric slipped under the canvas to find Bryan approaching him. Despite the support of the orb and the network Victoria had establish, Alaric could see the exhaustion on his face.

"Zero says we have some time. She says the compound is still reeling."

Alaric nodded. From what he'd seen from Evan, they'd left chaos in their wake. "Do we have a plan?"

Bryan nodded. "Yeah. It's ten hours to get us to Rapid City, South Dakota, provided we can get through. Zero seems to think we should be safe enough there."

"Okay. Is Mom still connected with Victoria?"

Bryan nodded, yeah, but she's going to need sleep soon."

"Yeah, we all will." He sighed and looked back at the truck. "Have Victoria reach out to anyone we have in South Dakota. I don't think I want to risk bluffing our way into a hotel, not with this many. I've got six Shades in my truck. Mason's in the worst shape, but they're all pretty beat up. My Shifter friend needs medical attention too."

He left Bryan to sort them out and headed to the van where he knew Raven was working. He climbed into the driver's seat to avoid bathing the back with sunlight.

Raven looked up from where she was bent over the teenager. She already looked tired. "I have a few Shades that might help take the load off." Alaric said. "We need you for Mason."

She yawned and stretched. "Yeah, I'm nearly finished her. She was close to gone. One of the others said she was rather defiant."

"We'll keep her here." Alaric said. "I'm going to get Mason in here for you, and check on the others. I hope to have us on the road soon."

He was feeling the wear, and knew if he didn't rest soon, he would fall over. As he exited the van, Zero and Maddie came toward them. Zero was showing the strain, but she had the advantage of her youth.

Zero pointed to vehicles. "Sahara, Maddie, me, and we have a few Shadows that have volunteered to drive."

"Are you going to be up for driving after everything?" Alaric asked, reaching across to assess her energy."

"I'm good. We need one more driver."

"Okay, go help Bryan. At least five of the folks in my trucks aren't Shades, see if any of them are up for driving." Alaric turned then to where his mother was, nodding to Sahara who seemed to be standing guard over the van. His mother wasn't alone. He could sense a few others with her.

Alaric brushed along her shields before he opened the passenger side door and climbed in. Her mind surged into his and she pulled him in to hug before he'd even pulled the door closed. She fed him energy from the network she was still connected to, then dumped information along behind it. He pulled back mentally and pressed a kiss to her cheek. He'd have time to dig through the information once they were on the road.

"Are you okay?" Alaric asked, glancing around him. There were five people all sitting in the back, looking stunned.

She cupped a hand to his face and smiled. "I am now. What about you?"

"Tired. But I'll live." He could feel her disconnecting from the network of other minds. She sagged a little and exhaled a bit shakily. "We

296

should get moving soon. We're just getting the last of the injured into vehicles."

The back door opened and the female Shade who'd volunteered to help climbed in, followed by two more. "The man said they're nearly ready."

"Okay, get settled in." Alaric kissed his mother's cheek again. "*Get some sleep.*"

Bryan was leaning on the side of Raven's van, his eyes closed. Gathered around him was a rag tag group of seven that included Sahara, Maddie and Zero, as well as Evan, who was wearing borrowed clothes and three others he could tell were his people, even if he didn't know them. "I want at least one Shadow in every vehicle." Alaric said as he approached. "That way we can keep in touch. We're heading for Rapid City, South Dakota. By the time we get there, we should all be in better shape, so we can regroup and plan from there. I don't need to remind you that we are not safe. Use any means necessary to get through checkpoints and roadblocks. We need to stagger our departure, so we don't show our hand. Go around the city if possible. Too many 8th Battalion troops and by now word has got to have gotten out about our escape." He rubbed his head where a low throb had started, yet another indication of his exhaustion.

"Take any route you need to, just stay in contact. Sahara, you head out first. Maddie, you're next. Evan, are you sure you can drive?"

Evan moved the arm that would have matched the wounded wing. "One of the Shades took care of me. I'm good."

Alaric nodded. "Okay, you'll follow Maddie. Zero, you're with me and Mason. Then the rest of you, follow at five-minute intervals."

"I'll ride with Maddie." Bryan offered, yawning.

"Good. Let's get moving."

Alaric couldn't stifle the yawn as he made his way to the van where Mason was waiting. He climbed into the passenger seat and from there into the crowded back of the van. Mason lay nearest the front seats, his body draped in a dark blanket. Raven sat beside him, her eyes closed and one hand on his head. She stirred as Alaric squatted beside them.

"I can't do much to heal him until we get that bullet out." Raven said softly. "The salt and gold are just contaminating everything. I don't know how he's still alive."

Alaric glanced at the others, from the teen she had been working on before to the tiny child currently being held by one of the others. They all looked shell-shocked and bloody, and there was little he could do for any of them until they got to safety.

He settled into the passenger seat and closed his eyes. Sleep pulled heavily on him and he barely noticed when Zero started the engine and got them moving.

* * *

He woke as the van came to a stop. Beside him, Zero stretched, yawning broadly. "*Gas.*" Zero sent to him before climbing from the truck. The sun was high in the sky, showing they had passed noon.

Alaric glanced behind him. Most of their passengers were asleep. He reached out for the rest of the vehicles. Familiar minds acknowledged him and sent him locations, and unfamiliar minds responded a little more slowly. So far, they all seemed to have cleared Utah and were working their way through Wyoming.

The last two cars were still in 8th Battalion territory, but should cross into the buffer zone soon, provided they managed to get through or around the last checkpoint.

Alaric slipped out of the van, stretching as he circled it. Zero was at the end of her endurance, looking like she was going to drop. She'd used her last reserves to bump the pump, making it think she'd used a credit card.

"I'll drive." Alaric said, holding out a hand for the keys. She didn't argue, just passed them over. "Go on, get some sleep."

He took over the task of pumping gas, while she went to the passenger side door. He wasn't fully rested, he'd need a full night in an actual bed to get there, but he could drive them the last of the way.

Once the van's tank was full, Alaric climbed in behind the wheel. Zero was already asleep, but he could feel eyes on him. He pulled the door shut and leaned into the back. Mason's eyes found his and the connection between them flared. Alaric rubbed against him, but Mason was already slipping back into the unconscious state that would help him survive until they reached help.

Raven cleared her throat and held up a cell phone. "Got ahold of Darvin. He's sending help to meet us in Rapid City."

"What kind of help?" Alaric asked as he started the engine.

"Didn't ask, didn't want to risk giving away our position."

He nodded. "Probably a good idea." He pulled them out of the gas station and pointed them east. "About two and a half hours from our destination, I think. Try to rest."

The roads were starting to be more populated, though most of the traffic was big rigs moving goods along the new borders. As they approached a border checkpoint so new it didn't even have proper facilities set up, just a manual barricade across the interstate, Alaric reached out around him for a sense of what would be needed to get through. To his surprise, he found a mind that bore a signature that said his mother had been there.

The man was clan, though not gifted with much in the way of active gifts. Alaric slowed on his approach and rolled down his window. The man smiled and stepped toward him. "I've been expecting you." He offered a hand and Alaric took it, reading what his mother had left behind. It was directions to a home where other clan members had offered assistance.

Alaric planted instructions and images of the others coming behind them and thanked the man, who stepped back and waved for the barricade to be moved. Alaric drove them through, hoping the others wouldn't be too far behind.

Zero stayed out until he could feel a nightmare bubbling just under her shields. She jerked awake and pulled into herself at Alaric's questing touch. "I'm okay." Her voice was rough with lack of sleep and remembered pain.

Some of that was his fault. He'd only begun to help her with those memories before their world has fallen apart.

She rubbed her eyes, shifting in her seat to glance behind them. "We're getting close."

He nodded. "We're just about to Rapid City."

She closed her eyes and he could sense her mind casting back behind them. "Evan is hurting, but not far behind us." She licked her lips. "The others are clear of the 8th Battalion." She shifted her focus closer to herself, then forward. "Oh, I didn't expect that."

"What?" he asked, glancing her way.

"Darvin. And Dr. Anthony. They haven't met up with your mother yet. She is on the east side of the city, has the people spread out in three different houses on the same street."

"Address?" Raven asked from behind them. Zero didn't speak, just passed the information mentally to Raven and Alaric at the same time. "I'll call Adam, get them to meet us."

Alaric knew she was exhausted. They all were. But they were close, and once he was sure Mason was safe, they could all sleep.

Chapter Twenty-One

Raven stretched as the van rolled to a stop. She was stiff and sore from sitting for so long, drained from keeping Mason's lungs working, his heart beating.

The van reversed, and darkness covered them from the glare of the setting sun. All around her Shades stirred. She kept one hand on Mason's shoulder as the back doors were opened and Alaric and Zero helped the more mobile out.

A few minutes later, she felt a familiar presence and looked up, smiling tiredly as Adam squatted beside her. "I was beginning to think I'd never see you again." He touched her shoulder, his eyes filled with concern. "You look exhausted."

She nodded. "We all are, I think. I can't rest yet, not until someone can take over here." She glanced down at Mason who was starting to stir again. His eyes opened, slowly focusing on Adam's face.

"We made it?" he asked, attempting to sit up.

Raven pushed him back down. "Stay still."

Adam reached over to touch his hand. "We thought we lost you too. I'm glad to see you still with us."

Mason closed his eyes. "Yeah, they tried."

"But you, young man, are as stubborn as they come." Dr. Anthony's voice came from the back door.

Raven felt him already following her energy tether as he climbed in. "I've got him." Dr. Anthony said, and she pulled back. "There is a bed waiting for you inside, and a bath for soaking when you're ready. I'll be in to check on you once I have our Mr. Jerah settled."

"I'm not injured." Raven said, sliding away from Mason. "Just need some soaking time and some sleep."

She wobbled a little as her feet touched the concrete floor of the garage, but she steadied herself on the van door. Adam was beside her a moment later, one arm sliding around her waist to support her. Together, they climbed the two steps into the house.

The place bustled with activity that swept around her. Adam kept her moving and as they reached a flight of stairs, someone else stepped in on her other side.

Emily, Raven realized belatedly. Together Adam and Emily helped her up the stairs. "Bed or bath?" Emily asked softly as they reached the top.

Raven wavered before deciding that sleep was the more pressing need. "Bed."

They moved into a room with bunk beds. Someone was already asleep on the top bunk. Adam kissed her cheek and stepped away as Emily helped her lay down and covered her with a blanket. "The bathroom is just across the hall. Fresh towels in the closet. Clean clothes will be here by the time you wake up.

Raven nodded her thanks. Her body was heavy with fatigue, but her mind was still stuck on the damage Mason had sustained. She'd never seen anything like it. The bullet had managed to miss any major organs on impact, but the gold and salt and chlorine had spread through the tissue and had begun to infiltrate his bloodstream. If they could get the bullet out, he would stand a chance, but even with Shade care, it would be touch and go for a while.

Even beyond the bullet though, he was riddled with the signs of torture, as she imagined most of them were. His memory of it was sparse, which she considered a blessing. The marks of it though, the scars on his skin would be there for the rest of his life.

Raven rolled toward the wall, closing her eyes and willing herself to let go of Mason, and her guilt. He was in good hands, and she could do nothing to change what he'd been through.

* * *

The house was quiet when she woke. Her roommate was no longer in the room. Dim light from a half moon let her see there was a pile of clothing on the dresser as she rose, and her duffle bag on the floor.

Raven moved as silently as possible across the hall to draw a bath. She needed a good long soak and something to eat. She looked in the closet while the tub filled, pulling out two towels and setting them on the floor beside the tub.

She stripped out of her clothes, the same ones she'd been wearing for longer than she could remember, and she sat on the toilet, relieving herself while she pulled the elastic from her hair, pulling the tight braid apart with her fingers.

She had last bathed at the motel in Utah, which was days behind her at this point, but it felt like longer. It had been months since the attack on Shady Lakes, since the last time she had felt safe. It felt like a lifetime.

The last of her family was gone, the people she'd known as a child were either dead or otherwise gone. She moved to the tub, sinking into the water and sliding until she could dunk her head.

She opened her mouth, drinking in the water, feeling it slowly rehydrate her dried out system. For a moment she thought about how easy it would be to just let go, let the water take her away.

It startled her how inviting it sounded and she forced herself to sit up. She sat for a long time trying to keep her mind blank while her body soaked in the water. When her stomach grumbled, she rose, letting the water out of the tub and reaching for the towels.

She wrapped the long locks of her hair in one, and wrapped the other one around her naked form. Her skin sucked in the water, leaving her only mildly damp as she crossed the hall back to the room where she had slept.

She dressed quietly and headed downstairs, where she assumed she would find a kitchen. The living room at the bottom of the stairs was filled with cots and sleeping bodies. She tiptoed through them until she could enter the dining room and from there the kitchen.

The clock above the stove told her it was almost three thirty in the morning as she pulled some lunchmeat from the refrigerator and set about finding what she needed to build a sandwich. She had just sat down with her food and a glass of water when Zero appeared, rubbing her eyes.

"Morning." Zero said softly. "You okay?"

Raven nodded. "You?"

"Aside from nightmares, I'm fine." She stretched and sat across from Raven. "I didn't want to keep waking Maddie, so I figured I should come downstairs."

"Did you get any decent sleep?" Raven asked before taking a bite.

Zero shrugged. "Some. Emily helped."

They were quiet for a long time before Zero shifted. "Now that we've rescued these people, I need to go after my father."

"Zero." Raven reached a hand for her, but she pulled away.

"No, he's got a plan. We need to stop it."

"You don't even know what his plan is, let alone how to stop it."

"I know enough." She bit her lip and picked at a hangnail. "I know we need to eliminate him." Her eyes lifted to Raven's. "Not just him either. Douglas, his vice president. Probably more."

Raven's chest tightened. "You're talking about assassinating a sitting president."

Zero nodded. "I know."

"She may not be wrong." Adam said softly from the archway. His arms were crossed as if he was cold and his hair was disheveled. He moved closer, sitting at the end of the table. "It's bad out there. Douglas is out of control."

"In what way?" Raven asked breathlessly. "I mean, how much worse could it be?"

"Well, aside from the camps for Shades? They're working on legislation to outlaw abortion, close the borders except for a very select

group of nations they consider safe, and a contact in DC says that they plan to spread the
camps to include Shadows, Shifters and Sages,
possibly Muslims, Jews, anyone not Christian or
willing to say that they are."

Raven shook her head. It was hard to believe
the country had fallen so far, so fast. In just under a year they had gone from no one believing
Shades existed to Shades being seen as some evil,
and now even beyond that.

"Still, we can't just...walk into Washington
and murder people."

"I can." Zero said coldly. "I will."

"We need a plan." Adam countered.

"I may have one." Alaric said, suddenly behind
Adam. "But we aren't ready for it. We all need
some time to get back into top shape." He met
Zero's gaze and held it until she nodded.

Raven couldn't tell what he said to her, but she
seemed to deflate a little. The room went quiet
for a long time, then Adam stirred, getting up and
heading into the kitchen. Alaric took his vacated
seat. "Thank you both, for your help getting us
out of there."

"We weren't going to leave those people in there either." Raven said. "How's Mason?"

He shrugged a bit. "He's not out of the woods. Dr. Anthony got the bullet out, but there's a lot of work to do. He should be stable enough to move in a few days though. Dr. Anthony wants to get him back to the facility in Chicago."

Raven could smell coffee as Adam returned to the dining room. "I think we could all do with a few days rest." Adam said. "And some good food. I'm going to get some breakfast started.

She stood after draining her glass of water. "Where's Mason?"

Alaric gestured toward the garage. "Dr. Anthony set up a clean room of sorts in the garage."

She nodded and headed toward the garage. Clear plastic walls formed an exterior and an interior wall, the space between them armed with fans and air cleaners. Inside the first flap, she pulled on a surgical gown and a mask. One of the Shades they had pulled from the prison was sitting beside a shallow bed of water where Mason lay with little but a towel covering his genitals. In the stark neon light, Mason's injuries stood out starkly against his pale skin.

The woman looked up as Raven entered, lifting her hand out of the water. "He's still under pretty deep. Dr. Anthony put him under with a combination of drugs and Shade work. I'm just monitoring while the doctor gets some rest."

Raven nodded as she moved closer. "I'm Raven Ivany."

"Elizabeth Waller. You were with the Shadows?"

Raven sighed and pulled a rolling stool closer. "In a manner of speaking."

"I was only in that place for a week or so, but I was pretty sure I was going to die there. Thank you."

"You don't owe us anything." Raven demurred, slipping a hand into the water surrounding Mason. The tingle of the mild current made the hairs on her arms stand up and the water resonated with Dr. Anthony's energy. "I can sit with him. Breakfast will be ready soon."

Elizabeth nodded and rose. "I take it you know him?"

She shrugged a little. "Not as well as I should, I guess. But yeah, we've worked together."

Elizabeth left, and Raven turned her attention to getting a better understanding of Mason's condition. She reached into the water, letting it guide her. The stomach wound was the worst of them, the poison of that bullet lingering inside him, but his skin was torn in many places, wounds from knives, from leather tongues wielded by angry men, from tools that served no purpose other than to cause pain.

His feet were welted and blistered and several of his toenails were missing. His back was criss-crossed with partially healed scars and newer wounds that were only just starting to heal with Dr. Anthony's ministration.

Raven stirred the water with her own energy, directing it toward his back and feet. She would leave the stomach to more experienced hands than her own.

Mason shifted some in the water and she could feel the nightmare moving in on him. Raven flushed the water with as much energy as she dared, hoping it would be enough to keep him under and the nightmare at bay.

Shades or not, this was not something they would heal easily.

Raven relinquished her spot at Mason's side as Alaric entered the room, with Dr. Anthony in tow. She moved past them and out into the garage, pulling off her mask and gown. The sun was up, she could sense it, so she couldn't run out into the night to find a wilder source of water.

She was restless, uneasy. She didn't want to admit that Zero was probably right. Didn't want to think that she'd wade right back into the battle when it was time. It wasn't even the killing that made her uneasy. She'd killed before, and with less cause.

Raven moved back to the room where she'd slept, ignoring the rest of the house as it woke. She sat on the bunk and pulled her duffle bag to her. It was her whole life in that bag.

No, that wasn't right. It wasn't even her life. It was a life she'd borrowed and stolen. A brush, a change of clothes, a few first aid supplies, random tools she'd found useful since leaving the reservation. She pulled the brush out and started working it through her still damp locks, through the inevitable snarls and knots.

She had nearly finished when she flushed with a sudden desire to cut it off. Her hand fished in the bag until she came back with a pair of shears. She wasn't sure where they had come from, but she didn't care either.

Raven lifted them, dropping the brush and hacking through a handful of hair, almost to her scalp. Tears fell hotly onto her face as she cut, dropping the long locks to the floor as she moved to the next. In a moment's time, fifteen years' worth of hair growth lay at her feet.

She stood and rain a hand through what was left, shaking a little as realization struck her. She'd get someone to clean it up for her later, even out the ends. She crossed to the dresser mirror, blinking a little.

It hadn't been that short since she was in her early teens. The loss of the length made her look older. Made her look like her mother.

Raven blinked back tears and shook her head. Her mother had been gone longer than she'd had most of that hair she had just lopped off.

She wiped her face and laid down on the bed. She needed more sleep. She needed to be prepared for what came next.

Chapter Twenty-Two

Mason was aware that he was laying in water and he could feel the touch of another Shade, but found he couldn't feel much beyond that as he came to.

He had no idea where he was, only that he was safe. He couldn't remember the last time that felt true. He was injured, though he couldn't tell where or how bad it was. Vague memories of pain and desperation made him struggle to open his eyes.

The light was too bright, and he closed them almost as fast, his hands lifting to grip the edges of the shallow bed. Hands dipped into the water, stirring it with energy. "Try again."

Mason blinked a few times before getting his eyes open. The light didn't seem as bright and he recognized the energy surrounding him. "Dr. Anthony?"

He leaned over the tub, his lips turned up in a smile. "Easy, now Mason, I've had you under for quite some time."

"What…" His head swam with images that were overwhelming.

Dr. Anthony's hand found his chest and it helped him focus. "Your injuries are severe. Better now that we've gotten the bullet out of you, but I'm afraid I may still need to go back in and cut out more of the tissue. It isn't healing as I'd like."

Mason frowned at him. "Bullet?"

"Mason?"

Alaric's presence suddenly filled him, filled the room and he fell to his knees beside the tub, his hand covering Mason's. He looked different, older somehow. His blond hair was shorn short, his blue eyes were dark and flooded with worry.

"Alaric." It felt like forever since Mason had seen him, a feeling echoing back to him from Alaric. "Where are we?"

"At the moment, South Dakota." Alaric said. "You have a long way to go." Alaric lifted his hand and kissed it lightly. "But Doctor Anthony said we could move you once you woke up."

"Yes, I'd like my next surgery to take place in an actual hospital, rather than on a kitchen table." Dr. Anthony said.

"Move me..." Mason frowned, trying to remember exactly where he was and how he got there. Flashes of memory sifted through the sluggish relays of his brain, faces and voices and pain. "What...what exactly happened?"

Alaric looked concerned as he responded. "We nearly lost you."

A flare of panic made his heart speed up and the monitor beside him beep louder. Mason shook his head. "I don't remember? Why are we in South Dakota?"

"Easy, it's okay. I'm right here." Alaric's thoughts rubbed against his, offering comfort.

Mason rubbed at his head, his eyes catching on the fading signs of restraints on his wrist. He frowned harder, his mind scrambling to figure out what had happened.

"What's the last thing you remember?" Alaric asked softly.

"I –Arizona. There was salt in the water." Something flashed through his head...screaming, fire...but it slipped away. "Someone..." He shook his head.

"Take it easy, Mr. Jerah." Dr. Anthony said, his hand returning to the water to stir it with a different energy pattern. "It isn't unusual to have some memory loss after an ordeal like yours."

"Memory of what?" Mason asked, catching Alaric's hand.

Alaric offered a soft smile and sighed. "Arizona was almost three months ago."

Mason could feel himself frowning, so hard it actually hurt. "Three months?"

Alaric nodded. "You were gone a long time, Mason. We thought…" He looked away, and Mason almost pulled away from the roiling grief, fear, anger, anguish that rolled off of him. "We thought you were dead."

He blinked, tears in his eyes in reaction to what he could feel in Alaric. "You gave your life so that Bryan could get away."

Mason licked his lips, a vague memory of fire inside him and turning that fire on others. "I killed…"

Alaric's hand cupped his face, his kiss soft and chaste. "You did it so Bryan could survive. You sent him to me with these." His hand left Mason's to pull familiar talisman's from inside his shirt. "You told him to tell me that you loved me."

320

"I think that is quite enough for now, Mr. Lambrecht." Dr. Anthony said. "Mr. Jerah needs his rest if we are to leave for Chicago by the end of the week."

Alaric nodded, leaning in to press a kiss to Mason's forehead. "I won't be far away." He rose, and disappeared behind plastic walls.

Mason turned his attention to Dr. Anthony. "Why can't I feel anything?"

Dr. Anthony smiled. "That's my doing. I didn't think you needed to wake up in pain. If you're ready, I'll ease back the shielding, let you get a feel for yourself."

Mason nodded, licking his lips and moving his hands to grip the edges of the tub again. He exhaled and something like the feeling of a sheet being peeled away from his body slowly let him feel the extent of his injuries.

He gasped a little. "Wow."

"You had us all pretty worried, young man." Dr. Anthony said. "The damage was pretty severe, especially in the tissues directly around the shrapnel pieces. We had to go in surgically to pull the bullet out. As you can tell, the tissue around it was necrotic. It's not responding to treatment.

But, we don't have adequate facilities here for me to operate again."

Mason could feel the incisions, the place in his stomach and side where they had removed the bullet fragments and dead tissue. There was still a lot of healing left to do though, places where salt and...something had been left to fester inside him. "I should have died." He knew that somehow. He wouldn't have given Bryan the talismans if he hadn't expected to die.

"Don't strain yourself. If it doesn't come back to you, you're probably better off. They kept you alive only to torture you." Dr. Anthony said. "Now, you're probably ready to try something more solid than IV nutrients. You stay in the water. I'll bring you out some food. And, if you're up to it later, I'll move you inside with the others."

Mason watched him go and turned his thoughts inside. His back was angry, healing scars crisscrossed his back in layers of what he could only imagine was part of the torture the doctor had spoken of. His wrists and even his ankles were still bruised from some sort of restraint, the skin around his wrist only recently closed up from where rope had scrubbed the skin off.

Dr. Anthony returned with a tray and set it on a stool before bringing it close to his tub. He helped Mason sit up. "It isn't much, I'm afraid. Chicken broth with some rice and a few crackers. Your stomach hasn't had solid food in a while, we want to take it slow."

Mason lifted the bowl of broth and rice, sipping at it. "I was a prisoner." He glanced up and Dr. Anthony nodded. "Alaric came for me."

"Yes. That man loves you very much." Dr. Anthony observed as Mason lifted the bowl of soup.

He smiled at the plastic flap where he'd last seen Alaric. "Yes. He does."

"He risked a lot to save you. But he risked even more when he thought you were dead."

Mason frowned up at him. "How so?"

"I don't know all the details, but I'm told he did some very…dark things as he sought revenge."

Mason blinked. "But…he's okay, right?"

Dr. Anthony smiled. "Physically, he's fine. Mentally…well, he won't let me in, so I don't know. He seems to be doing well, but time will tell." He moved to check the settings on the tubs controls. "Now then, eat up and rest. No getting up without help."

Honestly, he was pretty sure he couldn't get up without help, so he wasn't going to argue, and he was already yawning, even though he'd only been awake a little while.

"Okay." He pushed the troubling lack of memory away and focused on eating and drinking the water that had come with the meal. He was only half way through when exhaustion began pulling him down. He set the bowl aside and slipped back down until he was once more laying in the shallow water, his eyes closing. He could hear Dr. Anthony moving around, but it didn't take long for even that to fade and sleep to sink in.

* * *

Mason settled in for the ride beside Alaric. The sun had only just gone down. It was just the three of them in the SUV, with Dr. Anthony behind the wheel. He was starting to feel stronger, but the stomach wound was still sapping him of strength. The sooner they got to Chicago, the sooner Dr. Anthony could operate.

He'd seen some of the others in the previous days: Emily and Zero, even a brief moment with Bryan and Sahara, but they were all gone, following Adam and Raven whom Mason never even saw. From what Alaric said, Adam had some sort of facility in Chicago.

His memory was improving as well, though he still didn't have much beyond the salt in the lake and the mad dash for freedom. There were moments about the night he was supposed to die, the fire, the bullet, but beyond that it was blank.

Alaric blanketed him with a soft covering that offered Mason a place to hide himself, a place of love where he wouldn't have to face the world they moved through, or the details of how much had changed.

For a long time, Mason let himself float there. It was easier somehow. They didn't really talk, just lived inside one another as the night wore on.

About eight hours in, Alaric took over driving, and Dr. Anthony moved to the back seat with Mason, producing a blanket to help protect them both as the sun would be rising soon, and while the windows were tinted, it wouldn't quite be enough.

Under the confining heat of the blanket, Mason drifted off, his head buzzing with the discomfort in his body. The miles fell behind them, and the heat in his body rose. He could vaguely hear Alaric and the doctor talking, but couldn't seem to bring himself up enough to understand them, even when the SUV came to a stop.

Hands moved him, gentle and urgent, from the seat into the cold, lifting him up and laying him down.

"*Hold on, Mason.*" Alaric's voice urged, his hand gripping Mason's as they started to move.

It was Dr. Anthony he felt though, his deft touch reaching inside Mason and pushing him into the dark.

* * *

He could tell before opening his eyes that he was in some sort of medical facility. Dr. Anthony wasn't far away, but he wasn't in water any more.

His stomach felt better than it had before. Mason opened his eyes, blinking a bit to bring the room into focus. For the moment he was alone.

Mason felt through his body, marking the healing that had happened since he'd passed out in the SUV. The bruises on his wrists and ankles were nearly gone, and all but the worst of the lash marks on his back were little more than scar tissue.

"You're awake."

Mason looked up at Alaric in the doorway, smiling. "So it seems."

"How do you feel?"

"Better." Mason shifted, sitting up and reaching a hand for Alaric.

He came, taking Mason's hand and kissing the back of it as he caught a stool with his foot and dragged it over. He was closed off though, his mind distant. Mason squeezed his hand. "Is everything okay?"

Alaric looked up, surprise in his eyes. "What? Yeah. Everything's better now that you're okay."

"But something is going on," Mason said.

Alaric nodded. "But it's nothing for you to worry about."

Mason shook his head. "Tell me anyway."

"No, you focus on getting better. There's time enough for the rest."

"I **am** better." Mason said, pulling his hand back so he could shift his position. It wasn't a lie, he was a lot better than he had been, but it was easy to tell he wasn't a hundred percent yet.

"I promise to tell you everything once Dr. Anthony releases you."

Mason rolled his eyes, but nodded. He could tell Alaric wouldn't be persuaded. "Yeah, okay, but I'm going to hold you to that promise."

Alaric smiled at him, his hand lifting to brush Mason's face. "My mother was here last night. She told me you would wake up today."

"We're in Chicago?" Mason asked.

The room he was in was similar to the medical rooms at the facility in D.C., but smaller.

"Yeah, in a secret facility Mr. Darvin had set up. We made it back here a few days ago."

"Who all is 'we'?" Mason asked.

Alaric sighed. "You, me and Dr. Anthony, of course. Raven, Zero and Darvin. My mother, Bryan, Sahara and Maddie."

"There were other prisoners too." Mason said, remembering Alaric coming for him. "There was a girl."

"Yes, she's okay. Somewhat developmentally delayed, and she was severely dehydrated and undernourished, but I'm told she's on the mend. She seems quite taken with my mother."

Mason smiled. "Good. From what I could tell, she hasn't had much mothering. They used her to control her mother, then her grandfather." Images and feelings fluttered through his head; a brutal flogging with something that left his back in shreds, a dirty mattress, and the girl, curling up against his body, her tiny body nearly vibrating until someone pulled her away and then drugs flooding him.

He shook his head and Alaric's hand found his, tugging him up out of the memory. "Hey, where'd you go?"

"Nowhere good." Mason responded, pushing the memory away. "She helped Damon keep me alive."

Damon. The Shade who had found him in the mountains. The Shade who had saved Alaric after Maddie's transformation in a van had nearly killed him.

He blinked and pulled back from the thought, smiling mildly at Alaric. "Just…memories. I'm okay."

"That's good to hear." Raven said from the doorway.

Mason looked up, shocked by her appearance. Her waist length locks of hair were gone, and what was left was shorn short. She rubbed a hand over her head subconsciously and shrugged. "I needed a change."

She stepped into the room, her eyes darting to Alaric. He nodded and stood, leaning over to kiss Mason lightly. "I'll be back. Get some rest."

"All I've done is rest." Mason called after him.

Raven came closer and lifted her hip up to sit on the bed beside him. "I was pretty sure I would never see you again."

"So I've been told." Mason said.

"Dr. Anthony says you should make a full recovery, with some additional scar tissue to tell the story."

"Not exactly a bedtime story." Mason said softly.

"No," Raven agreed. "When you're up for it, Adam wants to debrief you, see if there's some intelligence we can glean from what you went through."

"Don't remember much." Mason admitted. "And what I do remember isn't going to be worth much."

"That's what I told him, but you know how he is."

She rested a hand on his arm. Their energies tingled against each other for a moment. "I'm going to let you get some sleep. We'll talk later."

Mason watched her leave, but his mind was on Alaric's exit. Something was happening, and Alaric was keeping it from him.

Chapter Twenty-Three

"I'm not planning to run off halfcocked." Alaric said. "Not this time. It's going to take all of us."

"Unite the tribes?" Sahara asked, her hand on Bryan's shoulder.

Alaric nodded, his eyes skimming the ragtag group settling around him. "I think I know what it means." He took a deep breath and held it for a moment before exhaling and standing up, raising his hands to draw the attention of the room.

"I think it's safe to say that a year ago none of us would have guessed we'd be here like this. Even when the trouble started. But here we are. And we need to decide what we're going to do."

Maddie and Zero sat on the floor, looking younger than he knew them to be. They were still kids, and he was about to ask them to go to war. Behind them on the sofa was Raven and Evan. Leaning against the wall nearest the door was Adam Darvin. To Alaric's right was Bryan and Sahara. Together, they represented all four tribes, well five, if he included Darvin.

Alaric had been inside the minds of every one of them. He knew what they were capable of, and it had helped him plan out what would come next.

"We aren't enough to go up against the 8th Battalion, we learned that the hard way." Alaric said. "But, they aren't our only problem. Right here in what's left of the USA, we have those who think like the 8th Battalion. We have a president under the control of a man who has been using him to round up our kind, providing him with a pool of victims for his experiments. If we have any hope of returning our country to sanity, we need to deal with him."

"His name is Lewis Rede." Darvin said, stepping closer to Alaric. "Our intelligence puts him in Washington with the President, and a man we believe is responsible for a campaign of disinformation about Shades and Shadows."

"We can't underestimate him." Alaric added. "He's killed at least five people that we know of, and instigated mobs to kill at least five more."

"His name is Rudolph Ranstein." Darvin said, holding up a grainy picture. "He is currently in charge of the largest of the Shade camps, just outside of DC."

"He's also probably got a few skills we don't know about." Alaric continued. "He's not one of us genetically, but we believe he's been altered, like our friend Zero here." He nodded, and she licked her lips.

"When I last saw him, he had been given at least some Shadow gifts. He was one of the agents that went with Rede to the west coast to create what became the 8th Battalion." Zero offered.

"From what we've been able to gather, Rede took a compliment of three individuals with Shadow gifts and used them to spark the fear, but one of them overinvested in the religious rhetoric, which then took over the movement. We aren't sure what happened to the second man, but Rede and Ranstein turned their attention back to this side of the divide, and Rede focused on a man he could control, Norman Douglas."

The room was quiet for a moment as people absorbed the information and shifted uncomfortably. "So, what exactly are we talking about here?" Evan asked.

"For starters, we need to eliminate Rede." Alaric said, his eyes on Zero. She met his gaze without blinking. In the days they'd been in the relative safety of Darvin's facility, they'd been able to work at stabilizing her memories and opening up her gifts. If she was anything to go by, Rede would not be easy to defeat.

"You should know that Rede's experiments have all been an effort to assume all of our collective gifts himself. So far, he's managed to acquire all of the Shadow clans, as well as a number of Sage clans and at least one Shade clan."

"How is that even possible?" Sahara asked.

"It's complicated." Zero answered. "It involves several steps. Painful and delicate steps. And he needs the right 'specimen' to match his profile. I don't really know the details, only what he did to me."

"So, you have a plan?" Evan asked when the silence had lingered.

Alaric nodded. "I do." Bryan didn't like the plan and Darvin was doubtful, but it was all they had. "Before all of this happened, and when I took up the leadership role vacated when my father died, I was told that I needed to unite the tribes. I think the only way we're going to accomplish what needs to be done if we are bonded together, so that we can use our combined gifts as one."

"Bonded how? Maddie asked.

Alaric exhaled. "It's complicated, but it involves a ritual of sorts, that will link our minds and even allow us to use each other's gifts." He held up a hand to forestall their questions.

"You will all get the details, I promise. There is some prep I need to do with each of you, I will give you the information then. And, I will need Bryan and Sahara to go get the orb, Mr. Darvin to find a place for the ritual, and where the sun can charge the orb safely."

"How many of us are you planning on bonding with?" Evan asked, his distaste showing on his face.

"Ideally? I would like two of each tribe." Alaric said.

"Then, you're going to need me."

Alaric turned sharply as Mason entered the room. He was pale and there was still dusty bruising under his eyes and along his jaw bone, but he was walking with only a little stiffness. He clapped a hand to Alaric's shoulder. "I got bored and I sensed there was a conspiracy happening." He grinned and moved to the empty seat on the sofa. "So…bonding, two of each tribe…go on."

Alaric blinked away from his face and tried to find his place to pick up. "Right. We are a bit short on Sages, so Zero will have to do." Alaric shook his head lightly. She had the skills, she just hadn't learned to use them, which could hinder them. "Currently, my bond is with Bryan, a Shadow and Sahara, a Shifter. This ritual would add the rest of you to the bond and allow us to work in tandem without relying on radios or other means of communication."

"What about me?" Maddie said, looking up at him. "You've already got two Shifters in Sahara and the falcon guy." She gestured at Evan.

"Don't worry, Maddie, we won't be leaving you out." Alaric assured.

Zero touched her knee and Alaric sensed she was filling the young Shifter in on what they had discussed privately. Zero was counting on her friend to be her body guard and keep her father's men off her.

"So, over the next couple of days, while Darvin and his team firm up our intelligence and Bryan and Sahara go get the orb, I will spend time with each of you, setting up the frame work we're going to need to do this. If, once you get the details of how and what we'll be doing, you want to back out, you can. No questions asked."

He nodded and watched them leave. Mason's hands found his waist and pulled his attention back. "So, if I understand correctly, we're going to assassinate a sitting president?"

Alaric nodded. "You sure you want to participate? It's more than one death we're after."

"I don't want to be left here waiting for you to come back." Mason replied.

Alaric nodded. "And what does Dr. Anthony have to say?"

Mason rolled his eyes. "I'm fine. A few more days soaking, and I'll be better than ever."

"Good. You should make sure Bryan knows that." He gestured toward where Bryan and Sahara were talking with Maddie. "His guilt is killing me."

Mason's face crinkled up. "Guilt? I nearly got him killed. He's got nothing to be guilty for."

"In his mind, he left you to die." Alaric countered. "And finding out you were alive and being tortured was worse."

Mason sighed and nodded. "Yeah, okay. I'll talk to him."

Alaric pulled him in to kiss, letting his senses extend, feeling his way through Mason's body to make sure he really was okay. He'd learned a lot watching Dr. Anthony work, and while he'd never be a Shade, the knowledge of how to read a body was invaluable.

Mason nudged him. "You done?"

"Just making sure you're okay."

"I told you, I'm fine." Alaric sensed his irritation, even with his amusement. "So, what's this plan of yours?"

"Still working out the details."

"Alaric, I need you for a minute." He looked up as Darvin stepped up beside them. "If you don't mind, Mason."

"You know, I think that's the first time you've used my first name." Mason said, pulling away.

"Go on. I'm going to go soak for a bit. I'll meet up with you later."

Alaric stepped out into the hall with Darvin and fell into step beside him as they left the lounge and headed for the elevator. "Did our people get through?" Alaric asked when the doors had closed.

"Yes, I got word just before the meeting. They've met up with the Canadian front just north of the border. They should be safe."

"Good." Most of the prisoners they had liberated had chosen to flee across the border into Canada rather than to stay to fight. Alaric couldn't blame them. None of them had had it easy.

"We have intercepted some intel I want to go over with you." The doors opened and Darvin led him into the communications center. He held out his hand and someone handed him a tablet. "This is the president's schedule for the next ten days. We've marked the days when we expect Rede to be with him. We're still working on where Rede is when he's not with the President."

"Honestly, I don't think we're going to need to worry about finding him. I think once Zero's in

Washington and I lift the obfuscation shielding I'm currently using to keep us hidden, we'll find him quickly."

"Don't you mean that he'll find you?"

"That would make it easier for us to pick the venue for the showdown." Alaric said, his eyes darting the map of Washington DC on one of the monitors. "Any progress in that area?"

Darvin crossed to the map and enlarged an area. "This is a research refuge. Very little traffic. There's a stream here, and this clearing has a decent distance from population areas. Obviously not ideal, but so far it's the best we've found that is still close enough to draw him in."

Alaric reached across the distance to see the area in his mind, nodding as he pulled back. "Should do. What about a place for us to do the ritual?"

Darvin crossed his arms. "You still don't want to use the roof?"

He shook his head. "It won't be safe, especially with so many who have never been exposed to the orb before. It can be very disorienting."

"Alright, we'll figure out something."

"Good, anything else?"

"You sure about this plan of yours?"

"No." Alaric admitted. "Got a better one?"

Darvin shook his head. "I agree with the basic concept, cut the head off of the snake, the snake should die. I'm just not sure putting all of you at risk like this is the best way to do it."

"I know, you'd rather send in a lone assassin and slink back into the shadows. My way is more showy, but it has a higher chance of success."

"You'll still need an assassin." Darvin said as Alaric headed for the door.

"I'm working on that." Alaric said. He wasn't sure who would end up with that job until they were on the ground in Washington, but at least one of them would be killing someone before it was over.

Chapter Twenty-Four

Mason floated in the small pool of water twenty floors down from the surface, fighting to keep his mind focused on his body and not the pit of dark inside him from which nightmares sought to grab him.

Fire races through his veins as salt burns its way into him. Hot sand is soaking with blood and he's unsure if it's his or if it belongs to the men he's killed as he dies. There are hands, dragging him over coals; fingers probing open wounds, words he cannot understand. Water is poured over his parched lips and he tries to tell them no. He is done, dead.

Then he is aware of light and the slow burning of his skin, blisters forming, salt on his tongue, fists that pound against his skin until he is sure that he will finally die, only to be denied again... with water and hands that urge angry wounds to calm. "Let me die," he begs in a voice no longer his own, words scraping over his tongue even as the beating begins anew. He screams and shakes in his chains, screams uncontrollably.

Mason pushed himself down, into the dark and cold of the water, willing it to separate him from the pain that was only an echo in his body, but lived on, vibrant and alive in his memory. When he felt a little more secure, he surfaced, exhaling slowly. His body bore the marks, told the story that he didn't fully remember.

His fingers walked over his skin, pausing as they found a scar on his side, a few inches up from the bullet wound and to the left. It was a thin strip a few inches long. His fingers played along the scar as his mind tried to place what had caused it.

He was so caught up in his own thoughts, he didn't hear the door open, so he was surprised to hear Raven's voice. "Counting scars?"

Mason looked up, just as Raven dropped a towel and her robe on the chair near the door. "What? No. Just trying to remember."

He moved his hand as she waded into the water. "Looks like a whip mark," she said, sinking under the water.

He remembered the whip. They used it several times, or so he thought. There was also something that was worse, tongues of fire and stone that ripped skin from his body with every blow. He knew his back was filled with scars from that torment. They had hit him with it over and over as he hung from his dislocated shoulder.

He didn't remember any questions. They just hurt him for the pleasure of his screaming. There was one in particular who had enjoyed hurting him.

Mason ducked back under the water. He couldn't remember what the man looked like and he'd never known his name... but he'd been there in Arizona. And again, on the journey to the place where they'd been planning on killing him.

"You shouldn't try so hard." Raven said quietly, pulling his attention out of his memory.

"What?"

"If you don't remember, there's probably a good reason. You shouldn't try so hard."

Mason nodded slowly. "You sound like Dr. Anthony."

"Maybe you should listen."

He climbed out of the water and reached for his towel. "It's hard not to pick at it." He dried the water that didn't absorb into his skin, a sure sign he was better than he'd been in a long time. He wrapped his towel around his waist, covering the swimming trunks, and lifted a hand in farewell. "I'll see you later."

He stepped out into the corridor, squinting at the florescent light reflecting off the white walls. He'd only been out of the infirmary a few days, and he was still learning his way around. He found his way back to the elevator and took it up a few floors to the residential floor. He had a room next to Alaric's, and it was a lot like the one he'd had in Washington, twin bed, small desk and a locker for the clothes he'd been given.

He was nearly to his door when he felt a familiar presence and stopped, his eyes lifting to find Bryan in his path. Bryan's eyes scanned over Mason's skin, his jaw tightening and his gaze never fully rising back to Mason's eyes. "I've been meaning to…" he trailed off, licking his lips uncomfortably.

"Alaric told me you came to see me when I was still under." Mason said, not really sure how to bridge the gap with the man he knew had never really approved of him.

Bryan nodded. "Least I could do. Alaric needed someone he trusted to keep an eye on you."

Bryan was uncharacteristically open, his guilt spilling out and filling up the space between them. It was uncomfortable.

Mason turned to open the door to his room and heard Bryan gasp. Heat rose in his face as Bryan's hand ghosted over the scarred skin, never really touching. Mason stepped into his room, leaving the door open for Bryan to follow.

He crossed to the locker to pull out clothes, keeping his back turned to Bryan as he dropped his towel and trunks and pulled on clean boxers and black uniform pants. Mason didn't know how to process the input he was getting from Bryan.

He turned to find Bryan watching him, his eyes wide. Mason stepped closer. "Bryan, I–"

Bryan surprised him, grabbing him and dragging him into an embrace. His breath was hot on Mason's skin and Bryan was shaking as Mason pulled back from the hug. "It's okay." Mason said softly.

He pulled a hand down his face and took a deep breath. "I left you. I–"

"You didn't leave me. Not...not really. I was as good as dead. If you hadn't left, if you hadn't run, you'd be dead, or broken."

Bryan shook his head, rubbing both hands over his face. "I could have..." he trailed off, looking up at Mason, then looking away. "Telling Alaric that you were gone was the hardest thing I've ever done." He paced to the door, then back to the bed. "It broke him. In ways I didn't expect. I'm his Keeper. I should have known."

Mason sighed and moved to finish getting dressed. "On some level, you did. You knew the moment Alaric helped me for the first time." He pulled a black t-shirt on and smoothed it over his chest. "He didn't listen."

Bryan was frowning at him when he turned around. "What are you saying?"

Mason sighed. "I don't know. You never wanted Alaric and I to get too close. You warned him I'd bring him pain."

"I'm the one that brought him pain." Bryan argued. "I left you alone in the desert to die."

Mason nodded. "I know, but if you'd never let him take me out of the cell with you in the first place, my dying wouldn't have broken him the way it did."

"Either way, it's still my fault." Bryan responded, guilt dripping from the words. "I'm responsible for leaving you, for telling him you were dead when you weren't, for not being a better Keeper, and for everything he did after I told him."

Mason moved a little closer. It wasn't the first time he'd heard allusions to Alaric's actions after he found out Mason was dead. "What did he do?" Mason asked breathlessly.

Bryan inhaled deeply and shook his head. "Not my story to tell. Besides, I wasn't there for most of it. I didn't catch up with him until he was pulling up in that truck with you in the back."

Mason could just about feel Bryan pulling himself together and closing his shielding. He took it to mean that the moment was over, and they would go back to their usual relationship, maybe with a slightly less antagonistic push from Bryan's side. "So, are we good?" Mason asked.

Bryan gave a short nod. "Sahara and I are leaving in a few hours to go get the orb. See you when I get back."

Mason watched him go and sighed. So much had changed in the months he'd been a prisoner, and he still didn't even know half of it. He sat and pulled on the boots he'd been given and pulled a hand through his damp hair. It had grown out a bit, and he probably needed to get it trimmed back into shape, but there were more pressing concerns.

He stretched as he stood, working the muscles in his back slowly before crossing to the door. He wasn't sure where he should start now that he'd been released from Dr. Anthony's care. If he shouldn't pick at his own memory of the last three months, maybe he should get caught up on current events elsewhere.

That decided, Mason left his room and headed back to the elevator. He took it up to the floor he was pretty sure held the communications center. Smiling to himself when he was right, Mason slipped into the large room set about with monitors, and stations where two men and two women manned keyboards and headsets, receiving and relaying information to whomever Darvin still had out in the field.

Judging from the relative calm, that list was small. One of the men looked up, his lips curling in a smile. Mason recognized him from Washington, but his name escaped him.

"Good to see you up and around, Jerah. Thought we lost you."

Mason nodded and chuckled a little. "Apparently I'm hard to kill."

"What can I do for you?"

"Well, I'm a little out of the loop. I was hoping to get caught up on what I missed while I was gone."

The man raised an eyebrow. "Yeah, okay. Take that station there." He pointed to an empty seat. "I'll throw you the highlights."

"Thanks." Mason sat and lifted the headset. The monitor filled with files, some written, some video sets. He put the headset on and pressed play on the earliest video.

* * *

Several hours later, Mason left the communications room and went in search of lighter company and food. He found the mess hall with little trouble and grabbed a tray of the meatloaf before sitting at table off to the side.

He'd only just started eating when Zero and Maddie sat on either side of him, giggling over something he couldn't begin to guess. He nodded in greeting. "Hello ladies."

Zero lifted a hand to straighten the plain brown wig she was wearing before lifting the sandwich off her tray. "So, you all recovered now?" Zero asked around the bite of her sandwich.

"As much as I can be, I guess." Mason answered, looking at her. There were dark circles under her eyes and her skin was drawn and pale. "What about you?"

She shrugged. "I'll survive. Better when we get moving. Sitting still is hard."

He understood that. Sitting still gave him too much time to pick at wounds, too many hours that filled with nightmares that ripped his sleep yet left no concrete memories of what or why behind. "Soon."

"Not soon enough." Maddie muttered, drawing his attention.

"You in a hurry for what's coming?"

Maddie rolled her eyes and looked across to Zero. "I'm in a hurry for it to be over."

"I think we're all ready for that." Mason agreed.

"Even if we succeed, it won't be over." Zero countered. "Take out my father, and R, the president, and we still have a congress that put the camps into effect, and a whole, okay, half a country that wanted them. Not all of them can be under my father's control. He's not that strong."

"One step at a time." Mason said softly. She wasn't wrong, but for the moment he had to cling to the idea that what they were about to do would solve something, that it wasn't just a stepping stone to something bigger. He needed some sort of resolution.

Zero sighed and seemed to deflate a little. "I know. I just feel…helpless right now."

Mason touched her shoulder. "You're far from helpless, if half of what Alaric says is true."

"And, you should have seen her earlier today. She's always said she didn't have control of all of her Sage powers, but I've never seen the stuff she was doing." Maddie said.

Zero sloughed off the praise. "I haven't practiced in ages. It felt good to stretch those muscles."

"I'll admit, I know very little about Sages." Mason said as he lifted his glass of water.

"What do you want to know?" Zero asked around her mouthful of sandwich.

Mason put his fork down and looked at her. "I don't even know what to ask." He thought about it a minute, then asked, "Alaric said you were 'initiated into' your clans. You're not born to them?"

Zero shrugged. "It's complicated? My mother seemed to think that at one time we were, but clans started mixing and pretty soon, you didn't know which gifts you'd get until you started puberty, sometimes sooner. I come by fire and water pretty naturally, but my father made sure I had the DNA for all four. So, when I initiated, I chose the fifth clan, those who initiate into all four and can learn to combine them."

"That's impressive," Mason said, "but how is that going to help us in the field?"

"A properly trained Earth Sage can open cracks in the ground, cause earthquakes, mudslides, bring down trees, and on and on." Zero took a drink from her soda. "An Air Sage can pull all of the oxygen out of a room or call up a wind strong enough to send your enemy rolling away.

"The real trick is when you can combine the gifts from the different clans." Zero said, toying with what was left of her sandwich. "Technically, I may be initiated into the fifth clan, but my mastery of Earth and Air are tentative at best, and I've never really been trained." She sighed and shook her head. "So, it comes down to, when a Sage, or group of Sages, can control all four elements, they can control storms, stop hurricanes. But, like the rest of the tribes, we're scattered, the bloodlines diluted. And we have to rely on our elders to teach us, but so few remain."

Even more so now that they were hunted, Mason mused to himself. Indeed, they might be among the last of their kind, at least here in what remained of the United States of America.

Chapter Twenty-Five

Zero collapsed to the ground, sweat soaking into her clothes. Her hands trembled, and she shoved them against the grass to still them. The circle where she had been practicing was scorched, wind-blown, soaked and torn.

She pushed herself over onto her back and slowly up to sitting. The trees around the clearing gave her a small sense of privacy, but she knew the wards she'd erected were far more protective of the space than the trees would ever be.

The park was walking distance from the tower that hid their collective secrets and small enough that it only attracted people escaping their offices at lunch time. It was still hours until lunch, in fact, the sun had only been up for a short time. Still, with daylight came danger and she knew she should be headed back.

She couldn't shake the restlessness or the nightmares. Her desire to repay her father for the pain he'd caused her would fill her up and her rage would leak out to anyone who was too close.

Other times, the whole thing seemed to be too much and no matter what they managed to do once they got to DC, it didn't seem it would matter at all. More than once she and Maddie had talked about just leaving, disappearing into Canada...go someplace where no one knew them.

She wouldn't, maybe couldn't, but that didn't stop her from thinking about it. Slowly, Zero stood, moving back to the ring that was the only evidence of how she had spent the last few hours. Her hands were still shaking as she held them out over the ripped up ground, reaching inside to summon the power over the earth and the words that went with it to repair the damage she had made.

It took longer than it should, but she was exhausted and needed sleep. When the ground looked nearly as it had before she started, she considered it good enough and turned to head back to the building, stopping to grab the small bag she'd brought with her. It held her ID to get into the building along with water and an apple.

She drained the bottle on the walk back and ate the apple to hold her over until she could get into the cafeteria for real food. Then she'd go down to the cinderblock room Darvin had given her to work in and try to get another couple of hours of work on honing her skills.

"You're going to wear yourself out."

Zero stopped suddenly, blinking up at Alaric's mother. "What?"

She smiled and slipped an arm around Zero pulling her close. "You need sleep. All of this frantic trying to prepare for everything is going to burn you out."

Zero wanted to pull away from the comfort Emily offered, but at the same time wanted to lean into it and accept it. She hadn't had a mother to lean on in a long time. "I need to be ready."

"I agree. But this…" She waved a hand gently. "Whatever it is you're doing, isn't getting you ready, it's wearing you out."

"I don't have time for sleep." Zero argued, pulling away. "I'll be fine."

"No, you won't." Emily countered, her hand on Zero's arm. "Alaric is worried about you, but he doesn't know how to help."

"And you do?" Zero asked, her tone harsher than she meant for it to be.

"I'd like to try. If you'll let me." Emily responded.

Zero closed her eyes and breathed in deep. "I don't know what you can do," she said after she'd let the breath out. "I need practice with these... things my father forced onto me, so I can use them."

Emily nodded. "I know. I have a little experience with those who have been separated from their gifts. I think I can help you without tearing you apart at the same time."

Zero squelched the bit of hope that flared inside her. "Okay, I'm willing to try anything at this point."

"Good. We'll start by getting you some breakfast, and then at least four hours of sleep."

Zero let Emily start them walking toward the cafeteria but held out little hope for sleep. "I don't sleep much these days."

Emily patted her arm. "Don't worry, you will today."

* * *

Zero woke in the dark of her room, surprised to find herself rested, at least more so than she had been in more time than she could remember. No nightmares had come to steal her sleep, and nothing else had intruded on her either.

The last part she was pretty sure she owed to Emily, who had blanketed her in layers of protection that slowly blocked off every single one of her senses and left her suspended in a soft cocoon, alone.

She stretched from head to toe, marveling at how much better she felt. Emily was still walling her off and it was peaceful, not hearing everything that was going on around her. No matter how strong she made her shields, it didn't seem to ever be enough, other people's thoughts seemed to always be leaking in.

Taking her time, Zero got dressed, grabbing the half a bagel still sitting on the small bedside table. She was hungry like she hadn't eaten in days.

"Not days." Emily said softly from the doorway, making Zero jump. "Only about seven hours. How do you feel?"

Zero nodded. "Better, thank you."

She smiled. "Good. You ready to work?"

"I am."

"Come on then, let's get started."

Zero followed her out the door and into the corridor. "Can you start with that shielding you're using? I can't seem to close up enough anymore. That was the first time since Alaric helped me access what my father did to me that I couldn't sense anything outside my room."

Emily smiled. "Well, for starters, it isn't like the shielding you use, it's more fluid, more like a blanket than a wall."

Zero considered that. "So it what? Fills the gaps better?"

"Something like that yes." Emily said.

"Okay, that makes sense." Zero pressed the button in the elevator that would take them down to the level for the room was she'd been practicing in. The ride was quiet, giving her space to think about how she would construct a blanket instead of a wall. "So what is it you want to teach me?" Zero asked as she opened the door into the room and flipped the lights on.

The long room was little more than a concrete floor and cinder block walls, marked in places with scorch marks or pock marks from her efforts.

"Well, let's start with letting me get a good look inside that head of yours." Emily said, closing the door behind them.

Zero licked her lips apprehensively. "Okay." She turned to face Emily and offered her a hand.

"Relax, I'm not going to hurt you." Emily said, cupping Zero's hand and petting over her palm. "Close your eyes and let me in."

She inhaled and closed her eyes, letting her shields fall with her exhale. Emily's touch was soft as she entered, exuding calm. Zero watched her get her first good look, her amusement echoing in the space. "*Good, Zero. Show me around.*"

At first, Zero wasn't sure what she meant, so she moved them to the series of rooms Alaric had helped her build to house her memories. Emily seemed to get distracted though, drifting to the place where Zero's father had built up the traps and walls that had kept her a prisoner for so long.

Zero was still tender there and she pulled back, but Emily didn't. She caressed over it, spilling soothing peace over the area. "*You have to let it heal, Zero,*" Emily said. "*Or you will never be free of it.*"

She moved a little, her attention moving to the center of Zero's Sage gifts. Zero could *feel* her smile. "*This is the problem.*" Emily drew her closer. "*Tell me what you see.*"

Zero shrugged. "*Fire, Water, Air, Earth.*" She pointed to each in turn.

"*And underneath?*"

"*Underneath?*"

"*Look closer, Zero.*" Emily instructed.

"*There's nothing underneath.*" Zero responded. At least not under Air and Water. Fire and water both seemed to twine around each other and down.

"*Exactly.*" She shifted them to the place where Zero's Shadow abilities were centered. "*And here?*"

Zero had never looked at herself this way before. The controls seemed more distinct than she remembered, the gifts interconnected: telepathy, empathy, telekinesis, prophecy and more, all moving together and underneath, they all flowed into her, out of her mind and into her body.

"Oh." Zero said out loud.

Emily slipped out of her head and Zero opened her eyes. "You are holding them as separate from yourself, which makes them difficult to control." Emily said.

Zero nodded. "Okay, so how do I...make them work?"

Emily bit her lip. "Let me see your back?"

Zero frowned at her, but turned and lifted her shirt. Emily's hand ghosted over her skin, settling over two of the squares of skin that were not Zero's own. "These two are the Sages your father took to give you those gifts. Can you sense the people they come from?"

"What? Like, reach out to them?" Zero asked. "They're probably dead now."

"That doesn't mean they are gone." Emily said softly. "Close your eyes and center. Feel my finger against your skin, feel the difference between the skin you were born with and this square that comes from another."

Zero followed her directions, pushing away the notion that this was a worthless exercise to try what Emily was asking. It took a minute to still her mind enough to sense the minute differences between one patch of skin and another.

"*Good. Tell me about the person this comes from.*" Emily said.

"Man, mid-twenties." Zero breathed. "Earth clan. Artist." She could almost picture him. He had been the first. She let herself into the memory of it, the feeling of another person invading her, no, not the person, but part of him. His DNA, his power. It had rushed into her, even though she was sedated. Even before the doctor had finished the stitching of the skin, the earth was shaking with her pain.

"*Very good, Zero. Now, this one.*" Emily's hand moved and Zero refocused her attention.

"Air clan. Woman in her sixties." Zero said aloud. She felt for the skin and the related memory. "She fought them. Even when... Oh."

The memory was strong, spilling out fast and hard.

The sedation is failing again, but she can't speak, her father's control on her mind is too strong. Zero turns her head, her eyes finding the woman on the next bed. Her grey eyes are filled with fury and the air around them is getting colder.

Zero wants to tell the woman that she's sorry, that this shouldn't be happening. Fire burns through her veins as they feed their serums into her and the knife that cuts her open only adds to the flames.

The woman screams as they cut into her and her screams come out Zero's mouth as they stitch the woman's skin into her back. Her father's hands are inside her head, stitching power the same way the surgeon stitches her skin and with it comes cooling wind, easing the burn, whipping around them. Zero can't tell if it's her or the woman, but her father's hand squeezes inside her head and everything goes black.

Emily's had caught her before she could fall down, and Zero clung to her arm while she tried to regain her balance. She'd never seen a memory so clearly, not of the experiments anyway. The pain, the torment that came after was all clear, but never that.

"Are you okay?" Emily asked softly.

Zero nodded. "I think so? I...that woman..." She was pretty sure that both Sages had died shortly after their contribution to the freak she had become.

Zero licked her lips and moved toward the center of the room. "Let me try something. You might want to stand back."

Closing her eyes, Zero reached into that center of Sage gifts and sank herself into the middle of them. Fire and water came to her easily, swirling around her core and moving easily when she lifted her hands. Breathing out, Zero beckoned earth and air the same way, willing them to permeate her body.

Air came first, sliding along the swirling tide of water and fire before it too came to her fingertips. Earth was more sluggish, but now that she understood better where it began, it sank into her body, making everything heavy. Beneath her feet, the ground rumbled.

Zero opened her eyes, directing the forces together. Clouds formed over her head, lightning and rain shooting in all directions.

"*Stop trying to control it.*" Emily said.

Zero glanced in her direction. Letting go control could bring the whole tower down on them. She licked her lips and exhaled. She murmured the words she'd memorized for her initiation and turned her back to Emily, hoping to spare her from what might follow.

"*Unite the tribes.*" That wasn't Emily. In a flash, Zero could see Alaric and Mason, Maddie and Sahara, Evan and Raven, Darvin and Bryan, and Zero in the middle of them. "*Unite the tribes.*"

Zero reached for the center of her Shadow gifts, pulling it toward her, pulling it into the center of her Sage gifts.

"*Unite the tribes*"

With a nearly audible click, her two power centers snapped together, and energy surged through her, exploding out through her hands. The room shook, and her body was pelted with rain and hail, lightning cracked the air and thunder boomed around her, shaking the room again.

Her mind filled the space, expanding out until it was filling the tower, and everyone within could feel it, feel her as she let go and gave herself over to what she was.

Zero was floating in the air when she opened her eyes again. Emily stood near the door, soaked through with rain, but smiling at her. Slowly, the energy stilled, and she sank to the floor, her knees giving out as her feet touched down. For a long, still moment, Zero knelt in the inch or so of water that soaked the floor.

When she lifted her head Alaric had joined them, his eyes wide. Zero stood unsteadily and licked her lips.

"I think I know how to defeat my father," she said, her voice sounding raspy in her ears. She took two steps and felt the world tilt. Alaric caught her before she hit the floor. "But maybe a nap first."

Chapter Twenty-Six

Alaric paced the hallway outside of Zero's room, his head spinning with possibilities. Even with Zero asleep, he could hear that same phrase in the same voice as his own visions echoing in his head, "*Unite the tribes.*"

"Stop with the pacing." Bryan said, interrupting his pattern. "You're going to wear out the floor."

Alaric stopped and leaned against the wall. "Sorry." His connection with his Keepers was buzzing with what he had witnessed when he responded to the call Zero had put out. He wasn't even sure she knew she'd called him, or how.

"So, what are you thinking?" Bryan asked, breaking through his replay of the scene.

"That you're not going to like what I'm thinking." Alaric responded. "To get to Rede, we need her."

"We already knew that." Bryan said, crossing his arms.

Alaric looked him over. In the time he'd been gone he'd gotten his hair trimmed and shaved off the growth of facial hair. His clothes fit him for the first time in a while, showing off the tight physique that had developed along the way. He looked better than Alaric remembered seeing him in a long time.

"Unite the tribes." Alaric said out loud. "Remember?"

Bryan nodded. "I remember you not really knowing what it meant."

"I think I do. What I witnessed down there...she's the answer."

"Do you hear yourself?" Bryan asked. "She's a child. What is she, seventeen?"

Alaric let the memory of what he'd seen play across his connection to Bryan. The older man stepped back. "That's impressive."

Alaric nodded. "Can you imagine if we were able to give her Shade and Shifter qualities too?"

Bryan's eyes narrowed. "Are you talking about stitching them into her, like Victoria did with me and Sahara?"

Alaric nodded. "Something like that. I mean, clearly, we can't do what her father did to her, even if we wanted to. We don't have the time or the equipment. But what if we could stitch ourselves into her, give her Raven and Mason's Shade gifts, and Sahara and Evan's Shifter ability, or some of them at least."

Bryan exhaled, shaking his head slowly. "It would be risky; do you think she could handle that much power?"

Alaric went back to pacing. "I don't know. I need to introduce her to the orb. See how she handles that. See if the ancestors have a trick or two hidden in our collective memory to make it easier. Either way, our bonding ritual is going to change quite a bit."

"We can prep here, but we shouldn't actually stitch into her until we're in DC." Bryan said. "A road trip while she's in that volatile state would be dangerous."

Alaric nodded. "Is the orb on the roof to charge?"

Bryan nodded. "Yeah, not quite back to full strength after the trip."

"Okay, stay here. I want to keep her safe and isolated until we're ready. Only you, me and my mother have access." Alaric headed down the corridor to go consult with the orb.

It was an insane idea, though he couldn't decide which part of it was the most insane. He'd first heard the words when he'd been in circle around the globe with his father and his father's other Keepers, trying to build something coherent out of the prophetic visions from the clans farseeing psychics.

The words had plagued him, right up until Mason. Then, like so much else, he'd let it go to grab onto something unexpected and wonderful. His love had blinded him to a lot, but now maybe he could finally make sense of it all.

Alaric emerged out onto the roof as the sun was setting. The orb pulsed in the center of the space, alone and unguarded. He approached it slowly. His last personal encounter with the orb had been the night he'd demanded it give him what he needed to avenge the death of the man he loved.

He'd learned a lot since then, and he had relinquished most of the power it had given him then. Zero on the other hand had never experienced the orb, and yet, she possessed much of what it had given him then. He had seen what she was capable of. It was terrifying.

Her father was sure to be as capable or more. He'd had the time and the resources to continue his experiments on himself.

Alaric stopped just shy of the orb and centered himself, putting his mind to order and calming himself before he reached out and slowly touched the surface of the energy barrier. Energy surged up his arm and drew him in, circling around him.

It was overwhelming for a moment, the pull and the wash of energy that swept through him. As it washed away, he was surrounded by the voices of the ancestors. He almost pulled back, shame for what he might have done with the power they had given him fighting against their acceptance.

Slowly, he let go of the man he almost became and let them buoy him, let the light scrub through him and reinvigorate him. When it had all settled, he offered up the image of Zero as she had been when he found her, floating in the air with her gifts manifesting in the air around her, along with the knowledge he had of how she had come to be that powerful.

For all they knew, Rede had managed to complete his experiments, and he possessed all of the gifts of all of the tribes. Their only hope of defeating him lay in giving Zero the power to fight him, and even then, there was no guarantee.

He was considering that when he became aware of someone trying to get his attention. Alaric reached out, connecting with a mind he did not know, but was clearly of his clan. She was in Washington, and up until very recently had worked in the White House. She sent a flurry of information, about Rede and Douglas, about the camps and the disinformation they were still spreading.

Alaric thanked her and filed it away to go over later, but before he could turn his attention to anything else, he could feel Mason hovering inside the door to the stairs.

Alaric separated himself from the orb, stepping back before opening his eyes and turning toward the door. Mason was agitated. "What?" Alaric asked, reaching for his mind as he crossed the roof.

"Darvin sent me to find you." Mason said. "We've got news coming in from multiple sources."

It wasn't good, that much was easy to read. He slipped a hand into Mason's and they headed down the stairs, ending up in the communications room, where Darvin was pacing. Zero sat in one of the chairs, knees drawn up to her chest, her eyes distant.

"Show me." Alaric said to the tech sitting at the nearest terminal. Headlines filled the screens around them. *Dog-Shifter at large in New York City. Witches in Alabama Trailer Park arrested in plot to assassinate President Douglas.* There were more, but he didn't need to see them. They were all ultimately the same.

"*President Norman Douglas presided over the swearing in of his new Vice President today. Relative unknown, Lewis Rede, a long-time associate of the President's is stepping into the role just vacated when it was discovered that the President's original choice for the role has Shade blood in his family history. Vice President Rede most recently worked in the President's staff, though it is unclear what position he held.*"

"I think we know what his end game is now." Darvin said dryly.

Zero stood suddenly, her eyes wide. "No, this isn't it." She pressed her lips together and looked at Alaric. "He's got something bigger up his sleeve."

Alaric could see the echo in her eyes and he nodded. "War."

"We're already at war." Darvin responded, his eyes darting between them.

"Not like this." Zero said. She paced a little. "He's going to do something big. Like…I don't know…This is the push though. He's going to put anyone and everyone in those camps."

"He's not done." Alaric realized suddenly. "He needs them for his experiments."

Zero stood, nodding. "He's making more."

"What are we talking about here?" Darvin asked, crossing his arms.

"He's going to make himself a small army of killers, then he's going to kill Douglas and declare himself President." Alaric said, his disbelief coloring his voice. "And he's going to get the rest of the country to accept his takeover with fear."

"I should have gone after him when I was still in DC." Zero said, pacing. "We need to get in there and stop him."

"One thing at a time." Alaric countered, intercepting her. "I have a plan, but it's going to take time."

"We don't have time." Zero responded, her voice tightly pitched.

"Then we make time." Alaric responded. "If we don't go in there prepared, he'll kill all of us."

* * *

It took a bit, but Alaric managed to talk her down, and he turned her over into his mother's care while he pulled the rest of the team together to talk through the changes in their plan.

The room wasn't as full as it had been for their last meeting. Zero and Darvin were both gone and Brian was seeing to some specific preparations they would need.

Alaric cleared his throat and let his eyes meet everyone's eyes one by one. "Thank you for being here. Most of you have probably heard at least rumors of our change in plans."

"Is Zero okay?" Maddie asked.

"She's fine. My mother is with her, helping her get some rest." Alaric responded. "We're going to need Zero to be at her best because we're going to try something that will take every ounce of strength she has. We believe that Lewis Rede has perfected his protocols and has accumulated power from all four tribes. We need to be able to match him."

"We outnumber him." Evan said. "Isn't that enough?"

Alaric shook his head. "No, I don't think it will be."

"So, what are we talking about?" Raven asked.

"It's a process called 'stitching' and if we can manage it, it should give Zero the power of all of those stitched into her."

Alaric let his gaze move through the room. "Now, obviously, it won't let her shift, but it can give her some of the skills of a Shifter, or two." He nodded to Sahara and Evan. "Those of us stitched into her will need to be close physically for the best transfer of power."

"Rede's just been sworn in as Vice President." Evan said when the room had gone quiet. "How do you propose to get close enough?"

"Still working on that." Alaric said. "We may only need to show him that Zero is in the city and he'll come to us, but I don't think a private showdown is going to work now. We need the public to see Rede for what he is."

"You want to challenge the Vice President of the United States to a duel?" Evan asked, his face clearly expressing what he thought of that idea.

"Want to? No." Alaric countered. "But if it helps us put an end to this? I will."

"Why Zero?" Raven asked. "She's just a girl. Wouldn't it be better if you were our center-piece?"

"If I could, I would, trust me." Alaric said. "I need to be outside of the stitch to help keep it strong. Bryan and my mother will be with me, regulating the wards we'll put up to try to contain the damage."

"It's what Zero wants." Maddie said. "She's wanted to go after him for what he did to her ever since she started to remember."

"What about our other targets?" Sahara asked. "Ramstein and Douglas?"

Alaric nodded. "We'll still need to deal with them, but Rede needs to be our focus. He's going to have people with him who are like him."

He waited until they all seemed to have accepted that this was how it was going to be, then he nodded. "Okay, for this to work, I'm going to need Mason, Sahara, Evan and Raven. Over the next few days I'm going to do some experimenting with each of you, so I can determine what each of you can contribute. Maddie, I want you with my mother and Zero. From this moment on, you're her bodyguard."

Chapter Twenty-Seven

Zero watched Alaric and Bryan setting up the space and tried to keep her attention from wandering. They couldn't let her father know they were there until they were ready and any thing she sent beyond the deep blanket of shielding Emily was holding over her could alert him.

Beside her, Maddie sat quietly on her haunches, her eyes tracking Alaric's movements. Zero dropped a hand to rub behind Maddie's ears, though she wasn't sure if the reassuring gesture was for Maddie or herself.

She knew the ritual inside and out; she and Alaric had walked through it over and over. It didn't mean she was comfortable with it though. It didn't help that the others weren't comfortable either.

Raven, in particular, seemed to be ill at ease with the idea. Zero watched her across the clearing. They'd talked briefly that morning, and Zero could tell there was something bothering the Shade, but Alaric had been clear about using any of her gifts before they were ready, so Zero hadn't tried to read beyond the general unease.

Mason, on the other hand seemed more himself than he had since she'd last seen him in Shady Lakes. He was healed and strong, and somewhere along the way, he had found a sense of purpose.

Both of them were dressed for a long day in the sun, long sleeves and gloves, scarves around their necks, wide brimmed hats pulled low. Still, they would need to keep to the shade as much as possible.

Sahara was approaching, her eyes on Maddie, though her words were for both of them. "You ready?"

Zero shrugged. "I guess. You?"

Sahara turned to watch Alaric and Bryan as they finished walking the circle and erecting the wards they would need for the ritual. "I'll tell you that it's a strange thing, to feel yourself using gifts that aren't yours, and from what I understand, we'll be stitched into you much more completely than what I went through."

Zero nodded. None of them were sure of what she'd be capable of, but Alaric seemed to think she'd have access to everything but the ability to shift. Her hand stroked Maddie's head absently until she heard her name. Alaric beckoned her to the opening of the ritual space. Around her, the others took their places.

Alaric took his face in her hands, drawing her attention to him. *"Close your eyes. Narrow your focus to my voice."*

It was harder than it needed to be, nervous energy fluttering around the perimeter of her senses, but she did as he asked, slowly rolling open her shields to his touch. She felt Emily's blanket protection pull back to encompass the entire circle, adding to the wards already pulsing around them. Once she had marshalled her senses, Alaric let his hands fall from her face to take her hands.

She kept her eyes closed as Alaric led her into the circle. She didn't need them to see the others, or the globe that hung in the middle of the space. It was a thing alive, and it had embraced her completely the first time Alaric brought her to the orb.

Its energy had scrubbed through her, clearing out the last vestiges of the walls and traps her father had filled her with, and helped her bring order to the memories that had been hidden from her for so long. It reached out to her now, even as Alaric led her around the circle, past Mason and Sahara, past Raven and Evan and back to the spot where they had started.

Bryan approached from behind her, reaching around her to settle a crystal the size of a child's fist against her chest. The weight of it surprised her, but the power of it did not. It was, after all, a part of the orb. Bryan murmured some words she didn't fully understand, and the pulse of the crystal matched the rhythm of the orb's pulse.

Alaric tugged on her hands and they moved toward the orb. She was half sure that the orb itself would broadcast her presence with the energy it was emitting, energy that drew her in, circled around her and filled her.

Zero slid to her knees, surrendering both to the globe and Alaric, for what came next. Alaric first reached into her and found the now joined centers where her Sage and Shadow powers were controlled. "*Open up as much as you can, like you did the other day.*" Alaric said.

Without responding, Zero sank her awareness into that center, letting her gifts flow into her body and out into the air around her.

Alaric moved so that he was behind her, his body offering her physical support even as he reached inside her to begin the work they had come to do. Mason was first, approaching her slowly and moving to stand between her and the orb. His shields dropped, and she was instantly aware of everything inside him.

A wave of *Mason* crashed through her; his strength, his pain, his desire to be a part of ending this, his energy filled with healing and warmth. Alaric gathered what he needed and worked it down into her power center, nearly literally stitching it into her, making Mason a part of who she was to become.

Raven was next, slightly more restrained, focused. Her energy was sharper and carried darker knowledge, ways to use that energy that wouldn't bring healing at all.

Again, Alaric stitched them together, then pulled back a little, giving her a few minutes to adjust, to work with her new power. Zero manipulated the Shade energy, let it infuse her, flow out into her physical body the same way her other power did.

It wasn't as strong, but it was still potent enough that she could use it. She would be able to heal herself if needed, and deal death if required. Not that she needed Shade power for that.

After a few moments, she signaled Alaric and felt Sahara approach. She was all cool fire and power as she took her place, shields dropping with practiced ease. Golden sparks and strength filled Zero as Sahara offered herself up and Alaric did his work.

It took longer than either Mason or Raven, Sahara's power different than any of the others. There was a roar and Zero realized belatedly that it had come from her mouth. Alaric was tiring, she could feel it, and she had to stop herself from offering him energy. The globe was there for him. She needed to keep her strength.

When Sahara finally moved away, Zero was trembling with the energy thrumming through her. Evan took Sahara's place, a solid column of locked up tension. Of all of them, she knew Evan the least, but that was about to change.

She expected something akin to Sahara when his shields opened, but Evan was so much more. His mind rivaled that of any Shadow she had ever known, ordered and neat and controlled. Rather then letting Alaric take what he needed, Evan very efficiently passed it across, keeping as much to himself as was possible with their minds connected the way they were.

There were flashes of memory, mostly moments when she and Evan had been together, a little spill over from his brother's death, then came the flush of the predator within him.

Alaric stitched Evan into place and again stepped back, leaving Zero to shake and stretch and find her new center. She knew that when she opened her eyes, she would see the world differently.

Zero wasn't ready for that, she needed time to adjust. This wasn't like waking up from one of her father's treatments. The person whose power she was about to access wasn't dead, or a prisoner in some cell. They were all there with her and they would feel everything she did.

"*Go on.*" Alaric encouraged, stepping back a bit mentally as well as physically.

She licked her lips and tried to just let go, drop into the center of all of that stitching and be. The sensation of foreign power inside her was daunting. *"Focus. Stop fighting. Just center yourself and let go."*

"Easy for you to say." Zero muttered, but she pulled her senses in and breathed in slowly, willing herself to release the fear. This wasn't what her father had created. This was not an abomination built through death and torture. This was a creation of trust, she was the center of their trust in each other. Her friends.

Fire exploded around her as she accepted that, pulling her deep into her core which was alive with contradiction. It swirled around her, filled her and she let it carry her for a long time.

The crystal on her chest pulsed louder, pulling her up toward it, toward Alaric who was kneeling beside her now, still in her head, stitching something of himself into her so he could monitor their union.

That left only one more step.

Maddie came easily, licking Zero's face once before sitting beside her. Alaric lifted Zero's hand and sliced across the palm with a knife, then made a small cut on Maddie's front leg. He pressed their wounds together, his voice lifting in a chant that was soon taken up by Bryan and Sahara.

In a flash, Maddie was *with her*, bound as guardian. As Keeper, she realized. The same way Bryan and Sahara were bound to Alaric.

Alaric stood. They would leave her there, in the protection of the circle until she was ready.

Then all they had to do was find her father, draw him out and kill him.

"*If only it were so simple.*" The voice had come from within the orb and Zero inched closer. "*Rest, child. Let us restore your strength.*"

Resting wasn't immediate on her list of things she was ready to do, but Zero could feel her body pulling her down. "*We will guard you while you sleep. When it is time, you will carry the united tribes to war.*"

Zero felt her body fall to the ground, but it wasn't darkness that swept over her, but light, filling her, blinding her and dropping her into a peaceful sleep.

* * *

Voices filled her head even before she was fully awake. New senses tingled with information and a sense of urgency drove her to sit up.

Zero found herself still in the circle, with Maddie laying tight to her side. The others were gathered around the cart that the orb had been loaded onto.

Beyond them, there was an air of expectation in the city, an announcement was due. She gathered herself and stood, sweeping her eyes around her. It was Evan's vision, sharp and detailed. It made things clear.

Maddie was up and at her side in an instant, green eyes checking in with Zero before they too began to survey around them.

Zero felt Alaric's eyes and attention and nodded to him. "We're ready."

Alaric spoke quietly to the others. For a moment Zero wondered how they felt, the ones who had been stitched into her brain. How odd must it be for a part of their consciousness to live in another's brain.

"There's a press conference in an hour." Alaric said as he approached. "They expect your father to announce sweeping new regulations for Sages and Shadows and Shifters."

She nodded. "He'll do it outside the camp. Security will be tight, and not just Secret Service."

Alaric gestured toward their waiting vehicle. "Evan and Raven will get us in, they've gone on ahead."

"Once we're in, we're going to need to get people to safety pretty fast." Zero said. "Once he sees me, he's going to know I came to fight. He won't waste time on niceties."

"You have a plan on how this plays out?" Alaric asked.

Zero climbed into the car and slid across the seat to make room for Maddie. "No, he'll anticipate anything I plan. I'm just going to go at him and hope I'm enough."

"You're not alone. We're all there to back you up."

She nodded. She knew that. She also knew that when it came right down to it, she would face her father alone. The others would need to deal with the other monsters he had created. "There are at least three others with powers he's given them." Zero said. "Keep them off of me."

"We will."

"And once we've engaged, we need to get the others. I can't get a good look at the camp without alerting my father, but we need to empty it, or there could be reprisals."

She vaguely knew the others had plans of how to get the others on their hit list, and she couldn't know them, because her father would find them in her mind. She also knew that they could call on her for help and she would be able to follow the stitched in tendrils to do what needed to be done.

The streets were busier than they had been as they nearer the prison camp where Shades had been hidden away from the world, only to become victims of her father's experiments. Alaric parked the car some ways back and they started the walk toward the spot in front of the prison where the press and public had gathered.

Zero extended a glamor over Maddie so she wouldn't draw attention and followed Alaric. The crowd was settling in and quieting.

A man in a suit stopped them and asked for press passes or invitations. Alaric was about to hand him their glamored pass when Evan appeared in uniform. "These people are with me."

The man in the suit looked Evan over and nodded. "Yes, sir."

Zero could feel Raven, also in uniform off to the right as Evan led them past the phalanx of guards and Secret Service. Mason was nearer to hand, standing behind the last row of chairs. Sahara was to the left, she would be the one to ensure that Ranstein and the others didn't get out alive.

She wasn't sure about Emily or Bryan, but she knew they were close. They stopped at the back of the middle aisle through the chairs just as a woman stepped up to the podium. Zero could see her father now, just waiting to be introduced. She would wait until he had begun his speech, to be sure all of the players were on the board.

Alaric stepped off to the right, leaving her with Evan and Maddie. Cheers went up as the woman at the podium introduced the vice president.

"Ladies and Gentlemen of the press, fellow Americans, today is a historic day. As we close my first week in office, the president has permitted me this opportunity to announce what we have been working toward since he took office, a sweeping slate of measures signed by President Douglas just this morning, that will make our country a safer place for all Americans. As of today, we will no longer be menaced by these extra-human monsters who possess gifts that kill and maim."

He held up a dark blue folder. "In my hand are new laws regulating all avenues these people have used to hide. From this point forward, there will be no fortune tellers, no psychics, no herbalist or 'healers' and no alternative medicines. All places of worship must be registered with the federal office of Clerical Authority. And finally, anyone found to possess gifts beyond the normal human being will be registered and sent to live in camps such as this to segregate them from the rest of us. We will use any means necessary to neutralize their gifts."

Zero took two steps into the aisle and pushed Emily's blanketing protection off, exposing herself. She dropped the glamor and lifted her bald head high. Her father's voice cracked.

"Does that include you, Mr. Vice President?" Zero asked, her voice echoing in the silence that followed. "Or have you forgotten to inform your new friends that you are a Shadow?"

"Alexis, where have you been?" He moved from behind the podium. All around him people were moving, coming toward her.

"Have you told them about how you tried to combine the gifts of these so called extra-humans?"

"Ladies and gentlemen, please stay calm. This troubled teenager is my daughter. She escaped a mental institution several months ago. We've been looking everywhere for you, darling."

"I'm right here. Why don't you come and get me?"

People were starting to move. She could sense men with guns on the periphery of the crowd. "You need armed guards to face me?" Zero taunted. With a mental push, everyone stepped back away from her.

"Are we going to fight, Alexis?" he asked, un-buttoning his suit jacket. "Is that what you came here for? Are you sure you're up to it?"

"One way to find out." She lashed out psychi-cally, even though it would barely be a glancing blow. She needed to goad him into the fight. "Come on, Daddy. Let's play."

Chapter Twenty-Eight

There was a sudden cacophony of people screaming and Zero got a strong surge of Sahara as she shifted and stalked toward the stage. Mason and Raven were ushering people out of the area and Bryan was working with Alaric to set up wards to protect those that couldn't get out.

"*I see you.*" Her father's voice filled her head and she reached for Maddie to steady herself. They were counting on his rage at her to override his reason. "*Did you think I didn't know you were coming?*

"*I see you too, **Daddy**. Been waiting to see you again.*" She sent out another blast of energy, which he deflected easily.

His laugh was haughty. "*I am going to teach you a lesson.*"

"*I've learned a few things since you saw me last. I'm not going to be easy to beat this time.*" Maddie growled beside her, as if she too wanted to goad the man.

"*Who's that with you, little girl? You make a friend? A Shifter. I need a few of those.*"

"*Can't have her.*" Zero slammed her shields against his just as the others got the wards up, locking the three of them in a bubble that the world would get to see. Zero blocked out the others and focused on him. She reached inside her for the first weapon that came to hand, fire dancing across her palms, fire that she flung at him.

Rage filled the air as he countered the spell, drenching the area in icy rain. "*Going to have to do better than that, Alexis.*"

"Oh, I'm just getting started." Zero growled out loud.

He stepped closer, lightning sparking along his fingers. "Good, I wouldn't want this to be easy." He shot the lightning toward her, the energy infused with both Sage and Shadow power. She shielded herself and Maddie from it and it shot out to the sides, knocking empty chairs around.

She pulled up Shade power, Raven's gift to her and pulled together a ball of disease that would strike down just about anyone who wasn't who wasn't a master Shade or Shadow. It struck him in the chest and she triggered the shielding that she'd bundled with it, containing the fever and disease and focusing it directly on him.

"I see you have more friends than the Shifter. Good. I can take them all away from you one at a time."

He burned away the disease and shook off the shielding. Her father was stronger than she was.

She couldn't get a good reading on the others, outside the wards, but they all had their roles to play. Hers was to expose her father for the fraud that he was, to get him to show his hand while the cameras rolled.

. "You think you're clever?" he asked, straightening and pulling his jacket off. "Do you think I can't explain this away to the public? Now that they know Shadows are real, I can make them believe anything I want them to."

"Keep telling yourself that." Zero said. She pulled energy from her core, whipping it into a storm she could hold in her hands. With a clap, it grew to fill the wards, raining down on him as wind tore at his clothes.

Alaric chose then to step inside the wards, Mason joining him on the opposite side.

"I see I have underestimated you." Rede said as he pulled up short, scanning the rough circle. His eyes found Alaric's and he straightened himself up. "Ah, I was beginning to wonder if you were real."

"So, you know who I am then?" Alaric asked, his voice calm.

"Yes. It's hard not to notice when a new power rises in the world. But surely, you've been far enough into her head that you know what you're up against here."

"I have a pretty good idea, yes." Alaric said.

"Pretty bright out here for your Shade friend, isn't it?"

"I wouldn't worry about him." Alaric stepped to the left as Mason moved to the right. Maddie took a few steps toward Rede, growling.

"I have to thank you for bringing the Shifter." Rede said, smiling. "They are getting mighty hard to find." He held out a hand and Maddie yelped, stepping back from the malignant energy that was eating its way toward her.

Mason responded, intervening and reversing the flow of energy. "*He's not fighting to kill. He genuinely wants her.*" Mason sent.

401

"*Yet.*" Zero countered, she pulled a ball of fire into being and launched it at her father.

He laughed as he caught it and squashed it. "I know you can do better than that, girl."

Zero growled, but Alaric warned her not to react. "*He's goading you. Don't let him.*" She nodded her agreement and took a step inward.

"I think it's adorable that you all came to help Alexis with her daddy issues." Rede said. "Two little girls and two men with issues of their own. If you surrender to me now, I promise not to hurt you. You might even survive the procedures." He turned to Maddie again, sniffing the air. "Come now, kitty, let's be friends."

Before he could attack Maddie, Zero sent a flash of bright light that wrapped around Rede's neck, dragging him toward her. He stumbled, laughing even as he fell and rolled on the ground. She pulled him close and knelt beside him, feeding a malignant force into him, stopping the laughter as Rede fought against it.

For a brief moment she thought she'd beat him, but he struggled to his feet, the black handprint she'd left behind already fading.

"My turn." Rede said, snarling at her. He closed his eyes and the ground shook as he pulled at the bedrock under them. He pulled energy from the air and fed it into the ground beneath them.

Zero knelt to counter it, pulling the energy back out of the ground and throwing it at her father. For a long time they were stuck in a loop, each feeding the other, but the ground finally stilled and Rede was the first to step back.

His face was a snarl of fury as he drew in a deep breath and his body began to contort.

"*He's shifting.*" Alaric said, though none of them had believed it was possible.

His skin turned dark, nearly black and his mouth elongated into a narrow snout filled sharp teeth. Gray fur covered some of his skin and his clothing shredded as his legs thickened. Great claws sprung from his hands and feet and the growl that came from him left Zero with a pit of fear in her stomach.

"*What is he?*" Maddie asked.

"*Who knows…bear, wolf…maybe more.*"

Zero back stepped as he came toward her, casting about for an obvious means of stopping him. Or maybe she needed something not obvious. She stopped, planting her feet and sinking herself into her center, pulling Evan and Sahara, Mason and Raven together.

She sidestepped his first attack, Sahara's instincts moving her. He turned, grabbing her around the waist and throwing her into a row of chairs. He bellowed and turned toward her, throwing himself at her. With his attention on Zero, he didn't see Maddie coming, and she sank her claws into his back, ripping skin before darting away.

Rede roared and grabbed Zero with his clawed hands, ripping her shirt and leaving bloody marks on her chest. He threw her again, this time toward the stage. Dropping to all fours he ran after her and she rolled to her feet. She leaped over him, slapping her hand down on his torn back and shoving infection into the open wounds before running back to the center of the area.

Sahara filled her senses, and Zero felt as though the cat had taken her over, turning to face him as he came. They crashed together, Zero using teeth and nails to rip at him as they tumbled down the aisle toward the barrier. Maddie was suddenly there, her claws digging into Rede's shoulder to pull him off of Zero. He slammed a hand into Maddie's face and she backed off, but it had been enough to get Zero back on her feet. She pulled energy to her and pummeled him with it, but he just countered with his own, pushing her backward until she could feel the energy of the barrier at her back. He shoved, and she abandoned everything but the energy to keep him from reaching her.

If there was anything left inside of her that he could control, he'd never reach it without skin contact. "*I should have killed you when you proved to be insufficient for my needs,*" he growled at her. "*Like I did your mother.*"

Zero pushed back, but she was losing the battle. She wanted to reach out to Alaric for strength, but he filled her senses, his deformed face so close to hers, his power blocking out everything outside of the space between them, a space that was closing rapidly.

"*You're weak and your friends can't save you,*" he taunted, pressing harder. "*This is my world, and I own you.*"

He was beating at her shielding with all of his collective power, Sage and Shadow, Shade and

Shifter, and he was going to win. Zero closed her eyes, determining that if this was it, she was going to make him pay for it. Digging into her reserves, Zero renewed her efforts.

The pressure suddenly stopped, then vanished as Rede fell backward. Mason was panting and moving out of reach, his hands bright red. Rede writhed on the ground, his hands trying to reach behind him. As he rolled to get to his feet, she could see why. Mason had doubled the infection in the wounds Maddie had given him.

Alaric approached then. "You should know, we are not your daughter's friends." His eyes met hers before returning to Rede's. "We're her family. She's one of us."

"What do you think you're going to win here?" Rede asked, pushing himself up straight. "You think you're going to be heroes for killing the big bad puppet master?" He snorted and moved to keep out of reach of Alaric's arms. "I've twisted this country in on itself so many times you won't ever set it right. Even if you succeed here, you'll never be free again."

Alaric shrugged a little. "Maybe. Maybe not."

From her spot near the barrier, Zero could feel their shields rubbing against each other, testing, looking for a way in. Swallowing her fear, she stepped in so that she was opposite Alaric, mimicking his positioning, the set of his shields. There was an electric zing as her shields made contact with her father's. There was a flash of surprise, but he didn't turn toward her. Alaric was the bigger threat in his mind.

"I should warn you, I'm stronger than you both." Rede said. He was starting to sweat from the exertion.

Alaric's eyes were cold as he leaned in a little harder. "I should warn you, you're not."

Her father was starting to really struggle now, his thoughts seeping over his shields as he started to realize he might not actually win the fight. Zero pushed in closer, fitting her shields to Alaric's to form a tight circle. "Besides, no matter how strong you are, **daddy**, cut a femoral artery, you're still going to die."

Zero *felt* Maddie's claw as it grabbed high up on his leg, near the groin, and dragged downward, opening up his upper leg quickly. Blood gushed out, covering Alaric's leg as Rede screamed and flailed. His shields stuttered as he fell, taking Zero down with him. She hit the ground seconds before he landed on top of her, his blood painting her clothes and the grass beneath them.

His mind flailed out at her, grabbing onto the part of her that was his and pulling energy into himself to replace what was draining with his blood. "*You belong to me. I will take you with me if I have to.*"

She pushed at him, at the invasion that seemed to not even acknowledge her shielding, just slid in under them like they didn't exist, and he kept coming. "*I made you.*" He loomed large inside her head, disembodied fingers digging into the walls she had been building, shredding them as he crawled inside her.

"Alaric!" She screamed, scrambling out from under him, shaking her head as she tried to dislodge him.

"*He can't save you.*"

Zero couldn't escape him, so she did the only thing she could, pulling herself deeper inside herself, like she used to when she had been his prisoner. She tunneled into herself, ripping up the order she had worked so hard to build, hoping it would stop him.

His mind crawled after her, as if he'd abandoned his body completely and was willing to take hers instead. Deftly, he cut through the stitching that bound her to Sahara and Raven. Zero flooded her mind-space with fire, hoping to burn him out, then dropped into her secret place, the one spot he'd never penetrated, to hide.

* * *

"*Zero.*" The voice echoed around in the empty spaces that lay in the wake of the fight to protect herself. Slowly, she uncurled, at least mentally, feeling through the dark for something familiar.

"That's it, come back." Alaric murmured in her ear. "You're safe. He's gone."

She let him lift her consciousness, though the damage she found there was nearly enough to send her diving back into the dark.

"*I don't mean to be pushy...*"

There was something she needed to do. Warmth flushed through her, something familiar. Mason. She belatedly recognized the hand of the Shade, healing the physical damage her father had done as he lay dying.

"*We're working on it, Evan,*" Alaric sent.

"*Work faster. We're almost out of time.*"

They needed her. Evan was flying, she could almost see what he saw. There were cars, a caravan of them. Sirens were blaring. They wanted her to stop them, destroy them.

Slowly, she climbed up enough to feel her body. She was laying in the sticky remnants of her father's life, curled up tight, with her head in Alaric's lap. She couldn't sense much beyond that, but she didn't need to, not for this.

Words evaded her, but she sent her intent well enough. Alaric helped her bridge the gap and that let her sink into Evan's bird shaped body.

The caravan was small, just three cars with no markings to indicate that it was a presidential caravan, but she knew it was. Douglas was trying to get back to the White House before he could be besieged with questions about what had happened.

All she needed to do was heat up the gas tank. It took her far too long to remember how to do that. Evan swooped in lower and she reached through him to the first tank. The spell burned through them both and sweat covered her face.

The resulting explosion propelled the vehicle into the next and it was even easier to guide the fire where they needed it to go. Evan barely escaped the flames when the third vehicle went up and Zero collapsed back into the safe dark spaces of her inner self.

Chapter Twenty-Nine

Chaos erupted around them as Alaric dropped the wards. Bryan and Sahara were on the heels of two of Rede's men who had gotten past them. Above them, the sky had started to darken. The television cameras were still recording, their operators long gone with the crowds. Mason moved among those who had fallen in the crush, healing as he could.

Maddie licked her lips, then licked at Zero's face. "She's okay for now." Alaric said soothingly.

Their immediate need was obviously to get to shelter. He and Zero were covered in blood, the ground around them slick with it.

Rede lay dead, a few feet away, his cold eyes staring out of his bloody face. Maddie hadn't been content with the killing blow. She'd done everything she could to pull the man off of Zero, leaving him in shreds.

Zero was deep within herself and wouldn't be coming out any time soon.

"You should find clothes." Alaric said to Maddie, shifting so he could stand. "Mason, get the car started." He scooped Zero up and headed toward the car, following Maddie. He reached out for the others, letting them know they were moving.

Alaric settled Zero into the back seat and climbed into the passenger seat. A few moments later, Maddie joined them, dressed in borrowed clothes. "Sahara and Bryan are making sure the camp is empty. Mom is already back at the hotel. Evan is our eye in the sky."

"What about Raven?" Mason asked, his eyes concerned.

"Rede cut the stitching, so I'm not sure." Alaric responded. He reached out to Evan. "*Do you have eyes on Raven?*" Mason sounded concerned.

"*I'm circling back to where I saw her last.*" Evan said.

"*Stay away.*" Raven's voice was distant, and it felt like she was blocking them. Alaric touched Mason's hand, bringing him into the link.

"*What are you doing?*" Mason asked.

"*Just stay away.*" Raven responded.

Alaric got the impression she was working on someone, a young man. His wounds were extensive, and she was pouring energy into him.

"*Evan, can you get to her?*" Alaric asked with a sense of urgency. "*She isn't safe.*"

"*I'm trying.*" Evan flew over her, and the sight filled their connection. With burning cars in the background, Raven was kneeling on the sidewalk, a circle of onlookers watching as she very clearly was rendering aid to a young man who had been caught in the blast. She was pulling energy from their connection, from the people around her, and using it to pull him back from the brink of death. The crowd around her was silent, until a shot rang out.

Raven fell to the ground, the bullet lodged firmly between her eyes, the energy spilling out of her hands and along the ground until it was finally stopped with her heart.

The connection went dark as Evan closed himself off, severing the stitching that had connected him with Zero.

Mason drove them in silence through dark streets that were swiftly closing down. The city was reeling from the day's events. By the time

414

morning came and the dust had settled, they would be a country in tatters.

Both Rede and Douglas were dead. Both died publicly at the hands of those they had sought to oppress. During the melee, Bryan and Evan had opened the doors of the prison camp and led the prisoners out with instructions to get low and stay low.

Raven's death was a shock, the sight of her face just before the bullet struck home filling his mind. She had abandoned fear of discovery in order to save a life, and she had paid the price for it. There was no way to know how that would affect the rest.

They may have eliminated their targets, but it was anybody's guess if they had won the war.

* * *

"Representatives say that it will be days before any official word is given regarding the cause of this tragedy that has claimed the lives of President Douglas, his wife, four secret service agents, an army general and several others. There is no word yet if this tragedy is related in any way to the showdown at the Shade camp just before the accident.

415

Recordings there seem to show newly sworn in Vice President Rede shifting into an animal that has yet to be identified.

The government is all but shut down right now as we face the death of the third United States President in nine months. The stress has been felt across Capitol Hill today, with several high-ranking officers resigning, and most of the president's cabinet in hiding."

Alaric looked up as the door opened and Mason slipped in with bags of take out food. His eyes darted to Zero's prone body on the bed farthest from the door, then back to Alaric who could only shake his head in answer to the unasked question. "No change."

Mason nodded and set the bags down on the table. Alaric started pulling food out, grabbing a burger and taking it to the far corner of the room where Maddie was tucked in between Zero's bed and the wall.

He squatted down and pitched his voice low. "Maddie, food."

Her eyes moved to him, but she didn't really see him. He put the burger in her hand and sighed. Neither of the young women had fared well. Both he and Mason had done what they could to help them, but he wasn't sure it amounted to much. The damage to Zero's mind was horrifying, but he wasn't sure if that wasn't Rede's point. He couldn't decipher how much of it was real, and how much was illusion, not without Zero's help and for the last seventy hours or so, Zero had been completely unreachable.

"*Meanwhile, in Virginia today, Pastor Andrew Elizabeth spoke at a gathering, encouraging Americans to search their hearts and know that God is speaking to us in these events.*" Alaric stood, moving to the table, though his eyes were on the television. The camera focused on a man in a black suit standing at a podium. "*We are reminded that Jesus told us that the greatest two commandments are to love God and love our neighbors. As a country we seem to have forgotten that. As a country we have let our fear lead us down some dark roads. We have allowed ourselves to hate our neighbors and pretend that we are acting in love. I call today for us to end that hate, to free our neighbors from these camps and welcome them home.*"

Mason snorted. "Right. Like that's going to happen."

Alaric shrugged. "It's anybody's guess right now."

"They shot Raven in the head while she was healing someone right in front of them. Her line dies with her." Mason countered, his tone bitter.

Alaric pulled him close, offering soothing comfort for the pain of losing a friend. "I know."

"*In related news, Jeremy Listo, the young man who is seen here on the ground with the purported Shade killed by secret service agents at the scene of the president's death, was released from the hospital today with a clean bill of health.*"

Alaric turned them so that Mason's face was turned away from the TV, having already seen the footage earlier. It had been taken by someone in the crowd of onlookers. The glow of energy could be clearly seen and there was no one who would argue that Raven was anything other than a Shade.

"*Mr. Listo, is a seventeen-year-old local boy was caught by the blast of the first car and thrown into the wall you see behind the Shade. People who saw the events say he was badly burned and bleeding from multiple wounds before the Shade reached him. He himself says he wouldn't be alive without*" *what the Shade did for him, insisting that she saved his life. Doctors will not comment beyond saying that Mr. Listo did have scar tissue from burns and that x-rays showed that bones had been broken."*

Alaric let Mason pull away and they both started to silently grab food, sitting and eating in silence for a few moments. "Anything from Darvin?" Mason asked softly after a while.

"More of the same. Stay put, stay low."

Mason nodded. "So, what do we do after this?" Mason asked after a long silence.

Alaric looked up. "What do you mean?"

Mason slumped down in his chair a little. "I mean, we still have Shades and others in these camps, the laws aren't going to change overnight. There's still the 8th Battalion. I'm not saying that what we did wasn't huge, but...now what?"

"Now, we rest." Alaric said. "We recover."

Mason's restlessness seeped into the air around him. It wasn't enough, even if he couldn't articulate it.

"Mason, we need to take care of Zero and Maddie. We need to get the orb back to Virginia."

Mason rolled his eyes. "I know. It feels like we're leaving the job half done."

Alaric couldn't argue that, but he was tired. He was tired down deep, the kind of tired that had him longing for the quiet country and a warm bed and days without obligation. Mason, on the other hand seemed to be amped up and unable to rest for more than a couple hours at a time. "Most of the Shades that Bryan and Evan got out are either hiding or running."

Mason nodded. "But we didn't get them all out." He got up and paced a little. "I know I'm being ridiculous."

Alaric got up and intercepted him. "No, you're not. But we need a break. We've been going nonstop since Arizona."

He froze up, his eyes closing. "I know."

Across the room, Maddie stood suddenly, her eyes on the door. Alaric felt someone outside and crossed to open it, only a little surprised to find Evan there. Alaric stood aside and let Evan in.

"Wasn't expecting you." Alaric said.

Evan nodded. "I know. I've been pacing my room for hours. I needed a change of scenery." He took in Maddie's expression and took a hesitant step toward her. Maddie blinked and shook her head, then darted for the bathroom. "Is she okay?"

Alaric sighed. "Honestly, I think she will be, but I can't really read past her shock without forcing myself on her."

Evan looked at him funny. "And that's actually stopping you?" He stepped toward the bathroom, then thought better of it. "We did ask an awful lot of both of them. Neither one of them is an adult."

"And she did help kill a man." Mason said softly. "That wasn't exactly according to plan."

"True." Alaric agreed. "But I think a lot of her shock is Zero's condition. I don't think even Zero realized how much she'd been relying on Maddie going into this."

"How is Zero?" Evan asked softly.

Alaric sighed and sank onto the bed beside her. "Rede made a mess before I pried him out of her. She had burrowed down deep to protect herself. We're doing what we can, but so far I haven't found her."

"How long are we planning to sit on our asses?" Evan asked, looking from Zero to Mason, then Alaric.

"You sound like Mason. What is it you want to do?"

"Something." Evan shifted his weight. "Anything."

"We're still waiting for Darvin."

"So, you're taking orders again?" Evan asked.

"He's tired." Mason interjected. "I think we can take a few days. See what happens from here?"

"We did that a lot of that at the beginning of this whole mess, look what it got us." Evan countered.

Alaric frowned as he stood. "Have you slept?"

"What?" Evan pulled away from him as Alaric reached for his shoulder.

Evan's shields were erratic, and they fell easily when Alaric finally grabbed his arm. His energy was jangled, and Alaric found the cause almost immediately. An endless loop of Raven's death was playing in his head, and he couldn't shut it down. Alaric gestured to Mason and pressed in on the controls that would knock the Shifter out.

Mason helped him catch Evan and move him toward the unoccupied bed. "Wow."

Mason lingered as Alaric stepped back, leaning over Evan's body to assess what could be done.

"Is he okay?"

Alaric turned, blinking in surprise. It was the first time Maddie had spoken since they had gotten back to the room. "He will be. He just needed a little help."

She nodded, her eyes on Evan's face. They were quiet as Mason helped ease Evan's pains from three days with next to no sleep and urged him into a deeper sleep. She felt Alaric's eyes and looked up, nodding slightly. "Me too. I'm going to be okay, I mean."

"I'm glad." Alaric said softly.

"Is it over?"

Alaric sighed and shook his head. "I don't know."

"We could go north." Mason said when he'd looked up from Evan. "It feels wrong though."

Alaric nodded. He looked at the television that was now showing images of one of the Shade camps, calling out the squalid conditions and the lack of food. Maybe that was where they needed to focus their efforts. Humanize the tribes that had been painted as inhuman.

He yawned and rubbed his hands over his face. "Virginia," he said after a few minutes. "We have room for everyone, we can rest, regroup."

They just had to wait until the roadblocks came down.

* * *

The room was quiet for the number of people in it. Alaric stood beside the chair where his mother sat. Sahara and Bryan huddled together on the far end of the couch. Maddie sat on the floor near the window and Evan leaned on the wall near her.

Darvin cupped his mug of coffee close to him, his eyes distant. He had just joined them a few hours before, after leaving behind a city still paralyzed by fear. He breathed in deep and lifted his head. "Her sacrifice wasn't lost. There's a growing movement starting to clamor for tolerance, led, I'm told, by that boy's mother."

"A little late." Mason murmured as he returned from the kitchen with a glass of water.

Darvin nodded and sipped at his coffee. "But a good sign. This isn't something that's just going to right itself in a few weeks."

"Which brings us back to, what do we do now." Evan said.

"Well, I still have the infrastructure." Darvin said. "We could organize our own movement."

Alaric frowned. "What do you mean?"

"He means resistance."

They all looked up as Zero stopped on the bottom step of the stairs. Her eyes were still haunted, and he knew she probably wasn't really ready to be in the company of others, but he offered her a smile. She rolled her eyes and came forward a few steps. She glanced at Darvin. "Sorry, you think loud."

He shrugged and gestured for her to continue. "If I'm reading his intent correctly, he means to form up an underground intelligence and resistance, work to disrupt the misinformation..."

Zero rubbed at her head. It had been nearly two weeks since they had succeeded in killing her father. She was starting to get her head back in order, but Alaric knew it would be a while before she was whole, if she ever was.

"Doctor Anthony has indicated a desire to found a medical center in Raven's name." Darvin added, putting his coffee cup on the side table. "Once we manage to find some stability."

He stood. "I know you're all tired and you deserve your rest, but the war is far from over. If we do this, we pull together all of the tribes to work for a common goal, it will be the first time since before recorded history."

"We have proven we work well together." Sahara said.

Darvin nodded. "I'm in contact with a number of other Shifters now as well, and Sages. Imagine what we could do." He buttoned his suit jacket and smoothed back his hair. "You all know where to find me. When you're ready."

They watched him go and for a long moment no one spoke. Emily broke the silence by standing and gathering Zero to her. They headed to the kitchen, where Alaric assumed his mother would ensure Zero ate well. He looked around the room, realizing that they were all looking to him.

"I'm not your leader." Alaric said softly. "This is a decision you each have to make for yourself."

Mason's hand slipped into his and tugged him toward the back door. They slipped out onto the porch and down onto the long grass in need of mowing. "You want to go with him."

Mason shrugged a little. "You don't?"

Alaric sighed. He was still tired, emotionally wrung out. "Not... right away."

Mason hooked a finger through his belt loop to pull him close enough to kiss lightly. His lips were warm and inviting. The stars above them were bright and even the sliver of a moon seemed to shine white down on them, making it feel like they were in their own personal spotlight. "I didn't plan on running after him to catch a ride." Mason whispered.

"Good. Because I need you right here with me for a while." Alaric responded, his hands sliding around Mason's waist.

Mason's restlessness was pushed back, and he was content for the moment, but Alaric knew that it wouldn't be long before he would be wanting to get out there to continue the fight. He imagined that they all would, eventually.

There was time though; time to grieve their dead, heal their wounds, find peace with what they had done. He pulled Mason in close and kissed him. And time to love what he'd thought he'd lost.

Dear reader,

We hope you enjoyed reading *Where Shadows Fall*. Please take a moment to leave a review, even if it's a short one. Your opinion is important to us.

Discover more books by Natalie J. Case at https://www.nextchapter.pub/authors/natalie-j-case

Want to know when one of our books is free or discounted? Join the newsletter at http://eepurl.com/bqqB3H

Best regards,
Natalie J. Case and the Next Chapter Team

About the Author

Natalie Case was born telling stories, or so she says when asked. Words were her first love and she grew up finding new ways to put words together to tell stories. Known to occasionally commit random acts of poetry, Natalie primarily dabbles in worlds where magic exists, where vampires and shape-shifters share page time with gods and demons and the characters that are born inside her head find themselves struggling in a world made real through the magic of words.

Refusing to be confined to a single genre, Natalie's current works in progress span, and sometimes combine, horror, fantasy, sci-fi and more. She currently calls the San Francisco Bay Area her home, splitting her time between her day job in the city and writing and photography in Walnut Creek.

Where Shadows Fall
ISBN: 978-4-86752-869-3 (Large Print)

Published by
Next Chapter
1-60-20 Minami-Otsuka
170-0005 Toshima-Ku, Tokyo
+818035793528
12th August 2021

Lightning Source UK Ltd.
Milton Keynes UK
UKHW040050010922
408147UK00002B/89